Grimms' Fairy Tales

GRIMMS'
Fairy Tales

BY THE BROTHERS GRIMM

Translated by

MRS. E. V. LUCAS, LUCY CRANE
AND MARIAN EDWARDES

Illustrated by

FRITZ KREDEL

Illustrated Junior Library

GROSSET & DUNLAP · PUBLISHERS

NEW YORK

Contents

Grimms' Fairy Tales

The Twelve Dancing Princesses

ONCE upon a time there was a king who had twelve daughters, each more beautiful than the other. They slept together in a hall where their beds stood close to one another. At night when they had gone to bed, the King locked the door and bolted it. But when he unlocked it in the morning, he noticed that their shoes had been danced to pieces, and nobody could explain how it happened.

So the King sent out a proclamation saying that anyone who could discover where the princesses did their night's dancing might choose one of them to be his wife and should reign after his death. But whoever presented himself, and failed to make the discovery after three days and nights, was to forfeit his life.

A prince soon appeared and offered to take the risk. He was well received, and at night was taken into a room adjoining the hall where the princesses slept. His bed was made up there, and he was to watch and see where they went to dance. The door of the room was left open, so that they could not do anything or leave without being seen. But the prince's eyes grew heavy and he fell asleep. When he woke in the morning, all the princesses had been dancing, for the soles of their shoes were full of holes. The second and third evenings passed with the same results.

The prince was then granted no mercy, and his head was cut off. Many others came after him and offered to take the risk, but they all forfeited their lives.

Now it happened that a poor soldier, who had been wounded and could no longer serve, found himself on the road to the town where the King lived. There he fell in with an old woman who asked him where he was going.

"I really don't know myself," he said. And he added in fun, "I should like to discover where the King's daughters dance their shoes into holes, and after that I should like to become king."

"That is not so difficult," said the old woman. "You must not drink the wine which will be brought to you in the evening, but must pretend to be fast asleep." Whereupon she gave him a short cloak, saying, "When you wear this you will be invisible, and then you can slip out after the twelve princesses."

When the soldier heard this good advice he considered it seriously, plucked up the courage to appear before the King, and offered himself as suitor. He was as well received as the others and was dressed in royal garments.

In the evening, when bedtime came, he was conducted to the anteroom. As he was about to go to bed the eldest princess appeared, bringing him a cup of wine. But he had fastened a sponge under his chin and let the wine run down into it, so that he did not drink one drop. Then he lay down, and when he had been quiet a little while he began to snore as though in the deepest sleep.

The twelve princesses heard him and laughed. The eldest said, "He too must forfeit his life."

Then they got up, opened cupboards, chests, and cases, and brought out their beautiful dresses. They decked themselves before the glass, skipping about and reveling in the prospect of the dance.

Only the youngest sister said, "I don't know what it is. You may rejoice, but I feel so strange. A misfortune is certainly hanging over us."

"You are a little goose," answered the eldest. "You are always frightened. Have you forgotten how many princes have come here in vain? Why, I need not have given the soldier a sleeping draught at all! The blockhead would never have awakened."

When they were all ready they looked at the soldier, but his eyes were shut and he did not stir. So they thought they would soon be quite safe. Then the eldest went up to one of the beds and knocked on it. It sank into the earth and they descended through the opening one after another, the eldest first.

The soldier, who had noticed everything, did not hesitate long, but threw on his cloak and went down behind the youngest. Halfway down he trod on her dress.

She was frightened and said, "What was that? Who is holding on to my dress?"

"Don't be so foolish. You must have caught it on a nail," said the eldest.

Then they went right down, and when they got quite underground they stood in a marvelously beautiful avenue of trees. All the leaves were silver, and glittered and shone.

The soldier thought, "I must take away some token with me." And as he broke off a twig, a sharp crack came from the tree.

The youngest cried out, "All is not well! Did you hear that sound?"

"Those are triumphal salutes because we have eluded our 'prince'!" said the eldest.

Next they came to an avenue where all the leaves were of gold, and at last into a third where they were of shining diamonds. From both these the soldier broke off a twig, and there was a crack each time which made the youngest princess start with terror. But the eldest maintained that the sounds were only triumphal salutes. They went faster and came to a great lake. Close to the bank lay twelve little boats and in every boat sat a handsome prince. They had expected the twelve princesses and each took one with him, but the soldier seated himself by the youngest.

Then said her prince, "I don't know why, but the boat

is much heavier today. I am obliged to row with all my strength to get it along."

"I wonder why it is," said the youngest, "unless perhaps it is the hot weather. It is strangely hot."

On the opposite side of the lake stood a splendid brightly lighted castle from which came the sound of the joyous music of trumpets and drums. They rowed across, and every prince danced with his love. And the soldier danced too, unseen. If one of the princesses held a cup of wine he drank out of it, so that it was empty when she lifted it to her lips. This frightened the youngest one, but the eldest always silenced her.

They danced till three next morning, when their shoes were danced into holes and they were obliged to stop. The princes took them back across the lake, and this time the soldier took his seat beside the eldest. On the bank they said farewell to their princes and promised to come again the next night.

When they got to the steps the soldier ran on ahead, lay down in bed, and when the twelve came lagging by, slowly and wearily, he began to snore again very loud, so that they said, "We are quite safe so far as he is concerned." Then they took off their beautiful dresses, put them away, placed the worn-out shoes under their beds, and lay down.

The next morning the soldier determined to say nothing, but to see the wonderful doings again. So he went with them the second and third nights. Everything was just the same as the first time, and they danced each time till their shoes were in holes. The third time the soldier took away a wine cup as a token.

When the appointed hour came for his answer, he took the three twigs and the cup with him and went before the

King. The twelve princesses stood behind the door listening to hear what he would say.

When the King put the question, "Where did my daughters dance their shoes to pieces in the night?" he answered, "With twelve princes in an underground castle." Then he produced the tokens.

The King sent for his daughters and asked them whether the soldier had spoken the truth. As they saw that they were betrayed and would gain nothing by lies, they were obliged to admit all.

Thereupon the King asked the soldier which one he would choose as his wife. He answered, "I am no longer young. Give me the eldest."

So the wedding was celebrated that very day, and the kingdom was promised to him on the King's death. But for every night which the underground princes had spent in dancing with the princesses, a day was added to their time of enchantment.

The Golden Bird

A LONG time ago there was a king who had a lovely pleasure garden around his palace, and in it stood a tree which bore golden apples. When the apples were nearly ripe they were counted, but the very next morning one was missing. This was reported to the King, and he ordered a watch to be set every night under the tree.

The King had three sons, and he sent the eldest into the garden at nightfall, but by midnight he was overcome with sleep, and in the morning another apple was missing.

On the following night the second son had to keep watch, but he fared no better. When the clock struck twelve, he too was fast asleep, and in the morning another apple was gone.

The turn to watch now came to the third son. He was quite ready, but the King had not much confidence in him and thought that he would accomplish even less than his brothers. At last, however, he gave his permission. So the youth lay down under the tree to watch, determined not to let sleep master him.

As the clock struck twelve, there was a rustling in the air, and by the light of the moon he saw a bird whose shining feathers were of pure gold. The bird settled on the tree and was just plucking an apple when the young Prince shot an arrow at it. The bird flew away, but the arrow hit its plumage and one of the golden feathers fell to the ground. The Prince picked it up, and in the morning took it to the King and told him all that he had seen in the night.

The King assembled his council, and everybody declared that a feather like that was worth more than the whole kingdom.

"If the feather is worth so much," said the King, "one will not satisfy me. I must and will have the whole bird."

The eldest son, relying on his cleverness, set out in search of the bird, thinking that he would find it soon. When he had gone some distance he saw a fox sitting by the edge of a wood. He raised his gun and aimed at it.

The fox cried out, "Do not shoot me, and I will give you some good advice. You are going to look for the Golden Bird. At nightfall you will come to a village where you will find two inns opposite each other. One of them will be brightly lighted and there will be noise and revelry going on in it. Be sure you do not choose that one, but go into the other, even if you don't like the looks of it so well."

"How can a stupid animal like that give me good advice?" thought the King's son, and he pulled the trigger. But he missed the fox, who turned tail and made off into the wood.

Thereupon the Prince continued his journey and at nightfall reached the village with the two inns. Singing and dancing were going on in the one, and the other looked poverty-stricken and decayed.

"I should be a fool," he said, "if I were to go to that miserable place when this good one is so near."

So he went into the noisy one and lived there in rioting and revelry, forgetting the bird, his father, and all his good counsels.

He raised his gun and aimed at it.

When some time had passed and the eldest son did not come back, the second started in quest of the Golden Bird. He met the fox, as the eldest son had done, and it gave him the same good advice, of which he took just as little heed.

He came to the two inns and saw his brother standing at the window of the one from which came the sounds of revelry. He could not withstand his brother's calling, so he went in and gave himself up to a life of pleasure.

Again some time passed and the King's youngest son wanted to go out to try his luck, but his father would not let him go.

"It is useless," he said. "He will be even less able to find the Golden Bird than his brothers. And when any ill luck overtakes him, he will not be able to help himself. He has no backbone."

But at last, because the son gave him no peace, the King let him go. The fox again sat at the edge of the wood, begged for its life, and gave its good advice. The Prince was good-natured and said, "Be calm, little fox, I will do thee no harm."

"You won't repent it," answered the fox. "And so that you may get along faster, come and mount on my tail."

No sooner had he seated himself than the fox began to run; and away they flew over stock and stone, at such a pace that his hair whistled in the wind.

When they reached the village, the Prince dismounted. And following the good advice of the fox, he went straight to the shabby inn without looking about him, and there he passed a peaceful night.

In the morning, when he went out into the fields, there sat the fox, who said, "I will now tell you what you must do next. Walk straight on till you come to a castle in front of which a whole regiment of soldiers is encamped. Don't be afraid of them—they will all be asleep and snoring. Walk through the midst of them straight into the castle, and walk through all the rooms. At last you will reach an apartment where the Golden Bird will be hanging in a common wooden cage. A golden cage stands near it for show, but beware! Whatever you do, you must not take the bird out of the wooden cage to put it into the other, or it will be the worse for you."

After these words the fox again stretched out his tail, the Prince took his seat on it, and away they flew over stock and stone, till his hair whistled in the wind.

When he arrived at the castle, he found everything just as the fox had said.

The Prince went to the room where the Golden Bird hung in the wooden cage. A golden cage was standing near by, and the three golden apples were scattered about the room. He thought it would be absurd to leave the beautiful bird in the common old cage, so he opened the door, caught it, and put it into the golden cage. But as he did it, the bird uttered a piercing shriek. The soldiers woke up, rushed in, and carried him away to prison. Next morning he was taken before a judge, and as he confessed all, he was sentenced to death. The King, however, said that he would spare his life on one condition: that he should bring him the Golden Horse which runs faster than the wind. In addition, he should have the Golden Bird as a reward.

So the Prince set off with many sighs. He was very sad, for where was he to find the Golden Horse? Then suddenly he saw his old friend the fox sitting on the road.

"Now you see!" said the fox. "All this has happened because you did not listen to me. All the same, keep up your spirits. I will protect you and tell you how to find the Golden Horse. You must keep straight along the road and you will come to a palace in the stable of which stands the Golden Horse. The grooms will be lying around the stable, but they will be fast asleep and snoring, and you can safely lead the horse through them. Only one thing you must beware of: put the old saddle of wood and leather upon it, and not the golden one hanging near, or you will rue it."

Then the fox stretched out his tail, the Prince took his seat, and away they flew over stock and stone, till his hair whistled in the wind.

Everything happened just as the fox had said. The Prince came to the stable where the Golden Horse stood. But when he was about to put the old saddle on its back, he thought, "Such a beautiful animal will be disgraced if I don't put the good saddle upon him, as he deserves." Hardly had the golden saddle touched the horse than he began neighing loudly. The grooms awoke, seized the Prince, and threw him into a dungeon.

The next morning he was taken before a judge and condemned to death, but the King promised to spare his life and give him the Golden Horse as well, if he could bring him the beautiful Princess out of the Golden Palace. With a heavy heart the Prince set out, but to his delight he soon met the faithful fox.

"I should leave you to your fate," said the fox, "but I will have pity on you and once more help you out of your trouble. Your road leads straight to the Golden Palace. You will reach it in the evening. And at night, when everything is quiet, the beautiful Princess will go to the bathroom to take a bath. As she goes along, spring forward and give her a kiss, and she will follow you. Lead her away with you. Only on no account allow her to bid her parents goodby, or it will go badly with you."

Again the fox stretched out his tail, the Prince seated himself upon it, and off they flew over stock and stone, till his hair whistled in the wind.

When he got to the Golden Palace, it was just as the fox had said. He waited till midnight, and when the whole palace was wrapped in sleep and the maiden went to take a bath, he sprang forward and gave her a kiss. She said she was quite willing to go with him, but she implored him to let her say good-by to her parents. At first he refused, but as she cried and fell at his feet, at last he gave her leave. Hardly had the maiden stepped up to her father's bed when he and everyone else in the palace woke up. The Prince was seized and thrown into prison.

Next morning the King said to him, "Your life is forfeited, and it can be spared only if you clear away from in front of my window the mountain which shuts out the view. It must be done in eight days, and if you accomplish the task in time, you shall have my daughter as a reward."

So the Prince began his labors, and he dug and shoveled without ceasing. On the seventh day, when he saw how little he had done, he became very sad and gave up all hope. In the evening, however, the fox appeared and said, "You do not deserve any help from me, but lie down and go to sleep. I will do the work." In the morning when he woke and looked out of the window, the mountain had disappeared.

Overjoyed, the Prince hurried to the King and told him that his condition was fulfilled, and whether he liked it or not he must keep his word and give him his daughter.

So the Prince and the King's daughter went away together, and before long the faithful fox joined them.

"You certainly have got the best thing of all," said he, "but the Golden Horse belongs to the maiden of the Golden Palace."

"How am I to get it?" asked the Prince.

"Oh, I will tell you that," answered the fox. "First take the beautiful maiden to the King who sent you to the Golden Palace. There will be great joy when you appear, and they will bring out the Golden Horse to you. Mount it at once and shake hands with everybody, but last of all with the beautiful maiden. And when you have taken her hand firmly, swing her up beside you and gallop away. No one will be able to catch you, for the horse goes faster than the wind."

All this was successfully done and the Prince carried off the beautiful maiden on the Golden Horse.

The fox was not far off and he said to the Prince, "Now I will help you to get the Golden Bird, too. When you approach the castle where the Golden Bird lives, let the maiden dismount and I will take care of her. Then ride with the Golden Horse into the courtyard of the castle. There will be great rejoicing when they see you, and they will bring out the Golden Bird to you. As soon as you have the cage in your hand, gallop back to us and take up the maiden again."

When these plans had succeeded, and the Prince was ready to ride on with all his treasures, the fox said to him, "Now you must reward me for my help."

"What do you want?" asked the Prince.

"When you reach that wood, shoot me dead and cut off my head and my paws."

"That would indeed be gratitude!" said the Prince. "I can't possibly promise to do such a thing."

The fox said, "If you won't do it I must leave you, but before I go I will give you one more piece of advice. Beware of two things: buy no gallows birds, and don't sit on the edge of a well." After saying this he ran off into the wood.

The Prince thought, "That is a strange animal. What whims he has! Who on earth would want to buy gallows birds? And the desire to sit on the edge of a well has never yet seized me."

He rode on with the beautiful maiden, and the road led him through the village where his two brothers had stayed behind. There was a great hubbub in the village, and when he asked what it was about he was told that two persons were going to be hanged. When he got nearer he saw that they were his brothers, who had wasted their possessions and done all sorts of evil deeds. He asked if they could not be set free.

"Yes, if you'll ransom them," answered the people. "But why will you throw your money away in buying off such wicked people?"

He did not stop to reflect, however, but paid the ransom for them. And when they were set free they all journeyed on together.

They came to the wood where they had first met the fox. It was deliciously cool there, though the sun was broiling outside. The two brothers said, "Let us sit down here by the well to rest a little and eat and drink." The Prince agreed, and during the conversation he forgot what he was about, and, never dreaming of any foul play, seated himself on the edge of the well. But his two brothers threw him backwards into it and went home to their father, taking with them the maiden, the horse, and the bird.

"Here we bring you not only the Golden Bird, but the Golden Horse and the maiden from the Golden Palace, as our booty."

Thereupon there was great rejoicing. But the horse would not eat, the bird would not sing, and the maiden sat and wept all day.

The youngest brother had not perished, however. Happily, the well was dry, and he fell upon soft moss without being harmed. Yet he could not get out.

Even in this great strait the faithful fox did not forsake him, but came leaping down and scolded him for not taking his advice. "I can't leave you to your fate, though. I must help you to get back to the light of day." He told him to take tight hold of his tail, and then he dragged him up. "You are not out of every danger even now," said the fox. "Your brothers were not sure of your death, so they have set watchers all over the wood to kill you if they see you."

A poor old man was sitting by the roadside and the Prince exchanged clothes with him, and by this means he succeeded in reaching the King's court.

Nobody recognized him; but the bird began to sing, the horse began to eat, and the beautiful maiden left off crying.

In astonishment the King asked, "What does all this mean?"

The maiden answered, "I do not know, but I was very sad and now I am gay. It seems to me that my true bridegroom must have come."

She told the King all that had happened, although the two brothers had threatened her with death if she betrayed anything. The King ordered every person in the palace to be brought before him. Among them came the Prince disguised as an old man in all his rags, but the maiden knew him at once and fell on his neck. The wicked brothers were seized and put to death, but the Prince was married to the beautiful maiden and proclaimed heir to the King.

But what became of the poor fox? Long afterwards, when the Prince went out into the fields one day, he met the fox, who said, "You have everything that you can desire, but there is no end to my misery. It still lies in your power to release me." And again he implored the Prince to shoot him dead and to cut off his head and his paws.

At last the Prince consented to do as he was asked. And no sooner was it done than the fox was changed into a man. He was no other than the brother of the beautiful Princess, at last set free from the evil spell which so long had lain upon him.

There was nothing now wanting to their happiness for the rest of their lives.

The Three Spinning Fairies

THERE was once upon a time a girl who was lazy and hated work, and nothing her mother could say would induce her to spin. At last the mother grew angry and, losing all patience with her, gave her a beating. At this the girl began to cry so loudly that the Queen, who was driving past at the time, heard her cries and stopped.

She went into the house and asked the mother why she was beating her daughter like that. "Her screams," she said, "can be heard outside in the street."

The mother was ashamed to confess the truth about her daughter's laziness, and so she answered, "I cannot get her to leave off spinning! She is forever at her wheel, and I am too poor to keep on buying her fresh flax."

"Is that all?" said the Queen. "There is nothing I like so much as the sound of spinning. I am never happier than when I can hear the humming of the wheels. Let me have your daughter and I will take her home with me to the castle. I have plenty of flax and she can go on spinning there to her heart's content."

The mother was heartily pleased at this proposal and so the Queen left, taking the girl with her. On their arrival at the castle, she took her upstairs and showed her three rooms filled from floor to ceiling with the most beautiful flax.

"Spin me all this," said the Queen, "and when it is finished, you shall have my eldest son for your husband. Your poverty is a matter of no consequence to me, for I consider that your unremitting industry is an all-sufficient dowry."

The girl dared not say anything but she inwardly trembled with fear, for she knew that she could never spin all that flax even if she were to sit at her spinning wheel from morning till night for three hundred years. As soon as she was alone she began to weep, and she sat like that for three days without doing a stroke of work.

When the Queen came again on the third day, she was surprised to find that the flax had not been touched. The girl excused herself by saying that she had felt so lonely and homesick that she had not been able to begin her spinning. The Queen was satisfied with this excuse, but as she was leaving she said, "Tomorrow, mind, I shall expect you to begin your work."

Alone once more, the girl was at her wit's end to know what to do, and in her distress of mind went and looked out of the window. There she saw three funny-looking women coming towards her. One had a big flat foot, another had a large underlip that hung over her chin, and the third had a very broad thumb. They stood still under the window and, looking up, they asked the girl what was the matter. She told them her trouble, and they offered to help her.

"If you will invite us to your wedding," they said, "and will not be ashamed of us, but will introduce us as your cousins and let us sit at your table, we will soon spin all that flax for you."

"That I will gladly promise," said the girl, "if you will but come in and begin working for me at once."

So she let in the three women, and what queer little figures they looked! She cleared a space for them in the first room, and they all sat down and began spinning. The first drew out the thread and turned the wheel, and the second moistened the thread. The third twisted it, striking with her fingers on the table; and every time she did this a beautiful skein of the finest spun yarn fell on the ground.

Whenever the Queen came, the girl hid the three women and then showed her skein upon skein of spun yarn, till the Queen did not know how to find words enough to praise her.

As soon as the first room was empty, the spinners went on to the second, and finally they went on to the third, which like the others was very quickly cleared of the flax. Then the three women took leave of the girl, saying to her as they parted, "Do not forget the promise you made us, for it will bring you good fortune."

When the Queen was shown the empty rooms and the great piles of yarn, she began at once to make preparations for the wedding. The bridegroom was delighted to think he should have such a clever and industrious wife, and showered his praises upon her.

"I have three cousins," said the girl, "and they have shown me such great kindness in the past that I should not like to forget them, now that I am happy and prosperous. Will you give me permission to invite them to the wedding, and allow them to sit at our table?" The Queen and the bridegroom both willingly consented to this request.

The wedding feast was beginning when in walked the three women, attired in the most wonderful dresses. The bride greeted them and said, "Welcome, dear cousins," but the bridegroom could not help exclaiming, "How came you to have such ugly friends?"

Then he went up to the first and asked her what had given her such a broad foot.

"Turning the wheel," she answered.

Then he went to the second and asked what had caused her to have such a large lip.

"Moistening the thread," she answered.

Then he went to the third and asked what made her thumb so broad.

"Twisting the thread," she answered.

"Then," cried the Prince, horrified at these answers, "my beautiful wife shall never go near a spinning wheel again as long as she lives." And so henceforth she was rid of the hated task of spinning.

The Three Children of Fortune

ONCE upon a time a father sent for his three sons and gave to the eldest a cock, to the second a scythe, and to the third a cat.

"I am now old," said he. "My end is approaching, and I would fain provide for you before I die. Money I have none, and what I give you seems of but little worth. It rests with yourselves alone to turn my gifts to good account. Only seek out a land where what you have is still unknown, and your fortune is made."

After the death of the father, the eldest set out with his cock. But wherever he went, in every town he saw from afar off a cock sitting upon the church steeple and turning round with the wind. In the villages he always heard plenty of them crowing, and his bird was therefore nothing new. So there did not seem much chance of his making his fortune.

At length it happened that he came to an island where the people who lived there had never heard of a cock, and knew not even how to reckon the time. They knew, indeed, if it were morning or evening, but at night, if they lay awake, they had no means of knowing how time went.

"Behold," said he to them, "what a noble animal this is! How like a knight he is! He carries a bright red crest upon his head and spurs upon his heels. He crows three times every night at stated hours, and at the third time the sun is about to rise. But this is not all. Sometimes he screams in broad daylight, and then you must take warning, for the weather is surely about to change."

This pleased the natives mightily. They kept awake one whole night and heard to their great joy how gloriously the cock called the hour at two, four, and six o'clock. Then they asked him whether the bird was for sale, and how much he would sell it for.

"About as much gold as an ass can carry," said he.

"A very fair price for such an animal," cried they with one voice, and they agreed to give him what he asked.

When he returned home with his wealth, his brothers wondered greatly, and the second said, "I will now set forth likewise and see if I can turn my scythe to as good an account."

There did not seem, however, much likelihood of this, for go where he would, he was met by peasants who had as good scythes on their shoulders as he had. But at last, as good luck would have it, he came to an island where the people had never heard of a scythe. There, as soon as the corn was ripe they went into the fields and pulled it up, but this was very hard work and a great deal of it was lost. The man then set to work with his scythe, and he mowed down their whole crop so quickly that the people stood staring openmouthed with wonder. They were willing to give him what he asked for such a marvelous thing, but he only took a horse laden with as much gold as it could carry.

Now the third brother had a great longing to go and see what he could make of his cat. So he set out, and at first it happened to him as it had to the others. So long as he

the wonderful animal.

The people besought their king to buy
the wonderful animal.

kept upon the mainland he met with no success. There were plenty of cats everywhere—indeed too many—so that most of the young ones were drowned in the water as soon as they came into the world.

At last he passed over to an island, where, as it chanced most luckily for him, nobody had ever seen a cat. And they were overrun with mice to such a degree that the little wretches danced upon the tables and chairs, whether the master of the house was at home or not. The people complained loudly of this grievance. The King knew not how to rid himself of them in his palace. In every corner mice were squeaking, and they gnawed everything that their teeth could lay hold of.

Here was a fine field for puss! She soon began her chase, and had cleared two rooms in the twinkling of an eye. The people then besought their king to buy the wonderful animal at any price, for the good of the public. The King willingly gave what was asked—a mule laden with gold and jewels. And thus the third brother returned home with a richer prize than each of the others.

Meantime the cat feasted away upon the mice in the royal palace and devoured so many that they were no longer in any great numbers. At length, quite spent and tired with her work, she became extremely thirsty. So she stood still, drew up her head, and cried, "Miau, Miau!"

The King gathered together all his subjects when they heard this strange cry, and many ran shrieking in a great fright out of the palace. But the King held a council to decide what was best to be done. It was at length decided to send a herald to the cat, to warn her to leave the castle forthwith, or else force would be used to remove her.

"For," said the counselors, "we would far more willingly

put up with the mice—since we are used to that evil—than get rid of them at the risk of our lives."

A page accordingly went and asked the cat whether she was willing to quit the castle. But puss, whose thirst became every moment more and more pressing, answered nothing but "Miau! Miau!"

The page interpreted this to mean "No! No!" and therefore carried this answer to the King.

"Well," said the counselors, "then we must try what force will do."

So the guns were planted and the palace was fired upon from all sides. When the fire reached the room where the cat was, she sprang out of the window and ran away, but the besiegers did not see her and went on firing until the whole palace was burnt to the ground.

King Thrushbeard

THERE was once a king who had a daughter. She was more beautiful than words can tell, but at the same time so proud and haughty that no man who came to woo her was good enough for her. She turned away one after another, and even mocked them.

One day her father ordered a great feast to be given and invited to it all the marriageable young men from far and near. They were all placed in a row, according to their rank and position. First came kings, then princes, then dukes, earls, and barons. The Princess was led through the ranks, but she had some fault to find with all of them.

One was too stout. "That barrel!" she said. The next was too tall. "Long and lean is no good!" The third was too short. "Short and stout, can't turn about!" The fourth was too white. "Pale as death!" The fifth was too red. "Turkey cock!" The sixth was not straight. "Oven-dried!"

So there was something against each of them. But she made specially merry over one good king who stood quite at the head of the row and whose chin was a little hooked.

"Why," she cried, "he has a chin like the beak of a thrush." After that he was always called "King Thrush-beard."

When the old King saw that his daughter only made fun of them, and that she despised all the suitors who were assembled, he was very angry. He swore that the first beggar who came to the door should be her husband. A few days afterwards, a wandering musician began to sing at the window, hoping to receive charity.

When the King heard him he said, "Let him be brought in."

The musician came in, dressed in dirty rags, and sang to the King and his daughter. And when he had finished, he begged alms of them.

The King said, "Your song has pleased me so much that I will give you my daughter for wife."

The Princess was horror-stricken, but the King said, "I have sworn an oath to give you to the first beggar who came, and I will keep my word."

No entreaties were of any avail. A parson was brought and she had to marry the musician there and then.

When the ceremony was completed, the King said, "Now that you are a beggar woman, you can't stay in my castle any longer. You must go away with your husband." The beggar took her by the hand and led her away, and she was obliged to go with him on foot.

When they came to a big wood she asked:

> "Ah, who is the lord of this forest so fine?"
> "It belongs to King Thrushbeard. It might
>   have been thine,
> If his queen you had been."
> "Ah, sad must I sing!
> I would I'd accepted the love of the King."

Then they reached a great meadow and she asked again:

> "Ah, who is the lord of these meadows so fine?"
> "They belong to King Thrushbeard, and would
>   have been thine,

If his queen you had been."
"Ah, sad must I sing!
I would I'd accepted the hand of the King."

They passed through a large town and again she asked:

"Ah, who is the lord of this city so fine?"
"It belongs to King Thrushbeard, and it might
*   have been thine,*
If his queen you had been."
"Ah, sad must I sing!
I would I'd accepted the heart of the King."

"It doesn't please me at all," said the musician, "that you are always wishing for another husband. Am I not good enough for you?"

At last they came to a miserable hovel and she said:

"Ah heavens! what's this house, so mean and small?
This wretched little hut's no house at all."

The musician answered, "This is my house and yours, where we are to live together." The door was so low that she had to stoop to get in.

"Where are the servants?" asked the Princess.

"Servants indeed!" answered the beggar. "Whatever you want done, you must do for yourself. Light the fire and put the kettle on to make my supper. I am very tired."

But the Princess knew nothing about lighting fires or cooking, and to get it done at all the beggar had to do it himself. When they had finished their humble fare they went to bed, but in the morning the man made her get up very early to do the housework. They lived like this for a few days, till they had eaten up all their store of food.

Then the man said, "Wife, this won't do any longer.

You can't live here without working. You shall make baskets." So he went out and cut some willow twigs and brought them home. She began to weave them, but the hard twigs bruised her tender hands.

"I see that won't do," said the beggar. "You had better spin. Perhaps you can manage that." So she sat down and tried to spin, but the harsh yarn soon cut her delicate fingers and made them bleed.

"Now you see," said the man, "what a good-for-nothing you are. I have made a bad bargain in you. But I will try to start a trade in earthenware. You must sit in the market and offer your goods for sale."

"Alas!" she thought, "if any of the people from my father's kingdom come and see me sitting in the market place offering goods for sale, they will scoff at me." But it was no good. She had to obey unless she meant to die of hunger.

All went well the first time. The people willingly bought her wares because she was so handsome, and they paid what she asked them—nay, some even gave her the money and left her the pots as well.

They lived on the gains as long as they lasted and then the man laid in a new stock of wares. She took her seat in a corner of the market, set out her crockery about her, and began to cry her wares. Suddenly a drunken Hussar came galloping up and rode right in among the pots, breaking them into thousands of bits. She began to cry, and was so frightened that she did not know what to do.

"Oh, what will become of me?" she cried. "What will my husband say to me?" She ran home and told him her misfortune.

"Who would ever think of sitting at the corner of the

market with crockery?" he said. "Stop that crying. I see you are no manner of use for any decent kind of work. I have been to our King's palace and asked if they do not want a kitchen wench, and they have promised to try you. You will get your victuals free, at any rate."

So the Princess became a kitchen wench and had to wait upon the cook and do all the dirty work. She tied a pot into each of her pockets and in them took home her share of the scraps and leavings, and upon these they lived.

It so happened that the marriage of the eldest Princess took place just then, and the poor girl went upstairs and stood behind the curtains to peep at all the splendor. When the rooms were lighted up and she saw the guests streaming in, one more beautiful than the other, and the scene grew more and more brilliant, she thought with a heavy heart of her sad fate. She cursed the pride and haughtiness which had been the cause of her humiliation, and of her being brought to such depths.

Every now and then the servants would throw her bits from the savory dishes they were carrying away from the feast, and these she put into her pots to take home.

All at once the King's son came in. He was dressed in silk and velvet and he had a golden chain round his neck. When he saw the beautiful girl standing at the door, he seized her by the hand and wanted to dance with her. But she shrank and refused, because she saw that it was King Thrushbeard, who had been one of the suitors for her hand, and whom she had most scornfully driven away.

Her resistance was no use and he dragged her into the hall. The string by which her pockets were suspended broke. Down fell the pots, and the soup and savory morsels were spilt all over the floor.

When the guests saw it they burst into shouts of mocking laughter. She was so ashamed that she would gladly have sunk into the earth. She rushed to the door and tried to escape, but on the stairs a man stopped her and brought her back. When she looked at him she saw that it was no other than King Thrushbeard again.

He spoke kindly to her and said, "Do not be afraid. I and the beggar man who lived in the poor little hovel with you are one and the same. For love of you I disguised myself. And I was also the Hussar who rode among your pots. All this I did to bend your proud spirit and to punish you for the haughtiness with which you mocked me."

She wept bitterly and said, "I was very wicked and I am not worthy to be your wife."

But he said, "Be happy! Those evil days are over. Now we will celebrate our true wedding."

The waiting-women came and put rich clothing upon her, and her father with all his court came and wished her joy on her marriage with King Thrushbeard.

Then in truth her happiness began. I wish we had been there to see it, you and I.

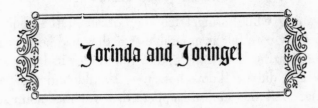

Jorinda and Joringel

THERE was once an old castle in the middle of a vast thick wood. In it there lived an old woman quite alone, and she was a witch. By day she made herself into a cat or a screech owl, but regularly at night she became a human being again. In this way she was able to decoy wild beasts and birds, which she would kill and boil or roast. If any man came within a hundred paces of the castle, he was forced to stand still; he could not move from the place till she gave the word of release. But if an innocent maiden came within the circle, she changed her into a bird and shut her up in a cage, which she carried into a room in the castle. She must have had seven thousand cages of this kind, all containing pretty birds.

Now there was once a maiden called Jorinda who was more beautiful than all other maidens. She had promised to marry a very handsome youth named Joringel, and it was in the days of their courtship, when they took the greatest joy in being alone together, that one day they wandered out into the forest. "Take care," said Joringel. "Do not let us go too near the castle."

It was a lovely evening. The sunshine glanced between the tree trunks of the dark greenwood, while the turtle-doves sang plaintively in the old beech trees. Yet Jorinda sat down in the sunshine and could not help weeping and bewailing, while Joringel, too, soon became just as mournful. They both felt as miserable as if they had been going to die. Gazing around them, they found they had lost their way and did not know how they should find the path home. Half the sun still appeared above the mountain; half had sunk below.

Joringel peered into the bushes and saw the old walls of the castle quite close to them. He was terror-stricken and became pale as death. Jorinda was singing:

> "My birdie with its ring so red
>   Sings sorrow, sorrow, sorrow;
> My love will mourn when I am dead,
>   Tomorrow, morrow, mor—jug, jug."

Joringel looked toward her, but she had changed into a nightingale who sang "Jug, jug." A screech owl with glowing eyes flew three times around her, and cried three times "Shu hu-hu." Joringel could not stir. He stood like a stone without being able to speak or cry, or to move hand or foot.

The sun had now set. The owl flew into a bush, out of which appeared almost at the same moment a crooked old woman, skinny and yellow. She had big red eyes and a crooked nose whose tip reached her chin. She mumbled something, caught the nightingale, and carried it away in her hand. Joringel could not say a word nor move from the spot, and the nightingale was gone.

At last the old woman came back, and said in a droning voice, "Greeting to thee, Zachiel! When the moon shines on the cage, unloose the captive, Zachiel."

Then Joringel was free. He fell on his knees before the witch and implored her to give back his Jorinda, but she said he should never have her again, and went away. He pleaded, he wept, he lamented, but all in vain. "Alas! what is to become of me?" said Joringel.

At last he went away, and arrived at a strange village where he spent a long time as a shepherd. He often wandered around about the castle, but did not go too near it. At last he dreamt one night that he found a blood-red flower in the middle of which was a beautiful large pearl. He plucked the flower and took it to the castle. Whatever he touched with it was made free of enchantment. He dreamt also that by this means he had found his Jorinda again.

In the morning when he awoke, he began to search over hill and dale in the hope of finding a flower like this. He searched till the ninth day, when he found the flower early in the morning. In the middle was a big dewdrop, as big as the finest pearl. This flower he carried day and night till he reached the castle. He was not held fast as before when he came within the hundred paces of the castle, but walked straight up to the door.

Joringel was filled with joy. He touched the door with the flower, and it flew open. He went in through the court and listened for the sound of birds. He went on and found the hall, where the witch was feeding the birds in the seven thousand cages. When she saw Joringel she was angry, very angry. She scolded him and spat poison and gall at him. He paid no attention to her but turned away and searched among the bird cages. Yes, there were many hundred nightingales, but how was he to find his Jorinda?

While he was looking about in this way he noticed that the old woman was secretly removing a cage with a bird inside, and was making for the door. He sprang swiftly towards her, touched the cage and the witch with the flower, and then she no longer had power to exercise her spells. Jorinda stood there, as beautiful as before, and threw her arms around Joringel's neck.

After that he changed all the other birds back into maidens again and went home with Jorinda, and they lived long and happily together.

The Wren and the Bear

ONCE upon a time a bear and a wolf were taking a walk in a wood. It was summer, and the bear heard a bird singing most beautifully. He said, "Brother Wolf, what kind of bird is that singing so beautifully?"

"That is the King of the birds, and we must bow down to it." But really it was a wren.

"If that is so," said the bear, "I should like to see his royal palace. Come, you must take me to it."

"That's not so easy," said the wolf. "You must wait till the Queen comes."

Soon afterwards the Queen made her appearance, bringing food in her beak, and the King came with her to feed their little ones. The bear would have liked to go in at once, but the wolf held him by the sleeve and said, "No, you must wait till the King and Queen fly away again."

So they marked the opening of the nest and trudged on. But the bear had no rest till he could see the royal palace, and before long he went back. The King and the Queen had gone out again. He peeped in and saw five or six young ones lying in the nest.

"Is that the royal palace?" cried the bear. "What a miserable place! And do you mean to say that you are royal children? You must be changelings."

When the young wrens heard this, they were furious.

They shrieked, "No, indeed we're not. Our parents are honest people. We must have this out with you."

The bear and the wolf were very much frightened. They turned around and ran home to their dens.

But the young wrens continued to shriek and scream aloud. And when their parents came back with more food, they said, "We won't touch so much as the leg of a fly, even if we starve, till you tell us whether we are really your lawful children or not. The bear has been here calling us names."

Then said the old King, "Only be quiet, and this shall be seen to."

Thereupon he and his wife flew off to the bear in his den and called in to him, "Old Bruin, why have you been calling our children names? It will turn out badly for you, and it will lead to a bloody war between us."

So war was declared, and all the four-footed animals were called together—the ox, the ass, the cow, the stag, the deer, and every other creature on the earth.

But the wren called together every creature which flew in the air. He called not only the birds both large and small, but also the gnats, the hornets, the bees, and the flies.

When the time came for the war to begin, the wrens sent out scouts to discover where the commanding generals of the enemy were to be found. The gnats were the most cunning of all. They swarmed into the wood where the enemy were assembled, and at last they hid themselves under a leaf of the tree where the orders were being given.

The bear called the fox up to him and said, "You are the slyest of all the animals, Reynard. You shall be our general and lead us."

"Very good," said the fox, "but what shall we have for a signal?" But nobody could think of anything. Then said the fox, "I have a fine, long, bushy tail which looks almost like a red feather brush. When I hold my tail erect, things are going well and you must march forward at once. But if it droops, you must all run away as hard as ever you can."

When the gnats heard this they flew straight home and told the wrens every detail.

When the day broke, all the four-footed animals came rushing to the spot where the battle was to take place. They came with such a tramping that the earth shook. The wren and his army also came swarming through the air. They fluttered and buzzed enough to terrify one.

And then they made for one another.

The wren sent the hornet down with orders to seat herself under the tail of the fox and to sting him with all her might.

When the fox felt the first sting, he quivered and raised one leg in the air. But he bore it bravely and kept his tail erect. At the second sting he was forced to let it droop for a moment. But the third time he could bear it no longer: he screamed, and down went his tail between his legs. When the animals saw this they thought all was lost, and off they ran helter-skelter as fast as they could go, each to his own den.

So the birds won the battle.

When it was over, the King and the Queen flew home to their children and cried, "Children, be happy! Eat and drink to your hearts' content. We have won the battle."

But the young wrens said, "We won't eat till the bear comes here to make an apology, and says that we are really and truly your lawful children."

The wren flew to the bear's den and cried, "Old Bruin, you will have to come and apologize to my children for calling them names, or else you will have all your ribs broken."

So in great terror the bear crept to the nest and apologized, and at last the young wrens were satisfied. They ate and drank and made merry till far into the night.

The Twelve Brothers

ONCE upon a time there lived a king and a queen very peacefully together. They had twelve children, all boys.

Now the King said to the Queen one day, "If our thirteenth child should be a girl the twelve boys shall die, so that her riches may be the greater and the kingdom fall to her alone."

Then he caused twelve coffins to be made, and they were filled with shavings and a little pillow laid in each, and they were brought and put into a locked-up room. And the King gave the key to the Queen and told her to say nothing about it to anyone.

But the mother sat the whole day sorrowing, so that her youngest son, who never left her and to whom she had given the Biblical name Benjamin, said to her, "Dear mother, why are you so sad?"

"Dearest child," answered she, "I dare not tell you."

But he let her have no peace until she went and unlocked the room and showed him the twelve coffins with the shavings and the little pillows.

Then she said, "My dear Benjamin, your father has caused these coffins to be made for you and your eleven brothers, and if I bring a little girl into the world you are all to be put to death together and buried therein."

She wept as she spoke, and her little son comforted her and said, "Weep not, dear mother. We will save ourselves and go far away."

Then she answered, "Yes, go with your eleven brothers out into the world, and let one of you always sit on the top of the highest tree that can be found and keep watch upon the tower of this castle. If a little son is born I will put out a white flag, and then you may safely venture back again. But if it is a little daughter I will put out a red flag, and then flee away as fast as you can, and the dear God watch over you. Every night will I arise and pray for you—in

winter that you may have a fire to warm yourselves by, and in summer that you may not languish in the heat."

After that, when she had given her sons her blessing, they went away out into the wood. One after another kept watch, sitting on the highest oak tree and looking towards the tower. When eleven days had passed and Benjamin's turn came, he saw a flag put out. It was not white, but blood red, to warn them that they were to die.

When the brothers learned this they were angry and said, "Shall we suffer death because of a girl? We swear revenge. Wherever we find a girl we will shed her blood."

Then they went deeper into the wood, and in the middle where it was darkest they found a little enchanted house standing empty.

Then they said, "Here will we dwell. And you, Benjamin, the youngest and weakest, shall stay at home and keep house. We others will go abroad and find food."

Then they went into the wood and caught hares, wild does, birds and pigeons, and whatever else is good to eat, and brought them to Benjamin for him to prepare and cook to satisfy their hunger. So they lived together in the little house for ten years and the time did not seem long.

By this time the Queen's little daughter was growing up. She had a kind heart and a beautiful face, and a golden star on her forehead.

Once when there was a great wash she saw among the clothes twelve shirts, and she asked her mother, "Whose are these? They are too small to be my father's."

Then the mother answered with a sore heart, "Dear child, they belong to your twelve brothers."

The little girl said, "Where are my twelve brothers? I have never heard of them."

And her mother answered, "God only knows where they are wandering about in the world." Then she led the little girl to the secret room, and unlocked it and showed her the twelve coffins with the shavings and little pillows.

"These coffins," said she, "were intended for your twelve brothers, but they went away far from home when you were born." And she related how everything had come to pass.

Then said the little girl, "Dear mother, do not weep. I will go and seek my brothers."

So she took the twelve shirts and went far and wide in the great forest. The day sped on, and in the evening she came to the enchanted house.

She went in and found a youth, who asked, "Whence do you come, and what do you want?" He marveled at her beauty, her royal garments, and the star on her forehead.

Then she answered, "I am a king's daughter and I seek my twelve brothers. I will go everywhere under the blue sky until I find them." And she showed him the twelve shirts which belonged to them.

Then Benjamin saw that it must be his sister and said, "I am Benjamin, your youngest brother."

And she began weeping for joy, and Benjamin also, and they kissed and cheered each other with great love.

After a while he said, "Dear sister, there is still a hindrance. We have sworn that any maiden whom we meet must die, as it was because of a maiden that we had to leave our kingdom."

Then she said, "I will willingly die, if by doing so I may benefit my twelve brothers."

"No," answered he, "you shall not die. Sit down under this tub until the eleven brothers get home and we come to an agreement about it." She did so, and as night came on they returned from hunting, and supper was ready.

And as they were sitting at table and eating, they asked, "What news?"

And Benjamin said, "Don't you know any?"

"No," answered they.

So he said, "You have been in the wood and I have stayed at home, and yet I know more than you."

"Tell us!" cried they.

He answered, "Promise me that the first maiden we see shall not be put to death."

"Yes, we promise," cried they all. "She shall have mercy. Tell us now."

Then he said, "Our sister is here." He lifted up the tub and the King's daughter came forth in her royal garments with her golden star on her forehead, and she seemed so beautiful, delicate, and sweet that they all rejoiced. And they fell on her neck and kissed her and loved her with all their hearts.

After this she remained in the house with Benjamin and helped him with the work. The others went forth into the woods to catch wild animals, does, birds, and pigeons for food for them all, and their sister and Benjamin took care that all was made ready for them. She fetched the wood for cooking, and the vegetables, and watched the pots on the fire, so that supper was always ready when the others came in. She also kept great order in the house, and the beds were always beautifully white and clean, and the brothers were contented and lived in unity.

One day the two got ready a fine feast, and when they were all assembled they sat down and ate and drank, and were full of joy. Now there was a little garden belonging to the enchanted house, in which grew twelve lilies. The maiden, thinking to please her brothers, went out to gather the twelve flowers, meaning to give one to each as they sat at meat. But as she broke off the flowers, the brothers were changed into twelve ravens and flew over the wood far away, and the house with the garden also disappeared. So the poor maiden stood alone in the wildwood.

And as she was looking around her she saw an old woman standing by her who said, "My child, what hast thou done? Why couldst thou not leave the twelve flowers standing? They were thy twelve brothers, who are now changed to ravens forever."

The maiden said, weeping, "Is there no means of setting them free?"

"No," said the old woman. "There is in the whole world no way but one, and that is difficult. Thou canst not release them but by being dumb for seven years. Thou must neither speak nor laugh, and wert thou to speak one single word, and it wanted but one hour of the seven years, all would be in vain. Thy brothers would perish because of that one word."

Then the maiden said in her heart, "I am quite sure that I can set my brothers free." And she went and sought a tall tree, climbed up, and sat there spinning, and never spoke or laughed.

Now it happened that a king who was hunting in the wood had with him a large greyhound, who ran to the tree where the maiden was, sprang up at it, and barked loudly. Up came the King and saw the beautiful Princess with the golden star on her forehead, and he was so charmed with her beauty that he prayed her to become his wife. She gave no answer, only a little nod of her head. Then he himself climbed the tree and brought her down, set her on his horse, and took her home. The wedding was held with great splendor and rejoicing, but the bride neither spoke nor laughed.

After they had lived pleasantly together for a few years, the King's mother, who was a wicked woman, began to slander the young Queen, and said to the King, "She is only a low beggar maid that you have taken to yourself. Who knows what mean tricks she is playing? Even if she is really dumb and cannot speak she might at least laugh. Not to laugh is the sign of a bad conscience."

At first the King would believe nothing of it, but the old woman talked so long and suggested so many bad things that he at last let himself be persuaded and condemned the Queen to death.

Now a great fire was kindled in the courtyard, and she was to be burned in it. And the King stood above at the window and watched it all with weeping eyes, for he had held her very dear. And when she was already bound fast to the stake and the fire was licking her garments with red tongues, the last moment of the seven years ended.

Then a rushing sound was heard in the air and twelve ravens came flying and sank downwards. And as they touched the earth they became her twelve lost brothers. They rushed through the fire and quenched the flames and set their dear sister free, kissing and consoling her.

And now that her mouth was opened and she might venture to speak, she told the King the reason of her dumbness and why she had never laughed. The King rejoiced when he heard of her innocence, and they all lived together in happiness until their death. But the wicked mother-in-law was very unhappy, and died miserably.

The Mouse, the Bird, and the Sausage

ONCE upon a time a mouse and a bird and a sausage lived and kept house together in perfect peace among themselves, and in great prosperity. It was the bird's business to fly to the forest every day and bring back wood. The mouse had to draw the water, make the fire, and set the table. And the sausage had to do the cooking. Nobody is content in this world: much will have more. One day the bird met another bird on the way, and told him of his excellent condition in life. But the other bird called him a poor simpleton to do so much work while the two others led easy lives at home.

When the mouse had made up her fire and drawn water, she went to rest in her little room until it was time to lay the cloth. The sausage stayed by the saucepans, looked to it that the victuals were well cooked, and just before dinnertime he stirred the broth or the stew three or four times well around himself, so as to enrich and season and flavor it. Then the bird used to come home and lay down his load, and they sat down to table; and after a good meal they would go to bed and sleep their fill till the next morning. It really was a most satisfactory life.

But the bird came to the resolution next day never again to fetch wood. He had, he said, been their slave long enough. Now they must change about and make a new arrangement. So in spite of all the mouse and the sausage could say, the bird was determined to have his own way. So they drew lots to settle it, and as the lot fell, the sausage was to fetch wood, the mouse was to cook, and the bird was to draw water and make the fire.

Now see what happened. The sausage went away after wood, the bird made up the fire, and the mouse put on the pot, and they waited until the sausage should come home, bringing the wood for the next day. But the sausage was absent so long that they thought something must have happened to him, and the bird went part of the way to see if he could see anything of him. Not far off he met a dog on the road, who, looking upon the sausage as lawful prey, had picked him up and made an end of him. The bird then lodged a complaint against the dog as an open and flagrant robber, but it was all no good, as the dog declared that he had found forged letters upon the sausage, so that he deserved to lose his life.

The bird then very sadly took up the wood and carried it home himself, and related to the mouse all he had seen and heard. They were both very troubled, but determined to look on the bright side of things and still to remain together. And so the bird laid the cloth, and the mouse prepared the food and finally got into the pot, as the sausage used to do, to stir and flavor the broth, but then she had to part with fur and skin and finally with life!

And when the bird came to dish up the dinner, there was no cook to be seen. And he turned over the heap of wood, and looked and looked, but the cook never appeared again. By accident the wood caught fire, and the bird hastened to fetch water to put it out, but he let fall the bucket in the well and himself after it, and as he could not get out again he was obliged to be drowned.

The Wolf and the Seven Goats

THERE was once an old nanny goat who had seven kids, and she was just as fond of them as a mother is of her children. One day she was going into the woods to fetch some food for them, so she called them all up to her and said, "My dear children, I am going out into the woods. Beware of the wolf! If once he gets into the house, he will eat you up—skin, and hair, and all. The rascal often disguises himself, but you will know him by his rough voice and his black feet."

The kids said, "Oh, we will be very careful, dear mother. You may be quite happy about us."

Bleating tenderly, the old goat went off to her work. Before long, someone knocked at the door and cried, "Open the door, dear children! Your mother has come back and brought something for each of you."

But the kids knew quite well by the voice that it was the wolf. "We won't open the door," they cried. "You are not our mother. She has a soft, gentle voice, but yours is rough, and we are quite sure that you are the wolf."

So he went away to a shop and bought a lump of chalk, which he ate, and it made his voice quite soft.

He went back, knocked at the door again, and cried, "Open the door, dear children. Your mother has come back and brought something for each of you."

But the wolf had put one of his paws on the window sill, where the kids saw it, and they cried, "We won't open the door. Our mother has not got a black foot as you have. You are the wolf."

Then the wolf ran to a baker and said, "I have bruised my foot. Please put some dough on it." And when the baker had put some dough on his foot, he ran to the miller and said, "Strew some flour on my foot."

The miller thought, "The old wolf is going to take somebody in," and refused.

But the wolf said, "If you don't do it, I will eat you up." So the miller was frightened, and whitened his paws. People are like that, you know.

Now the wretch went for the third time to the door, and knocked and said, "Open the door, children. Your dear mother has come home and has brought something for each of you out of the wood."

The kids cried, "Show us your feet first, so that we may be sure you are our mother."

He put his paws on the window sill, and when they saw that they were white they believed all he said and opened the door.

Alas, it was the wolf who walked in. They were terrified and tried to hide themselves. One ran under the table, the second jumped into bed, the third into the oven. The fourth ran into the kitchen, the fifth got into the cupboard, the sixth into the washtub, and the seventh hid in the tall clockcase. But the wolf found them all but one and made short work of them. He swallowed one after the other, except the youngest one in the clockcase, whom he did not find. When he had satisfied his appetite, he took himself off and lay down in a meadow, where he soon fell asleep.

Not long afterwards the old nanny goat came back from the woods. Oh, what a terrible sight met her eyes! The house door was wide open. Tables, chairs, and benches were overturned. The washing bowl was smashed to atoms, the covers and pillows torn from the bed. She searched all over the house for her children, but nowhere were they to be found. She called them by name, one by one, but no one answered.

At last when she came to the youngest, a tiny voice cried, "I am here, dear mother, hidden in the clockcase."

She brought him out and he told her that the wolf had come and eaten all the others. You may imagine how she wept over her children.

At last in her grief she went out, and the youngest kid ran by her side. When they went into the meadow, there lay the wolf under a tree, making the branches shake with his snores. They examined him from every side, and they could plainly see movements within his distended body.

"Ah, heavens!" thought the goat, "is it possible that my

poor children, whom he has eaten, should be still alive?"

She sent the kid running to the house to fetch scissors, needles, and thread. Then she cut a hole in the monster's side, and hardly had she begun when a kid popped out its head. And as soon as the hole was big enough, all six jumped out, one after the other—all alive and without having suffered the least injury, for in his greed the monster had swallowed them whole. You may imagine the mother's joy! She hugged them and skipped about like a tailor on his wedding day.

At last she said, "Go and fetch some big stones, children, and we will fill the brute's body while he sleeps."

Then the seven kids brought a lot of stones as fast as they could carry them, and stuffed the wolf with them till he could hold no more. The old mother quickly sewed him up, without his having noticed anything or even moved.

At last when the wolf had had his sleep out he got up, and as the stones made him feel very thirsty he wanted to go to a spring to drink. But as soon as he moved, the stones began to roll about and rattle inside him. Then he cried:

> *"What's the rumbling and tumbling*
> *That sets my stomach grumbling?*
> *I thought 'twas six kids, flesh and bones,*
> *Now I find it's nought but rolling stones."*

When he reached the spring and stooped over the water to drink, the heavy stones dragged him down, and he was drowned miserably.

When the seven kids saw what had happened, they came running up and cried aloud, "The wolf is dead! The wolf is dead!" And they and their mother capered and danced around the spring in their joy.

Thumbling the Dwarf and Thumbling the Giant

AN honest husbandman once upon a time had a son born to him who was no bigger than my thumb, and who for many years did not grow one hair's breadth taller.

One day as the father was going to plow in his field, the little fellow said, "Father, let me go too."

"No," said his father, "stay where you are. You can do no good out of doors, and if you go I am afraid I may lose you."

Then little Thumbling began to cry, and his father, to quiet him, at last said he might go. So he put him in his pocket, and when he was in the field pulled him out and set him upon the top of a newly made furrow, that he might be able to look about him. While he was sitting there, a great giant came striding over the hill.

"Do you see that huge man?" said the father. "If you don't take care he will run away with you."

Now he only said this to frighten the little boy and keep him from straying away. But the giant had long legs, and with two or three strides he really came close to the furrow and picked up Master Thumbling to look at him as he would at a beetle or a cockchafer. Then he let him run about his broad hand, and taking a liking to the little chap went off with him. The father stood by all the time, but could not say a word for fright. He thought his child was really lost, and that he should never see him again. But the giant took care of him at his house in the woods, and laid him in his bosom, and fed him with the same food that he lived upon himself. So Thumbling, instead of being a little dwarf, became like the giant—tall, and stout, and strong.

At the end of two years, when the old giant took him into the woods to try him and said, "Pull up that birch tree for yourself to walk with," the lad was so strong that he tore it up by the root. The giant thought he would make him a still stronger man than this, so after taking care of him two years more he took him into the wood to try his strength again. This time he took hold of one of the thickest oaks and pulled it up as if it were mere sport to him. Then the old giant said, "Well done, my man, you will do now." So he carried him back to the field where he first found him.

His father happened just then to be plowing his field again, as he was when he lost his son. The young giant went up to him and said, "Look here, father, see who I am! Don't you know your own son?"

But the husbandman was frightened and cried out, "No, no. You are not my son. Begone about your business."

"Indeed, I am your son. Let me plow a little. I can plow as well as you."

"No, go your way," said the father. But as he was afraid of the tall man, he at last let go the plow and sat down on the ground beside it. Then the youth laid hold of the plowshare, and though he only pushed with one hand he drove it deep into the earth.

The plowman cried out, "If you must plow, pray do not push so hard. You are doing more harm than good."

But his son took off the horses and said, "Father, go home and tell my mother to get ready a good dinner. I'll go round the field meanwhile." So he went on driving the plow without any horses till he had done two mornings' work by himself. Then he harrowed it. And when all was over, he took up plow, harrow, horses, and all, and carried them home like a bundle of straw.

When he reached the house he sat himself down on the bench, saying, "Now, mother, is dinner ready?"

"Yes," said she, for she dared not deny him anything. So she brought two large dishes full, enough to have lasted herself and her husband eight days. However, he soon ate it all up and said that was but a taste.

"I see very well, father, that I shall not get enough to eat at your house, so if you give me an iron walking stick, so strong that I cannot break it against my knees, I will go away again."

The husbandman very gladly put his two horses to the cart and drove them to the forge, and brought back a bar of iron as long and as thick as his horses could draw. But the lad laid it against his knee, and snapped it like a beanstalk.

"I see, father," said he, "you can get no stick that will do for me, so I'll go and try my luck by myself."

Then away he went and turned blacksmith, and traveled till he came to a village where lived a miserly smith who earned a good deal of money, but kept all he got to himself and gave nothing away to anybody. The first thing he did was to step into the smithy and ask if the smith did not want a journeyman.

"Aye," said the cunning fellow, as he looked at him and thought what a stout chap he was and how lustily he would work and earn his bread. "What wages do you ask?"

He took up plow, harrow, horses and all, and carried them home like a bundle of straw.

"I want no pay," said he. "But every fortnight when the other workmen are paid, you shall let me give you two strokes over the shoulders, just to amuse myself." The old smith thought to himself he could bear this very well and reckoned on saving a great deal of money, so the bargain was soon struck.

The next morning the new workman was about to begin to work but at the first stroke that he hit, when his master brought him the iron red-hot, he shivered it to pieces and the anvil sank so deep into the earth that he could not get it out again. This made the old fellow very angry.

"Holla!" cried he, "I can't have you for a workman. You are too clumsy. We must put an end to our bargain."

"Very well," said the other, "but you must pay for what I have done. So let me give you only one little stroke and then the bargain is all over." So saying, he gave him a thump that tossed him over a load of hay that stood near. Then he took the thickest bar of iron in the forge for a walking stick and went on his way.

When he had journeyed some way, he came to a farmhouse and asked the farmer if he wanted a foreman.

The farmer said, "Yes," and the same wages were agreed for as before with the blacksmith.

The next morning the workmen were all to go into the wood, but the giant was found to be fast asleep in his bed when the rest were all up and ready to start.

"Come get up," said one of them to him. "It is high time to be stirring. You must go with us."

"Go your way," muttered he, sulkily. "I shall do my work and get home long before you." So he lay in bed two hours longer and at last got up and cooked and ate his breakfast, and then at his leisure harnessed his horses to go to the wood.

Just before the wood was a hollow way through which all must pass, so he drove the cart on first and built up behind him such a mound of faggots and briars that no horse could pass. This done, he drove on. And as he was going into the wood he met the others coming out on their road home.

"Drive away," said he, "I shall be home before you still." However, after going only a very little way into the wood he tore up one of the largest timber trees, put it into his cart, and turned about homewards. When he came to the pile of faggots he found all the others standing there, not being able to pass by. "So," said he, "you see if you had stayed with me, you would have been home just as soon and might have slept an hour or two longer."

Then he took his tree on one shoulder and his cart on the other, and pushed through as easily as though he were laden with feathers. And when he reached the yard he showed the tree to the farmer, and asked if it was not a fine walking stick.

"Wife," said the farmer, "this man is worth something. If he does sleep longer, he works better than the rest."

Time rolled on, and he had worked for the farmer his whole year. So when his fellow laborers were paid, he said he also had a right to take his wages. But great dread came upon the farmer at the thought of the blows he was to have, so he begged him to give up the old bargain and take his whole farm and stock instead.

"Not I," said he. "I will be no farmer. I am foreman, and so I mean to stay and to be paid as we agreed."

Finding that he could do nothing with him, the farmer

begged one fortnight's respite, and called together all his friends to ask their advice in the matter. They bethought themselves for a long time and at last agreed that the shortest way was to kill this troublesome foreman. The next thing was to settle how it was to be done, and it was agreed that he should be ordered to carry into the yard some great millstones and put them on the edge of the well. Then he should be sent down to clean it out, and when he was at the bottom the millstones should be pushed down upon his head.

Everything went right, and when the foreman was safe in the well the stones were rolled in. As they struck the bottom, the water splashed to the very top. Of course they thought his head must be crushed to pieces, but he only cried out, "Drive away the chickens from the well! They are scratching about in the sand above, and they throw it into my eyes so that I cannot see."

When his job was done, up he sprang from the well, saying, "Look here! See what a fine neckcloth I have!" And he pointed to one of the millstones that had fallen over his head and hung about his neck.

The farmer was again overcome with fear and begged another fortnight to think of it. So his friends were called together again and at last gave this advice: that the foreman should be sent and made to grind corn by night at the haunted mill, whence no man had ever yet come out alive in the morning. That very evening he was told to carry eight bushels of corn to the mill and grind them in the night. Away he went to the loft, put two bushels into his right pocket, two into his left, and four into a long sack slung over his shoulders, and then set off to the mill. The miller told him he might grind there in the daytime but not by night, for the mill was bewitched and whoever went in at night had been found dead in the morning.

"Never mind, miller, I shall come out safe," said he. "Only make haste and get out of the way, and look out for me in the morning."

So he went into the mill and put the corn into the hopper, and about twelve o'clock sat down on the bench in the miller's room. After a little time the door all at once opened of itself and in came a large table. On the table stood wine and meat and many good things besides. All seemed placed there by themselves—at any rate there was no one to be seen. The chairs next moved themselves around it but still neither guests nor servants came, till all at once he saw fingers handling the knives and forks and putting food on the plates, but still nothing else was to be seen. Now our friend felt somewhat hungry as he looked at the dishes, so he sat himself down at the table and ate whatever he liked best.

"A little wine would be well after this cheer," said he. "But the good folks of this house seem to take but little of it." Just as he spoke, however, a flagon of the best moved on, and our guest filled a bumper, smacked his lips, and drank "Health and long life to all the company, and success to our next merry meeting!"

When they had had enough and the plates and dishes, bottle, and glasses, were all empty, of a sudden something unseen blew out the lights. "Never mind!" thought he. "One wants no candle to go to sleep by." But now that it was pitch dark he felt a huge blow fall upon his head. "Foul play!" cried he. "If I get such another box on the ear I shall just give it back again." And this he really did when the next blow came. Thus the game went on all night and he never let fear get the better of him, but kept dealing his blows, till at daybreak all was still.

"Well, miller," said he in the morning, "I have had some little slaps on the face but I've given as good, I warrant you. And meantime I have eaten just as much as I liked." The miller was glad to find the charm was broken and would have given him a great deal of money. "I want no money. I have quite enough," said he, as he took his meal on his back and went home to his master to claim his wages.

But the farmer was in great trouble, knowing there was now no help for him. He paced the room up and down, while the drops of sweat ran down his forehead. Then he opened the window for a little fresh air, and before he was aware his foreman gave him the first blow, and such a blow that off he flew over the hills and far away. The next blow sent his wife after him, and for aught I know they may not have reached the ground yet. But without waiting to find out the young giant took up his iron walking stick and walked off.

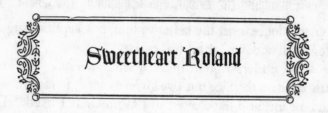

Sweetheart Roland

ONCE upon a time there was a woman who was a real witch, and she had two daughters. One was ugly and wicked, but she loved her because she was her own daughter. The other was good and lovely, but she hated her for she was only her foster child.

Now this foster child had a beautiful apron which the other daughter envied, and she said to her mother that she must and would have it.

"Just wait quietly, my child," said her mother. "You shall have it. Tonight when she is asleep I will go and chop off your sister's head. Only take care to lie on the farther side of the bed, against the wall, and push her well to this side."

Now all this would certainly have come to pass if the poor girl had not been standing in a corner and heard what they said. She was not even allowed to go near the door all day, and when bedtime came the witch's daughter got into bed first, so as to lie at the farther side. But when she was asleep the other gently changed places with her and put herself next the wall.

In the middle of the night the witch crept in, holding an ax in her right hand, while with her left she felt to find if anyone was there. Then she seized the ax with both hands, struck—and struck off her own child's head.

When she had gone away, the maiden got up and went to the house of her sweetheart, Roland, and knocked at his door. When he came out, she said to him, "Listen, dear Roland, we must quickly fly. My foster mother tried to kill me, but she hit her own child instead. When day comes and she sees what she has done, we shall be lost."

"But," said Roland, "you must first get her magic wand, or we shall not be able to escape if she comes after us."

The maiden fetched the magic wand, and then she took her foster sister's head and dropped three drops of blood from it—one by the bed, one in the kitchen, and one on the stairs. After that, she hurried away with her sweetheart, Roland.

When the old witch got up in the morning she called her daughter in order to give her the apron, but she did not come. Then she called, "Where art thou?"

"Here on the stairs," answered one drop of blood.

The witch went to the stairs but saw nothing. So she called again, "Where art thou?"

"Here in the kitchen warming myself," answered the second drop of blood.

The witch went into the kitchen but found nothing. Then she called again, "Where art thou?"

"Here in bed, sleeping," answered the third drop of blood.

So she went into the bedroom, and there she found her own child, whose head she had chopped off herself.

The witch flew into a violent passion and sprang out of the window. As she could see for many miles around, she discovered the maiden hurrying away with Roland.

"That won't do you any good!" she cried. "However far you may go, you won't escape me."

She put on her seven-league boots, and before long she overtook them. When the maiden saw her coming, with the magic wand she changed her sweetheart into a lake, and changed herself into a duck swimming in it. The witch stood on the shore and threw bread crumbs into the water, and did everything she could think of to entice the duck ashore. But it was all to no purpose, and she was obliged to go back at night without having accomplished her object.

When she had gone away, the maiden and Roland resumed their own shapes, and they walked the whole night till break of day.

Then the maiden changed herself into a beautiful rose in the middle of a briar hedge, and Roland into a fiddler. Before long the witch came striding along and said to the fiddler, "Good fiddler, may I pick this beautiful rose?"

"By all means," he said, "and I will play to you."

As she crept into the hedge in great haste to pick the flower (for she knew well who the flower was), Roland began to play. And she had to dance, whether she liked or not, for it was a magic dance. The faster he played, the higher she had to jump, and the thorns tore her clothes to ribbons and scratched her till she bled. He would not stop a moment, so she had to dance till she fell down dead.

When the maiden was freed from the spell, Roland said, "Now I will go to my father and order the wedding."

"Then I will stay here in the meantime," said the maiden. "And so that no one shall recognize me while I am waiting, I will change myself into a common stone."

So Roland went away and the maiden stayed in the field as a stone, waiting his return.

But when Roland reached home he fell into the snares of another woman, who made him forget all about his love. The poor maiden waited a long, long time, but when he did not come back, she became very sad and changed herself into a flower. "Somebody at least will tread upon me," she thought.

Now it so happened that a shepherd was watching his sheep in the field, and he saw the flower and picked it because he thought it was so pretty. He took it home and put it carefully away in a chest. From that time forward a wonderful change took place in the shepherd's hut. When he got up in the morning, all the work was done. The tables and benches were dusted, the fire was lighted, and the water was carried in. At dinnertime, when he came home, the table was laid and a well-cooked meal stood ready. He could not imagine how it all came about, for he never saw a creature in his house, and nobody could be hidden in the tiny hut. He was much pleased at being so well served, but at last he got rather frightened and went to a wise woman to ask her advice.

The wise woman said, "There is magic behind it. You

must look carefully about the room early in the morning, and whatever you see, throw a white cloth over it and the spell will be broken."

The shepherd did what she told him, and next morning just as the day broke he saw his chest open and the flower come out. So he sprang up quickly and threw a white cloth over it. Immediately the spell was broken and a lovely maiden stood before him, who confessed that she had been the flower and that it was she who had done all the work of his hut. She also told him her story, and he was so pleased with her that he asked her to marry him.

But she answered, "No, I want my sweetheart Roland. Though he has forsaken me I will always be true to him."

She promised not to go away, however, but to go on with the housekeeping for the present.

Now the time came for Roland's marriage to be celebrated. According to old custom, a proclamation was made that every maiden in the land should present herself to sing at the marriage in honor of the bridal pair.

When the faithful maiden heard this she grew very sad, so sad that she thought her heart would break. She had no wish to go to the wedding but the others came and fetched her. But each time as her turn came to sing, she slipped behind the others till she was the only one left and she could not help herself.

As soon as she began to sing and her voice reached Roland's ears, he sprang up and cried, "That is the true bride and I will have no other."

Everything that he had forgotten came back, and his heart was filled with joy. So the faithful maiden was married to her sweetheart, Roland. All her grief and pain were over, and only happiness lay before her.

The Goose Girl

THERE was once an old queen whose husband had been dead for many years, and she had a very beautiful daughter. When she grew up she was betrothed to a prince in a distant country. When the time came for the maiden to be sent into this distant country to be married, the old Queen packed up quantities of clothes and jewels, gold and silver, cups and ornaments, and in fact everything suitable to a royal outfit, for she loved her daughter very dearly.

She also sent a waiting-woman to travel with her and to put her hand into that of the bridegroom. They each had a horse. The Princess' horse was called Falada, and it could speak.

When the hour of departure came, the old Queen went to her bedroom and with a sharp little knife cut her finger and made it bleed. Then she held a piece of white cambric under it and let three drops of blood fall on it. This cambric she gave to her daughter and said, "Dear child, take good care of this. It will stand you in good stead on the journey."

They then bade each other a sorrowful farewell. The Princess hid the piece of cambric in her bosom, mounted her horse, and set out to her bridegroom's country.

When they had ridden for a time, the Princess became

very thirsty and said to the waiting-woman, "Get down and fetch me some water in my cup from the stream. I must have something to drink."

"If you are thirsty," said the waiting-woman, "dismount yourself, lie down by the water, and drink. I don't choose to be your servant."

So in her great thirst the Princess dismounted and stooped down to the stream and drank, since she could not have her golden cup. The poor Princess said, "Alas!" And the drops of blood answered, "If your mother knew this it would break her heart."

The royal bride was humble, so she said nothing, but mounted her horse again. Then they rode several miles further, but the day was warm, the sun was scorching, and the Princess was soon very thirsty again.

When they reached a river she called out again to her waiting-woman, "Get down and give me some water in my golden cup." She had forgotten all about the rude words which had been said to her.

But the waiting-woman answered more haughtily than ever, "If you want to drink, get the water for yourself. I won't be your servant."

Being very thirsty, the Princess dismounted and knelt by the flowing water. She cried, "Ah me!" And the drops of blood answered, "If your mother knew this it would break her heart."

While she stooped over the water to drink, the piece of cambric with the drops of blood on it fell out of her bosom and floated away on the stream, but she never noticed this in her great fear. The waiting-woman, however, had seen it and rejoiced at getting more power over the bride, who by losing the drops of blood had become weak and powerless.

Now when she was about to mount her horse Falada again, the waiting-woman said, "By rights, Falada belongs to me. This jade will do for you!"

The poor little Princess was obliged to give way. Then the waiting-woman in a harsh voice ordered her to take off her royal robes, and to put on her own mean garments. Finally she forced her to swear before heaven that she would not tell a creature at the court what had taken place. Had she not taken the oath she would have been killed on the spot. But Falada saw all this and marked it.

The waiting-woman mounted Falada and put the real bride on her poor jade, and they continued their journey.

There was great rejoicing when they arrived at the castle. The Prince hurried towards them and lifted the waiting-woman from her horse, thinking that she was his bride. She was led upstairs, but the real Princess had to stay below.

The old King looked out of the window and saw the delicate, pretty little creature standing in the courtyard. So he went to the bridal apartment and asked the bride about her companion who was left standing in the courtyard, and wished to know who she was.

"I picked her up on the way and brought her with me for company. Give the girl something to do to keep her from idling."

But the old King had no work for her and could not think of anything. At last he said, "I have a little lad who looks after the geese. She may help him."

The boy was called little Conrad, and the real bride was sent with him to look after the geese.

Soon afterwards, the false bride said to the Prince, "Dear husband, I pray you do me a favor."

He answered, "That will I gladly do."

"Well then, let the knacker be called to cut off the head of the horse I rode. It angered me on the way."

Really she was afraid that the horse would speak and tell of her treatment of the Princess. So it was settled, and the faithful Falada had to die.

When this came to the ear of the real Princess, she promised the knacker a piece of gold if he would do her a slight service. There was a great dark gateway to the town, through which she had to pass every morning and evening. Would he nail up Falada's head in this gateway so that she might see him as she passed?

The knacker promised to do as she wished, and when the horse's head was cut off he hung it up in the dark gateway. In the early morning, when she and Conrad went through the gateway, she said in passing:

> *"Alas! dear Falada, there thou hangest."*

And the head answered:

> *"Alas! Queen's daughter, there thou gangest.*
> *If thy mother knew thy fate,*
> *Her heart would break with grief so great."*

Then they passed on out of the town and right into the fields with the geese. When they reached the meadow, the Princess sat down on the grass and let down her hair. It shone like pure gold, and when little Conrad saw it he

was so delighted that he wanted to pluck some out. But
she said:

> "Blow, blow, little breeze,
> And Conrad's hat seize.
> Let him join in the chase
> While away it is whirled,
> Till my tresses are curled
> And I rest in my place."

Then a strong wind sprang up which blew away Conrad's hat right over the fields, and he had to run after it.
When he came back, she had finished combing her hair
and it was all put up again, so he could not get a single
hair. This made him very sulky and he would not say another word to her. And they tended the geese till evening,
when they went home.

Next morning when they passed under the gateway,
the Princess said:

> "Alas! dear Falada, there thou hangest."

Falada answered:

> "Alas! Queen's daughter, there thou gangest.
> If thy mother knew thy fate,
> Her heart would break with grief so great."

Again when they reached the meadows, the Princess
undid her hair and began combing it. Conrad ran to pluck
some out, but she said quickly:

> "Blow, blow, little breeze,
> And Conrad's hat seize.
> Let him join in the chase

While away it is whirled,
Till my tresses are curled
And I rest in my place."

The wind again sprang up and blew Conrad's hat far away over the fields, and he had to run after it. When he came back, the hair was all put up again and he could not pull out a single hair. And they tended the geese till the evening.

When they got home Conrad went to the old King and said, "I won't tend the geese with that maiden again."

"Why not?" asked the King.

"Oh, she vexes me every day."

The old King then ordered him to tell what she did to vex him.

Conrad said, "In the morning when we pass under the dark gateway with the geese, she talks to a horse's head which is hung up on the wall. She says:

Alas! Falada, there thou hangest.

And the head answers:

Alas! Queen's daughter, there thou gangest.
If thy mother knew thy fate,
Her heart would break with grief so great."

Then Conrad went on to tell the King all that had happened in the meadow, and how he had to run after his hat in the wind.

The old King ordered Conrad to go out next day as usual. Then he placed himself behind the dark gateway and heard the Princess speaking to Falada's head. He also followed her into the field and hid himself behind a bush. And with his own eyes he saw the Goose Girl and the lad come driving the geese into the field. Then after a time he saw the girl let down her hair, which glittered in the sun. Directly after this, she said:

> *"Blow, blow, little breeze,*
> *And Conrad's hat seize.*
> *Let him join in the chase*
> *While away it is whirled,*
> *Till my tresses are curled*
> *And I rest in my place."*

Then came a puff of wind which carried off Conrad's hat, and he had to run after it. While he was away, the maiden combed and did up her hair, and all this the old King observed. Thereupon he went away unnoticed, and in the evening when the Goose Girl came home, he called her aside and asked why she did all these things.

"I may not tell you that, nor may I tell any human creature, for I have sworn it under the open sky. If I had not done so, I should have lost my life."

He pressed her sorely and gave her no peace, but he could get nothing out of her. Then he said, "If you won't tell me, then tell your sorrows to the iron stove there." And he went away.

She crept up to the stove and, beginning to weep and lament, unburdened her heart to it and said, "Here I am, forsaken by all the world, and yet I am a princess. A false waiting-woman brought me to such a pass that I had to take off my royal robes. Then she took my place with my bridegroom, while I have to do mean service as a goose girl. If my mother knew it, it would break her heart."

The old King stood outside by the pipes of the stove and heard all that she said. Then he came back and told her to go away from the stove. He caused royal robes to be put upon her, and her beauty was a marvel. The old King called his son and told him that he had a false bride —she was only a waiting-woman, but the true bride was here, the so-called Goose Girl.

The young Prince was charmed with her youth and beauty. A great banquet was prepared to which all the courtiers and good friends were bidden. The bridegroom sat at the head of the table with the Princess on one side and the waiting-woman at the other, but she was dazzled and did not recognize the Princess in her brilliant apparel.

When they had eaten and drunk and were all very merry, the old King put a riddle to the waiting-woman. "What does a person deserve who deceives his master?" Then he told the whole story and ended by asking, "What doom does he deserve?"

The false bride answered, "No better than this: he must be put stark naked into a barrel stuck with nails, and be dragged along by two white horses from street to street till he is dead."

"That is your own doom!" said the King, "and the judgment shall be carried out."

When the sentence was fulfilled, the young Prince married his true bride, and they ruled their kingdom together in peace and happiness.

The Cat and Mouse
in Partnership

 A CAT, having made acquaintance with a mouse, professed such great love and friendship for her that the mouse at last agreed that they should live and keep house together.

"We must make provision for the winter," said the cat, "or we shall suffer hunger. And you, little mouse, must not stir out, or you will be caught in a trap."

So they took counsel together and bought a little pot of fat. Then they could not tell where to put it for safety, but after long consideration the cat said there could not be a better place than the church, for nobody would steal there. And they decided to put it under the altar and not touch it until they were really in want. So the little pot was placed in safety. But before long the cat was seized with a great desire to taste it.

"Listen to me, little mouse," said he. "I have been asked by my cousin to stand godfather to a little son she has brought into the world. He is white with brown spots, and they want to have the christening today. So let me go to it, and you stay at home and keep house."

"Oh yes, certainly," answered the mouse. "Pray go, by all means. And when you are feasting on all the good things, think of me. I should so like a drop of the sweet red wine."

But there was not a word of truth in all this. The cat had no cousin and had not been asked to stand godfather. He went to the church, straight up to the little pot, and licked the fat off the top. Then he took a walk over the roofs of the town, saw his acquaintances, stretched himself in the sun, and licked his whiskers as often as he thought of the little pot of fat. And then when it was evening he went home.

"Here you are at last," said the mouse. "I expect you have had a merry time."

"Oh, pretty well," answered the cat.

"And what name did you give the child?" asked the mouse.

"Top-off," answered the cat dryly.

"Top-off!" cried the mouse. "That is a singular and wonderful name. Is it common in your family?"

"What does it matter?" said the cat. "It's not any worse than Crumb-picker, like your godchild."

A little time after this the cat was again seized with a longing for the pot of fat.

"Again I must ask you," said he to the mouse, "to do me a favor and keep house alone for a day. I have been asked a second time to stand godfather, and as the little one has a white ring round its neck, I cannot well refuse."

So the kind little mouse consented, and the cat crept along by the town wall until he reached the church, where he went straight to the little pot of fat and ate half of it.

"Nothing tastes so well as what one keeps to oneself," said he, feeling quite content with his day's work. When he reached home, the mouse asked what name had been given to the child.

"Half-gone," answered the cat.

"Half-gone!" cried the mouse. "I never heard such a name in my life. I'll bet it's not to be found in the calendar."

Soon after that the cat's mouth began to water again for the fat.

"Good things always come in threes," said he to the mouse. "Again I have been asked to stand godfather. The little one is quite black with white feet, and not any white hair on its body. Such a thing does not happen every day, so you will let me go, won't you?"

"Top-off, Half-gone," murmured the mouse. "They are such curious names, I cannot but wonder at them."

"That's because you are always sitting at home," said the cat, "in your little gray frock and hairy tail, never seeing the world, and fancying all sorts of things."

So the little mouse cleaned up the house and set it all in order. Meanwhile the greedy cat went and made an end of the little pot of fat.

"Now all is finished one's mind will be easy," said he, and came home in the evening quite sleek and comfortable. The mouse asked at once what name had been given to the third child.

"It won't please you any better than the others," answered the cat. "It is called All-gone."

"All-gone!" cried the mouse. "What an unheard-of name! I never met with anything like it. All-gone! Whatever can it mean?" And shaking her head, she curled herself round and went to sleep. After that the cat was not again asked to stand godfather.

When the winter had come and there was nothing more to be had out of doors, the mouse began to think of their store.

"Come, cat," said she, "we will fetch our pot of fat. How good it will taste, to be sure!"

"Of course it will," said the cat. "Just as good as if you stuck your tongue out of the window."

So they set out, and when they reached the place they found the pot, but it was standing empty.

"Oh, now I know what it all meant," cried the mouse. "Now I see what sort of partner you have been! Instead of standing godfather you have eaten it all up. First Top-off! Then Half-gone! Then—"

"Hold your tongue!" screamed the cat. "Another word, and I eat you too!"

And the poor little mouse, having "All-gone" on her tongue, out it came, and the cat leaped upon her and made an end of her. And that is the way of the world.

The White Snake

A LONG time ago there lived a king whose wisdom was celebrated far and wide. Nothing was unknown to him, and the news of the most secret transactions seemed to reach him through the air.

Now he had one very odd habit. Every day at dinner, when the courtiers had withdrawn and he was quite alone, a trusted servant had to bring in another dish. It was always covered. Even the servant did not know what it contained, nor anyone else, for the King never uncovered it till he was alone. This had gone on for a long time, when one day the servant who carried the dish was overcome by his curiosity and took the dish to his own room.

When he had carefully locked the door, he took the cover off the dish and saw a white snake in it. At the sight of it, he could not resist tasting it, so he cut a piece off and put it into his mouth. Hardly had he tasted it, however, when he heard a wonderful whispering of delicate voices.

He went to the window and listened, and he noticed that the whispers came from the sparrows outside. They were chattering away and telling each other all kinds of things that they had heard in the woods and fields. Eating the snake had given him the power of understanding the language of birds and animals.

Now it happened on this day that the Queen lost her most precious ring, and suspicion fell upon this trusted servant who went about everywhere. The King sent for him, and threatened that if it was not found by the next day, he would be sent to prison. In vain he protested his innocence; but he was not believed.

In his grief and anxiety he went down into the court-yard and wondered how he should get out of his difficulty. A number of ducks were lying peaceably together by a stream, stroking down their feathers with their bills, while they chattered gaily. The servant stood still to listen to them. They were telling each other of their morning's walks and experiences.

Then one of them said somewhat fretfully, "I have something lying heavy on my stomach. In my haste I swallowed the Queen's ring this morning."

The servant quickly seized it by the neck, carried it off into the kitchen, and said to the cook, "Here's a fine fat duck. You had better kill it at once."

"Yes, indeed," said the cook, weighing it in her hand. "It has spared no pains in stuffing itself. It should have been roasted long ago." So she killed it and cut it open, and there, sure enough, was the Queen's ring.

The servant now had no difficulty in proving his innocence. The King, to make up for his injustice, gave the servant leave to ask any favor he liked, and promised him the highest post about the court which he might desire. The servant, however, declined everything but a horse and some money to travel with, as he wanted to wander about for a while to see the world.

His request being granted he set off on his travels, and one day came to a pond where he saw three fishes caught among the reeds, gasping for breath. Although it is said that fishes are dumb, he understood their complaint at perishing thus miserably. As he had a compassionate heart, he got off his horse and put the three captives back into the water. They wriggled in their joy, stretched up their heads above the water, and cried, "We will remember that you saved us and will reward you for it."

He rode on again, and after a time he seemed to hear a voice in the sand at his feet. He listened, and heard an ant king complain, "I wish these human beings and their animals would keep out of our way. A clumsy horse has just put his hoof down upon a number of my people in the most heartless way."

He turned his horse into a side path, and the ant king cried, "We will remember and reward you."

The road now ran through a forest, and he saw a pair of ravens standing by their nest throwing out their young.

"Away with you, you gallows birds," they were saying. "We can't feed you any longer. You are old enough to look after yourselves."

The poor little nestlings lay on the ground, fluttering

and flapping their wings and crying: "We poor helpless children must feed ourselves, and we can't even fly! We shall die of hunger. There is nothing else for it."

The good youth dismounted, killed his horse with his sword, and left the carcass as food for the young ravens. They hopped up to it and cried, "We will remember and reward you."

Now he had to depend upon his own legs, and after going a long way he came to a large town. There was much noise and bustle in the streets, where a man on horseback was making a proclamation.

"The King's daughter seeks a husband, but anyone who wishes to sue for her hand must accomplish a hard task. And if he does not bring it to a successful issue, he will forfeit his life." Many had already attempted the task, but they had risked their lives in vain.

When the youth saw the Princess, he was so dazzled by her beauty that he forgot all danger, at once sought an audience of the King, and announced himself as a suitor.

He was immediately led out to the seashore, and a golden ring was thrown into the water before his eyes. Then the King ordered him to fetch it out from the depths of the sea, adding, "If you come to land without it, you will be thrown back every time till you perish in the waves."

Everyone pitied the handsome youth, but they had to go and leave him standing solitary on the seashore.

He was pondering over what he should do when all at once he saw three fishes swimming towards him. They were no others than the very ones whose lives he had saved. The middle one carried a mussel shell in its mouth, which it laid on the sand at the feet of the youth. When he picked it up and opened it, there lay the ring.

Full of joy, he took it to the King, expecting that he would give him the promised reward. The proud Princess, however, when she heard that he was not her equal, despised him and demanded that he should perform yet another task. So she went into the garden herself, and strewed ten sacks of millet seeds among the grass.

"He must pick up every one of the seeds before the sun rises tomorrow morning," said she. "Not even a grain must be missing."

The youth sat miserably in the garden, wondering how it could possibly be done. But as he could not think of a plan, he remained sadly waiting for the dawn which would bring death to him.

But when the first sunbeams fell on the garden, he saw the ten sacks full to the top, and not a grain was missing. The ant king had come in the night with thousands and thousands of his ants, and the grateful creatures had picked up the millet and filled the sacks.

The Princess came into the garden herself, and saw with amazement that the youth had completed the task.

But still she could not control her proud heart, and she said, "Even if he has accomplished these two tasks, he shall not become my husband till he brings me an apple from the tree of life."

The youth had no idea where to find the tree of life. He started off, however, meaning to walk as far as his legs would carry him, but he had no hope of finding it.

When he had traveled through three kingdoms, he was passing one night through a great forest, and he lay down under a tree to sleep. He heard a rustling among the branches, and a golden apple fell into his hand.

At the same time three ravens flew down and perched

on his knee, and said, "We are the young ravens you saved from death. When we grew big and heard that you were looking for the golden apple, we flew across the sea to the end of the world, where the tree of life stands, and brought you the apple."

The youth, delighted, started on his homeward journey and took the golden apple to the beautiful Princess, who had now no further excuse to offer.

They divided the apple of life and ate it together, and then her heart was filled with love for him, and they lived happily to a great age.

The Frog Prince

IN the old times, when it was still of some use to wish for the thing one wanted, there lived a king whose daughters were all handsome, but the youngest was so beautiful that the sun himself, who has seen so much, wondered at her beauty each time he shone over her. Near the royal castle there was a great dark wood, and in the wood under an old linden tree was a well. When the day was hot, the King's daughter used to go forth into the wood and sit by the brink of the cool well. And if the time seemed long, she would take out a golden ball and throw it up and catch it again, and this was her favorite pastime.

Now it happened one day that the golden ball, instead of falling back into the maiden's little hand which had sent it aloft, dropped to the ground near the edge of the well and rolled in. The King's daughter followed it with her eyes as it sank, but the well was deep—so deep that the bottom could not be seen. Then she began to weep, and she wept and wept as if she could never be comforted.

And in the midst of her weeping she heard a voice saying to her, "What ails you, King's daughter? Your tears would melt a heart of stone."

And when she looked to see where the voice came from, there was nothing but a frog stretching his thick ugly head out of the water.

"Oh, is it you, old waddler?" said she. "I weep because my golden ball has fallen into the well."

"Never mind. Do not weep," said the frog. "I can help you. But what will you give me if I fetch up your ball?"

"Whatever you like, dear frog," said she. "Any of my clothes, my pearls and jewels, or even the golden crown that I wear."

"Your clothes, your pearls and jewels, and your golden crown are not for me," answered the frog. "But if you would love me, and have me for your companion and play-fellow, and let me sit by you at table and eat from your plate and drink from your cup, and sleep in your little bed —if you would promise all this, then would I dive below the water and fetch you your golden ball again."

"Oh yes," she answered, "I will promise it all, whatever you want, if you will only get me my ball again."

But she thought to herself, "What nonsense he talks! As if he could do anything but sit in the water and croak with the other frogs, or could possibly be anyone's companion!"

But the frog, as soon as he heard her promise, drew his head under the water and sank down out of sight. But after a while he came to the surface again with the ball in his mouth, and he threw it on the grass.

The King's daughter was overjoyed to see her pretty plaything again, and she caught it up and ran off with it.

"Stop, stop!" cried the frog. "Take me up too. I cannot run as fast as you!"

But it was of no use, for croak, croak after her as he might, she would not listen to him. Instead, she hastened home and very soon forgot all about the poor frog, who had to betake himself to his well again.

The next day, when the King's daughter was sitting at table with the King and all the court, and was eating from her golden plate, there came something pitter-patter up the marble stairs, and then there came a knocking at the door and a voice crying, "King's youngest daughter, let me in!"

And she got up and ran to see who it could be, but when she opened the door, there was the frog sitting outside. Then she shut the door hastily and went back to her seat, feeling very uneasy.

The King noticed how quickly her heart was beating and said, "My child, what are you afraid of? Is there a giant standing at the door ready to carry you away?"

"Oh no," answered she. "No giant, but a horrid frog."

"And what does the frog want?" asked the King.

"Oh, dear father," answered she, "when I was sitting by the well yesterday playing with my golden ball, it fell into the water. And while I was crying for the loss of it, the frog came and got it again for me on condition I would let him be my companion. I never thought that he could leave the water and come after me, but there he is now outside the door, and he wants to come in to me."

And then they all heard him knocking the second time and crying:

> "King's youngest daughter,
> Open to me!
> By the well water
> What promised you me?
> King's youngest daughter,
> Now open to me!"

"That which you have promised must you perform," said the King sternly. "So go now and let him in."

The frog feasted heartily, but every morsel
seemed to stick in her throat.

So she went and opened the door and the frog hopped in, following at her heels till she reached her chair.

Then he stopped and cried, "Lift me up to sit by you." But she delayed doing so until the King ordered her.

When once the frog was on the chair, he wanted to get on the table, and there he sat and said, "Now push your golden plate a little nearer so that we may eat together."

And so she did, but everybody could see how unwilling she was. And the frog feasted heartily, but every morsel seemed to stick in her throat.

"I have had enough now," said the frog at last. "And as I am tired, you must carry me to your room and make ready your silken bed, and we will lie down and go to sleep."

Then the King's daughter began to weep and was afraid of the cold frog, whom nothing would satisfy but he must sleep in her pretty clean bed.

Now the King grew angry with her and said, "What you have promised in your time of necessity, you must now perform."

So she picked up the frog with her finger and thumb, carried him upstairs, and put him in a corner. And when she had lain down to sleep, he came creeping up, saying, "I am tired and want sleep as much as you. Take me up or I will tell your father."

Then she felt beside herself with rage and, picking him up, she threw him with all her strength against the wall, crying, "Now will you be quiet, you horrid frog?"

But as he fell he ceased to be a frog, and became all at once a prince with beautiful kind eyes. And it came to pass that with her father's consent they became bride and bridegroom. And he told her how a wicked witch had bound him by her spells, and how no one but she alone could have released him, and that they two would go together to his father's kingdom.

And there came to the door a carriage drawn by eight white horses, with white plumes on their heads and with golden harness, and behind the carriage, faithful Henry, the servant of the young Prince, was standing. Now, faithful Henry had suffered such care and pain when his master was turned into a frog that he had been obliged to wear three iron bands over his heart, to keep it from breaking with trouble and anxiety. When the carriage started to take the Prince to his kingdom, and faithful Henry had helped them both in, he got up behind and was full of joy at his master's deliverance.

And when they had gone a part of the way, the Prince heard a sound at the back of the carriage as if something had broken, and he turned round and cried, "Henry, the wheel must be breaking!"

But Henry answered:

> "The wheel does not break;
> 'Tis the band round my heart
> That, to lessen its ache,
> When I grieved for your sake,
> I bound round my heart."

Again and yet once again there was the same sound, and the Prince thought it must be the wheel breaking, but it was the breaking of the other bands from faithful Henry's heart, because it was now so relieved and happy.

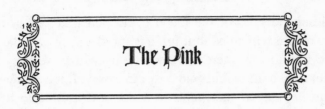

The Pink

THERE was once a queen who had not been blessed with children. She prayed every morning as she walked in her garden that a son or daughter might be given to her. Then one day an angel came, and said to her, "Be content. You shall have a son, and he shall be endowed with the power of wishing, so that whatsoever he wishes for shall be granted to him." She hurried to the King and told him the joyful news. When the time came, a son was born to them and they were filled with delight.

Every morning the Queen used to take her little son into the gardens where the wild animals were kept, to bathe him in a clear sparkling fountain. It happened one day, when the child was a little older, that as she sat with him on her lap she fell asleep.

The old cook, who knew that the child had the power of wishing, came by and stole it. He also killed a chicken and dropped some of its blood on the Queen's garments. Then he took the child away to a secret place where he placed it out to be nursed. Then he ran back to the King and accused the Queen of having allowed her child to be carried off by a wild animal.

When the King saw the blood on the Queen's garments, he believed the story and was overwhelmed with anger. He caused a high tower to be built, into which neither the sun nor the moon could penetrate. Then he ordered his wife to be shut up in it and the door walled up. She was to stay there for seven years without eating or drinking, so she would gradually pine away. But two angels from heaven, in the shape of white doves, came to her, bringing food twice a day till the seven years were ended.

Meanwhile the cook thought, "If the child really has the power of wishing, and I stay here, I might easily fall into disgrace." So he left the palace and went to the boy, who was then old enough to talk, and said to him, "Wish for a beautiful castle, with a garden and everything belonging to it." Hardly had the words passed the boy's lips than all that he had asked for was there.

After a time the cook said, "It is not good for you to be so much alone. Wish for a beautiful maiden to be your companion."

The Prince uttered the wish and immediately a maiden stood before them, more beautiful than any painter could paint. So they grew very fond of each other and played together, while the old cook went out hunting like any grand gentleman. But the idea came to him one day that the Prince might wish to go to his father some time, and he would thereby be placed in a very awkward position. So he took the maiden aside, and said to her, "Tonight when the boy is asleep, go and drive this knife into his heart. Then bring me his heart and his tongue. If you fail to do it you will lose your own life."

Then he went away, but when the next day came the maiden had not yet obeyed his command. She said, "Why should I shed his innocent blood, when he has never done harm to any creature in his life?"

The cook again said, "If you do not obey me you will lose your own life."

When he had gone away, she ordered a young hind to be brought and killed. Then she cut out its heart and its tongue and put them on a dish. When she saw the old man coming, she said to the boy, "Get into bed and cover yourself completely."

The old scoundrel came in and said, "Where are the tongue and the heart of the boy?"

The maiden gave him the dish, but the Prince threw off the coverings and said, "You old sinner, why did you want to kill me? Now hear your sentence. You shall be turned into a black poodle with a gold chain round your neck, and you shall be made to eat live coals so that flames of fire will come out of your mouth."

As he said the words, the old man was changed into a black poodle with a gold chain round his neck, and the scullions brought live coals which he had to eat till the flames poured out of his mouth.

The Prince stayed on at the castle for a time, thinking of his mother, and wondering if she were still alive. At last he said to the maiden, "I am going into my own country. If you like, you can go with me. I will take you."

She answered, "Alas, it is so far off, and what should I do in a strange country where I know no one?"

As she did not wish to go, and yet they could not bear to be parted, he changed her into a beautiful pink which he took with him.

Then he set out on his journey, and the poodle was made to run alongside till the Prince reached his own country. There, he went straight to the tower where his mother was imprisoned, and as the tower was so very high, he wished for a ladder to reach the top. Then he climbed up, looked in, and cried, "Dearest mother, lady Queen, are you still alive?"

She, thinking it was the angels who brought her food, said, "I have just eaten. I do not want anything more."

Then he said, "I am your own dear son whom the wild animals were supposed to have devoured. But I am still alive and I shall soon come and rescue you."

Then he got down and went to his father. He had himself announced as a strange huntsman, anxious to take service with the King. The King said, "Yes, if he is skilled in game preserving, and can procure plenty of venison, I will engage him. But there has never before been any game in the whole district."

The huntsman promised to procure as much game as the King could possibly require for the royal table.

Then he called the whole hunt together and ordered them all to come into the forest with him. He caused a great circle to be enclosed, with only one outlet. Then he took his place in the middle and began to wish as hard as he could. Immediately, over two hundred head of game came running into the enclosure. These the huntsmen had to shoot, and then they were piled onto sixty country wagons and driven home to the King. So for once he was able to load his board with game, after having had none for many years.

The King was much pleased and commanded his whole court to a banquet on the following day. When they were all assembled, he said to the huntsman, "You shall sit by me because you are so clever."

He answered, "My lord and King, may it please Your Majesty, I am only a poor huntsman!"

The King, however, insisted and said, "I command you to sit by me."

As he sat there, his thoughts wandered to his dear mother, and he wished one of the courtiers would speak of her. Hardly had he wished it than the Lord High Marshal said, "Your Majesty, we are all rejoicing here. How fares it with Her Majesty the Queen? Is she still alive in the tower or has she perished?"

But the King answered, "She allowed my beloved son to be devoured by wild animals, and I do not wish to hear anything about her."

Then the huntsman stood up and said, "Gracious father, she is still alive, and I am her son. I was not devoured by wild animals, but I was taken away by the scoundrel of a cook. He stole me while my mother was asleep, and sprinkled her garments with the blood of a chicken." Then he brought up the black poodle with the golden chain and said, "This is the villain."

He ordered some live coals to be brought, which he

made the dog eat in the sight of all the people till the flames poured out of his mouth. Then he asked the King if he would like to see the cook in his true shape, and wished him back, and there he stood in his white apron with his knife at his side.

The King was furious when he saw him and ordered him to be thrown into the deepest dungeon. Then the huntsman said further, "My father, would you like to see the maiden who so tenderly saved my life when she was ordered to kill me, although by so doing she might have lost her own life?"

The King answered, "Yes, I will gladly see her."

Then his son said, "Gracious father, I will show her to you first in the guise of a beautiful flower."

He put his hand into his pocket and brought out the pink. It was a finer one than the King had ever seen before. Then his son said, "Now I will show her to you in her true form."

The moment his wish was uttered, she stood before them in all her beauty, which was greater than any artist could paint.

The King sent ladies and gentlemen-in-waiting to the tower to bring the Queen back to his royal table. But when they reached the tower they found that she would no longer eat or drink. She said, "The merciful God, who has preserved my life so long, will soon release me now."

Three days afterwards she died. At her burial the two white doves which had brought her food during her captivity followed and hovered over her grave.

The old King caused the wicked cook to be torn into four quarters, but his own heart was filled with grief and remorse, and he died soon after.

His son married the beautiful maiden he had brought home with him as a flower, and for all I know they may be living still.

The Queen Bee

TWO king's sons once started to seek adventures, and they fell into a wild, reckless way of living and gave up all thoughts of going home again. Their third and youngest brother, who was called Witling, had remained behind, and now he started off to seek them. When at last he found them, they jeered at his simplicity in thinking that he could make his way in the world, when they who were so much cleverer were unsuccessful.

But they all three went on together until they came to an anthill. This the two eldest brothers wished to stir up, to see the little ants hurrying about in their fright and carrying off their eggs. But Witling said, "Leave the little creatures alone. I will not suffer them to be disturbed."

And they went on farther until they came to a lake where a number of ducks were swimming about. The two elder brothers wanted to catch a couple and cook them, but Witling again would not allow it.

He said, "Leave the creatures alone. I will not suffer them to be killed."

And then they came to a bees' nest in a tree, and there was so much honey in it that it overflowed and ran down the trunk. The two elder brothers then wanted to make a fire beneath the tree, that the bees might be stifled by the smoke and then they could get at the honey.

But Witling prevented them, saying, "Leave the little creatures alone. I will not suffer them to be stifled."

At last the three brothers came to a castle where there were many horses standing in the stables, all of stone. The brothers went through all the rooms until they came to a door at the end, secured with three locks, and in the middle of the door was a small opening through which they could look into the room. There they saw a little gray-haired man sitting at a table.

They called out to him once, twice, and he did not hear, but at the third time he got up, undid the locks, and came out. Without speaking a word he led them to a table loaded with all sorts of good things, and when they had eaten and drunk he showed to each his bedchamber.

The next morning the little gray man came to the eldest brother and, beckoning him, brought him to a table of stone on which were written three things, directing by what means the castle could be delivered from its enchantment. The first thing was that in the wood under the moss lay the pearls belonging to the Princess—a thousand in number. And they were to be sought for and collected; and if he who should undertake the task had not finished it by sunset, if but one pearl were missing, he must be turned to stone.

So the eldest brother went out and searched all day, but at the end of it he had found only one hundred. And just as it was said on the table of stone it came to pass, and he was turned into stone.

The second brother undertook the adventure next day, but it fared no better with him than with the first: he found two hundred pearls and was turned into stone.

And so at last it was Witling's turn, and he began to

search in the moss. But it was a very tedious business to find the pearls and he grew so out of heart that he sat down on a stone and began to weep. As he was sitting thus, up came the ant king with five thousand ants whose lives had been saved through Witling's pity, and it was not very long before the little insects had collected all the pearls and put them in a heap.

Now the second thing ordered by the table of stone was to get the key of the Princess' sleeping chamber out of the lake. And when Witling came to the lake, the ducks whose lives he had saved came swimming, and they dived down and brought up the key from the bottom.

The third thing that had to be done was the most difficult, and that was to choose out the youngest and loveliest of the three princesses as they lay sleeping. All bore a perfect resemblance each to the other, and differed only in this: that before they went to sleep each one had eaten a different sweetmeat—the eldest a piece of sugar, the second a little syrup, and the third a spoonful of honey. Now the queen bee of those bees that Witling had protected from the fire came at this moment and, trying the lips of all three, settled on those of the one who had eaten honey, and so it was that the King's son knew which to choose. Then the spell was broken. Everyone awoke from stony sleep and took his right form again.

And Witling married the youngest and loveliest princess and became king after her father's death. But his two brothers had to put up with the two other sisters.

Briar Rose (Sleeping Beauty)

A LONG time ago there lived a king and a queen, who said every day, "If only we had a child!" But for a long time they had none.

It happened once as the Queen was bathing that a frog crept out of the water onto the land and said to her, "Your wish shall be fulfilled. Before a year has passed you shall bring a daughter into the world."

The frog's words came true. The Queen had a little girl who was so beautiful that the King could not contain himself for joy, and he prepared a great feast. He invited his relatives, friends and acquaintances, and also the fairies, in order that they might be favorably and kindly disposed towards the child. There were thirteen of them in the kingdom, but as the King had only twelve golden plates for them to eat from, one of the fairies had to stay at home.

The feast was held with all splendor, and when it came to an end the fairies all presented the child with a magic gift. One gave her virtue, another beauty, a third riches, and so on, with everything in the world that she could wish for.

When eleven of the fairies had said their say, the thirteenth suddenly appeared. She wanted to revenge herself for not having been invited.

Without greeting anyone or even glancing at the company, she called out in a loud voice, "The Princess shall prick herself with a distaff in her fifteenth year and shall fall down dead." And without another word she turned and left the hall.

Everyone was terror-stricken, but the twelfth fairy, whose wish was still unspoken, stepped forward. She could not cancel the curse but could only soften it, so she said, "It shall not be death, but a deep sleep lasting a hundred years, into which your daughter shall fall."

The King was so anxious to guard his dear child from the misfortune that he sent out a command that all the distaffs in the whole kingdom should be burned.

As time went on, all the promises of the fairies came true. The Princess grew up so beautiful, modest, kind, and clever that everyone who saw her could not but love her. Now it happened that on the very day when she was fifteen years old, the King and Queen were away from home and the Princess was left quite alone in the castle. She wandered about over the whole place, looking at rooms and halls as she pleased, and at last she came to an old tower. She ascended a narrow winding staircase and reached a little door. A rusty key was sticking in the lock, and when she turned it the door flew open. In a little room sat an old woman with a spindle, spinning her flax busily.

"Good day, Granny," said the Princess. "What are you doing?"

"I am spinning," said the old woman, and nodded her head.

"What is the thing that whirls around so merrily?" asked the Princess. And she took the spindle and tried to spin too. But she had scarcely touched it before the curse was fulfilled, and she pricked her finger with the spindle. The instant she felt the prick she fell upon the bed which was standing near, and lay still in a deep sleep which spread over the whole castle.

The King and Queen, who had just come home and had stepped into the hall, went to sleep, and all their courtiers with them. The horses went to sleep in the stable, the dogs in the yard, the doves on the roof, the flies on the wall. Yes, even the fire flickering on the hearth grew still and went to sleep, and the roast meat stopped crackling. The cook, who was pulling the scullion's hair because he had made some mistake, let him go and went to sleep. The wind dropped, and on the trees in front of the castle not a leaf stirred.

But round the castle a hedge of briar roses began to grow up. Every year it grew higher, till at last it surrounded the whole castle so that nothing could be seen of it, not even the flags on the roof.

But there was a legend in the land about the lovely sleeping Briar Rose, as the King's daughter was called. And from time to time princes came and tried to force a way through the hedge into the castle. They found it impossible; for the thorns, as though they had hands, held them fast, and the princes remained caught in them without being able to free themselves. And so they died a miserable death.

After many, many years a prince came again to the country and heard an old man tell of the castle which stood behind the briar hedge, in which a most beautiful maiden called Briar Rose had been asleep for the last hundred years, and with her the King, the Queen, and all their courtiers. He knew also from his grandfather that many princes had already come and sought to pierce the briar hedge, and had remained caught in it and died a sad death.

Then the young Prince said, "I am not afraid. I am determined to go and look upon the lovely Briar Rose."

The good old man did all in his power to dissuade him, but the Prince would not listen to his words.

Now, however, the hundred years were just ended, and the day had come when Briar Rose was to wake up again. When the Prince approached the briar hedge it was in blossom, and was covered with beautiful large flowers which made way for him of their own accord and let him pass unharmed, and then closed up again into a hedge behind him.

In the courtyard he saw the horses and brindled hounds lying asleep. On the roof sat the doves with their heads under their wings. And when he went into the house, the flies were asleep on the walls. And near the throne lay the King and Queen. In the kitchen was the cook, with his hand raised as though about to strike the scullion, and the maid sat with the black fowl in her lap, which she had been about to pluck.

He went on farther, and all was so still that he could hear his own breathing. At last he reached the tower and opened the door into the little room where Briar Rose was asleep. There she lay, looking so beautiful that he could not take his eyes off her. He bent down and gave her a kiss.

As he touched her, Briar Rose opened her eyes and looked lovingly at him. Then they went down together,

and the King woke up, and the Queen, and all the courtiers, and looked at each other with astonished eyes. The horses in the stable stood up and shook themselves, the hounds leaped about and wagged their tails, the doves on the roof lifted their heads from under their wings, looked around, and flew into the fields. The flies on the walls began to crawl again; the fire in the kitchen roused itself and blazed up and cooked the food. The meat began to crackle, and the cook boxed the scullion's ears so soundly that he screamed aloud, while the maid finished plucking the fowl.

Then the wedding of the Prince and Briar Rose was celebrated with all splendor, and they lived happily till they died.

The Six Swans

ONCE upon a time a king was hunting in a great wood, and he pursued a wild animal so eagerly that none of his people could follow him. When evening came he stood still; then looking round him he found that he had lost his way, and seeking a path, he found none. Then all at once he saw an old woman with a nodding head coming up to him, and she was a witch.

"My good woman," said he, "can you show me the way out of the wood?"

"Oh yes, my Lord King," answered she. "Certainly I can, but I must make a condition. And if you do not fulfill it, you will never get out of the wood again, but will die there of hunger."

"What is the condition?" asked the King.

"I have a daughter," said the old woman, "who is as fair as any in the world. If you will take her for your bride and make her your Queen, I will show you the way out of the wood."

The King consented because of the difficulty he was in, and the old woman led him into her little house, where her daughter was sitting by the fire.

She received the King just as if she had been expecting him. And though he saw that she was very beautiful, she did not please him, and he could not look at her without an inward shudder. Nevertheless he took the maiden before him on his horse, and the old woman showed him the way, and soon he was in his royal castle again, where the wedding was held.

The King had been married before and his first wife had left seven children, six boys and one girl, whom he loved better than all the world. And as he was afraid the stepmother might not behave well to them, and perhaps would do them some mischief, he took them to a lonely castle standing in the middle of a wood.

There they remained hidden, for the road to it was so hard to find that the King himself could not have found it had it not been for a ball of yarn with wonderful properties, which a wise woman had given him. When he threw this down before him, it unrolled itself and showed him the way.

But the King went so often to see his dear children that the Queen was displeased at his absence. She became curious and wanted to know why he went out alone into the wood so often. She bribed his servants with much money, and they showed her the secret and told her of the ball of yarn, which alone could point out the way. Then she gave herself no rest until she had found out where the King kept the ball. Then she made some little white silk shirts and sewed a charm in each, since she had learned witchcraft from her mother. And once when the King had ridden to the hunt, she took the little shirts and went into the wood, and the ball of yarn showed her the way. The children, who saw someone in the distance, thought it was their dear father coming to see them and came jumping for joy to meet him. Then the wicked Queen threw over each of them one of the little shirts, and as soon as the shirts touched their bodies, they were changed into swans and flew away through the wood.

So the Queen went home much pleased to think she had got rid of her stepchildren, but since the maiden had not run out with her brothers the Queen knew nothing about her. The next day the King went to see his children, but he found nobody but his daughter.

"Where are your brothers?" asked the King.

"Ah, dear father," answered she, "they have gone away and have left me behind." Then she told him how from her window she had seen her brothers in the guise of swans fly away through the wood. And she showed him the feathers which they had let fall in the courtyard, and which she had picked up. The King was grieved, but he never dreamt that it was the Queen who had done this wicked deed. And as he feared lest the maiden also should be stolen away from him, he wished to take her away with him. But she was afraid of the stepmother and begged the

King to let her remain one more night in the castle in the wood.

Then she said to herself, "I must stay here no longer, but go and seek my brothers." And when night came, she ran away straight into the wood.

She went on all that night and the next day, until she could go no longer for weariness. At last she saw a rude hut, and she went in and found a room with six little beds in it. She did not dare to lie down in one, but she crept under one and lay on the hard boards and wished for night. When it was near sunset she heard a rustling sound and saw six swans come flying in at the window. They alighted on the ground and blew at one another until they had blown all their feathers off, and then they stripped off their swan skins as if they had been shirts. When the maiden looked at them and knew them for her brothers, she was very glad and crept out from under the bed. The brothers were not less glad when their sister appeared, but their joy did not last long.

"You must not stay here," they said to her. "This is a robbers' haunt, and if they were to come and find you here they would kill you."

"And cannot you defend me?" asked the little sister.

"No," answered they, "for we can only get rid of our swan skins and keep our human shape every evening for a quarter of an hour. After that we must be changed again into swans."

Their sister wept at hearing this and said, "Can nothing be done to set you free?"

"Oh no," answered they, "the work would be too hard for you. For six whole years you would be obliged never to speak or laugh, and during that time you would have to make six little shirts out of aster flowers. If you were to let fall a single word before the work was ended, all your work would be of no avail."

And just as the brothers had finished telling her this, the quarter of an hour came to an end and they changed into swans and flew out of the window.

But the maiden made up her mind to set her brothers free, even though it should cost her her life. She left the hut and went into the middle of the wood, where she climbed a tree and there passed the night. The next morning she set to work and gathered asters and began sewing them together. As for speaking, there was no one to speak to. And as for laughing, she had no mind to laugh. So she sat there and looked at nothing but her work.

When she had been going on like this for a long time, it happened that the King of that country went hunting in the wood, and some of his huntsmen came up to the tree in which the maiden sat.

They called out to her, "Who are you?" But she gave no answer.

"Come down," they cried. "We will do you no harm." But she only shook her head.

When they tormented her further with questions, she threw down to them her gold necklace, hoping they would be content with that, but they would not leave off. So she threw her sash down to them, and when that did no good she threw down her garters; and one after another everything she had on and could possibly spare, until she had nothing left but her smock. But it all did no good; the huntsmen would not be put off any longer. And they climbed the tree, carried the maiden off, and brought her to the King.

The King asked, "Who are you? What were you doing in the tree?" But she answered nothing.

He spoke to her in all the languages he knew, but she remained dumb. But, since she was very beautiful, the King felt a great love rise up in his heart towards her, and casting his mantle round her, he put her before him on his horse and brought her to his castle. Then he caused rich clothing to be put upon her, and her beauty shone as bright as the morning, but no word would she utter.

He seated her by his side at table, and her modesty and gentle mien so pleased him that he said, "This maiden I choose for wife, and no other in all the world." And accordingly after a few days they were married.

But the King had a wicked mother, who was displeased with the marriage, and spoke ill of the young Queen.

"Who knows where this maid can have come from," said she, "who is not able to speak a word? She is not worthy of a king!"

After a year had passed and the Queen brought her first child into the world, the old woman carried it away, and marked the Queen's mouth with blood as she lay sleeping. Then she went to the King and declared that his wife was an eater of human flesh. The King would not believe such a thing and ordered that no one should do her any harm. And the Queen went on quietly sewing the shirts and caring for nothing else. The next time that a fine boy was born, the wicked woman used the same deceit, but the King would give no credence to her words.

He said, "She is too tender and good to do any such thing, and if she were only not dumb, and could defend herself, then her innocence would be as clear as day."

When for the third time the old woman stole away the

newborn child and accused the Queen, who was unable to say a word in her own defense, the King could do nothing else but give her up to justice, and she was sentenced to suffer death by fire.

The day on which her sentence was to be carried out was the very last day of the six years during which she was neither to speak nor laugh, in order to free her dear brothers from the evil spell. The six shirts were ready, all except one which lacked the left sleeve. And when she was led to the pile of wood, she carried the six shirts on her arm. When she mounted the pile and the fire was about to be kindled, all at once she cried out aloud, for there were six swans coming flying through the air. She saw that her deliverance was near, and her heart beat for joy.

The swans came close up to her with rushing wings and stooped round her, so that she could throw the shirts over them. And when that had been done the swan skins fell off them, and her brothers stood before her in their own bodies quite safe and sound. But as one shirt wanted the left sleeve, so the youngest brother had a swan's wing instead of a left arm. They embraced and kissed each other, and the Queen went up to the King, who looked on with astonishment, and began to speak to him.

"Dearest husband," she said, "now I may dare to speak and tell you that I am innocent, and have been falsely accused." And she related to him the treachery of the old woman who had taken away the three children and hidden them. And she was reconciled to the King with great joy, and the wicked mother was bound to the stake on the pile of wood and burnt to ashes.

And the King and Queen lived many years with their six brothers in peace and joy.

The Fisherman and His Wife

THERE was once a fisherman who lived with his wife in a miserable little hovel close to the sea. He went to fish every day, and he fished and fished, and at last one day as he was sitting looking deep down into the shining water, he felt something on his line. When he hauled it up, there was a big flounder on the end of the line.

The flounder said to him, "Listen, fisherman, I beg you not to kill me. I am no common flounder. I am an enchanted prince! What good will it do you to kill me? I shan't be good to eat. Put me back into the water and leave me to swim about."

"Ho! ho!" said the fisherman. "You need not make so many words about it. I am quite ready to put back a flounder that can talk." And so saying, he put back the flounder into the shining water and it sank down to the bottom, leaving a streak of blood behind it. Then the fisherman got up and went back to his wife in the hovel.

"Husband," she said, "have you caught anything today?"

"No," said the man. "All I caught was one flounder. And he said he was an enchanted prince, so I put him back into the water."

"Did you not wish for anything then?" asked the goodwife.

"No," said the man. "What was there to wish for?"

"Alas," said his wife, "isn't it bad enough always to live in this wretched hovel? You might at least have wished for a nice clean cottage. Go back and call him! Tell him I want a pretty cottage. He will surely give us that."

"Alas," said the man, "what am I to go back there for?"

"Well," said the woman, "it was you who caught him and let him go again. He will certainly do that for you. Be off now."

The man was still not very willing to go, but he did not want to vex his wife and at last he went back to the sea.

He found the sea no longer bright and shining, but dull and green. He stood by it and said:

> "Flounder, flounder in the sea,
> Prythee, hearken unto me:
> My wife, Ilsebil, must have her own will,
> And sends me to beg a boon of thee."

The flounder came swimming up and said, "Well, what do you want?"

"Alas," said the man, "I had to call you, for my wife said I ought to have wished for something as I caught you. She doesn't want to live in our miserable hovel any longer. She wants a pretty cottage."

"Go home again then," said the flounder. "She has her wish fully."

The man went home and found his wife no longer in the old hut, but a pretty little cottage stood in its place and his wife was sitting on a bench by the door.

She took him by the hand and said, "Come and look in here. Isn't this much better?"

They went inside and found a pretty sitting room, a bedroom with a bed in it, a kitchen, and a larder furnished with everything of the best in tin and brass and every possible need. Outside there was a little yard with chickens and ducks and a little garden full of vegetables and fruit.

"Look!" said the woman. "Is not this nice?"

"Yes," said the man, "and so let it remain. We can live here very happily."

"We will see about that," said the woman. With that they ate something and went to bed.

Everything went well for a week or more, and then the wife said, "Listen, husband, this cottage is too cramped and the garden is too small. The flounder could have given us a bigger house. I want to live in a big stone castle. Go to the flounder and tell him to give us a castle."

"Alas, wife," said the man, "the cottage is good enough for us. What should we do with a castle?"

"Never mind," said his wife. "You just go to the flounder and he will manage it."

"No, wife," said the man. "The flounder gave us the cottage. I don't want to go back. As likely as not he'll be angry."

"Go, all the same," said the woman. "He can do it easily enough and willingly into the bargain. Just go!"

The man's heart was heavy and he was very unwilling to go. He said to himself, "It's not right." But at last he went. He found the sea was no longer green: it was still calm, but dark violet and gray. He stood by it and said:

> "Flounder, flounder in the sea,
> Prythee, hearken unto me:
> My wife, Ilsebil, must have her own will,
> And sends me to beg a boon of thee."

"Now what do you want?" said the flounder.

"Alas," said the man, half scared, "my wife wants a big stone castle."

"Go home again," said the flounder. "She is standing at the door of it."

Then the man went away thinking he would find no house; but when he got back he found a great stone palace, and his wife was standing at the top of the steps waiting to go in. She took him by the hand and said, "Come in with me."

With that they went in and found a great hall paved with marble slabs, and numbers of servants in attendance who opened the great doors for them. The walls were hung with beautiful tapestries and the rooms were furnished with golden chairs and tables, while rich carpets covered the floors and crystal chandeliers hung from the ceilings. The tables groaned under every kind of delicate food and the most costly wines. Outside the house there was a great courtyard, with stables for horses and cows, and many fine carriages. Beyond this there was a great garden filled with the loveliest flowers and fine fruit trees. There was also a park half a mile long, and in it were stags and hinds and hares, and everything that one could wish for.

"Now," said the woman, "is not this worth having?"

"Oh yes," said the man, "and so let it remain. We will live in this beautiful palace and be content."

"We will think about that," said his wife, "and sleep upon it."

With that they went to bed.

Next morning the wife woke up first. Day was just dawning, and from her bed she could see the beautiful country around her. Her husband was still asleep, but she pushed him with her elbow and said, "Husband, get up and peep out of the window. See here, now, could we not be King over all this land? Go to the flounder. We will be King."

"Alas, wife," said the man, "why should we be King? I don't want to be King."

"Ah," said his wife, "if you will not be King, I will. Go to the flounder. I will be King."

"Alas, wife," said the man, "why do you want to be King? I don't want to ask the flounder."

"Why not?" said the woman. "Go you must. I insist I will be King."

So the man went, but he was quite sad because his wife would be King.

"It is not right," he said. "It is not right."

When he reached the sea, he found it dark, gray, and rough, and evil-smelling. He stood there and said:

> "Flounder, flounder in the sea,
> Prythee, hearken unto me:
> My wife, Ilsebil, must have her own will,
> And sends me to beg a boon of thee."

"Now what does she want?" said the flounder.

"Alas," said the man, "she wants to be King now."

"Go back. She is King already," said the flounder.

So the man went back, and when he reached the palace he found that it had grown much larger and a great tower had been added with handsome decorations. There was a sentry at the door and numbers of soldiers were playing drums and trumpets. As soon as he got inside the house he found everything was marble and gold, and the hangings were of velvet with great golden tassels. The doors of the salon were thrown wide open, and he saw the whole court assembled. His wife was sitting on a lofty throne of gold and diamonds. She wore a golden crown and carried in one hand a scepter of pure gold. On each side of her stood her ladies in a long row, every one a head shorter than the next.

He stood before her and said, "Alas, wife, are you now King?"

"Yes," she said. "Now I am King."

He stood looking at her for some time, and then he said, "Ah, wife, it is a fine thing for you to be King. Now we will not wish to be anything more."

"No, husband," she answered, quite uneasily, "I find that time hangs very heavy on my hands. I can't bear it any longer. Go back to the flounder. King I am, but I must also be Emperor."

"Alas, wife," said the man, "why do you now want to be Emperor?"

"Husband," she answered, "go to the flounder. Emperor I will be."

"Alas, wife," said the man, "Emperor he can't make you, and I won't ask him. There is only one emperor in the country, and Emperor the flounder cannot make you. That he can't."

"What?" said the woman. "I am King, and you are but my husband. To him you must go and that right quickly. If he can make a king, he can also make an emperor. Emperor I will be, so go quickly."

He had to go, but he was quite frightened. And as he went he thought, "This won't end well. Emperor is too shameless. The flounder will make an end of the whole thing."

With that he came to the sea, but now he found it quite black and heaving up from below in great waves. It tossed to and fro and a sharp wind blew over it, and the man trembled. So he stood there and said:

> "Flounder, flounder in the sea,
> Prythee, hearken unto me:
> My wife, Ilsebil, must have her own will,
> And sends me to beg a boon of thee."

"What does she want now?" said the flounder.

"Alas," he said, "my wife wants to be Emperor."

"Go back," said the flounder. "She is Emperor."

So the man went back, and when he got to the door he found that the whole palace was made of polished marble, with alabaster figures and golden decorations. Soldiers marched up and down before the doors, blowing their

The flounder came swimming up, and said,
"Well, what do you want?"

trumpets and beating their drums. Inside the palace, counts, barons, and dukes walked about as attendants, and they opened to him the doors, which were of pure gold.

He went in and saw his wife sitting on a huge throne made of solid gold. It was at least two miles high. She had on her head a great golden crown set with diamonds three yards high. In one hand she held the scepter, and in the other the orb of empire. On each side of her stood the gentlemen-at-arms in two rows, each one a little smaller than the other, from giants two miles high down to the tiniest dwarf no bigger than my little finger. She was surrounded by princes and dukes.

Her husband stood still and said, "Wife, are you now Emperor?"

"Yes," said she. "Now I am Emperor."

Then he looked at her for some time and said, "Alas, wife, how much better off are you for being Emperor?"

"Husband," she said, "what are you standing there for? Now I am Emperor, I mean to be Pope! Go back to the flounder."

"Alas, wife," said the man, "what won't you want next? Pope you cannot be. There is only one pope in Christendom. That's more than the flounder can do."

"Husband," she said, "Pope I will be, so go at once! I must be Pope this very day."

"No, wife," he said, "I dare not tell him. It's no good. It's too monstrous altogether. The flounder cannot make you Pope."

"Husband," said the woman, "don't talk nonsense. If he can make an emperor, he can make a pope. Go immediately. I am Emperor, and you are but my husband, and you must obey."

So he was frightened and went, but he was quite dazed. He shivered and shook and his knees trembled.

A great wind arose over the land, the clouds flew across the sky, and it grew as dark as night. The leaves fell from the trees, and the water foamed and dashed upon the shore. In the distance the ships were being tossed to and fro on the waves, and he heard them firing signals of distress. There was still a little patch of blue in the sky among the dark clouds, but towards the south they were red and heavy, as in a bad storm. In despair, he stood and said:

> "Flounder, flounder in the sea,
> Prythee, hearken unto me:
> My wife, Ilsebil, must have her own will,
> And sends me to beg a boon of thee."

"Now what does she want?" said the flounder.

"Alas," said the man, "she wants to be Pope!"

"Go back. Pope she is," said the flounder.

So back he went, and he found a great church surrounded with palaces. He pressed through the crowd, and inside he found thousands and thousands of lights. And his wife, entirely clad in gold, was sitting on a still higher throne with three golden crowns upon her head, and she was surrounded with priestly state. On each side of her were two rows of candles, from the biggest as thick as a tower down to the tiniest little taper. Kings and emperors were on their knees before her, kissing her shoe.

"Wife," said the man, looking at her, "are you now the Pope?"

"Yes," said she. "Now I am Pope."

So there he stood gazing at her, and it was like looking at a shining sun.

"Alas," he said, "are you better off for being Pope?"

At first she sat as stiff as a post, without stirring. Then he said, "Now, wife, be content with being Pope. Higher you cannot go."

"I will think about that," said the woman, and with that they both went to bed. Still she was not content and could not sleep for her inordinate desires. The man slept well and soundly, for he had walked about a great deal in the day. But his wife could think of nothing but what further grandeur she could demand. When the dawn reddened the sky she raised herself up in bed and looked out of the window, and when she saw the sun rise she said, "Ha! Can I not cause the sun and the moon to rise? Husband!" she cried, digging her elbow into his side, "wake up and go to the flounder. I will be Lord of the Universe."

Her husband, who was still more than half asleep, was so shocked that he fell out of bed. He thought he must have heard wrong. He rubbed his eyes and said, "Alas, wife, what did you say?"

"Husband," she said, "if I cannot be Lord of the Universe, and cause the sun and moon to set and rise, I shall not be able to bear it. I shall never have another happy moment."

She looked at him so wildly that it caused a shudder to run through him.

"Alas, wife," he said, falling on his knees before her. "The flounder can't do that. Emperor and Pope he can make, but this is indeed beyond him. I pray you, control yourself and remain Pope."

Then she flew into a terrible rage. Her hair stood on end. She kicked him and screamed, "I won't bear it any longer. Now go!"

Then he pulled on his trousers and tore away like a madman. Such a storm was raging that he could hardly keep his feet. Houses and trees quivered and swayed, and mountains trembled, and the rocks rolled into the sea. The sky was pitchy black. It thundered and lightened, and the sea ran in black waves mountains high, crested with white foam. He shrieked out, but could hardly make himself heard:

> *"Flounder, flounder in the sea,*
> *Prythee, hearken unto me:*
> *My wife, Ilsebil, must have her own will,*
> *And sends me to beg a boon of thee."*

"Now what does she want?" asked the flounder.

"Alas," he said, "she wants to be Lord of the Universe."

"Now she must go back to her old hovel," said the flounder, "and there she is!" So there they are to this very day.

Rumpelstiltskin

THERE was once a miller who was very poor, but he had a beautiful daughter. Now it once happened that he had occasion to speak with the King, and in order to give himself an air of importance he said, "I have a daughter who can spin gold out of straw."

The King said to the miller, "That is an art in which I am much interested. If your daughter is as skillful as you say she is, bring her to my castle tomorrow, and I will put her to the test."

Accordingly, when the girl was brought to the castle, the King conducted her to a chamber which was quite full of straw, gave her a spinning wheel and a reel, and said, "Now set to work. And if between tonight and to-morrow at dawn you have not spun this straw into gold, you must die." Thereupon he carefully locked the door of the chamber, and she remained alone.

There sat the unfortunate miller's daughter, and for the life of her did not know what to do. She had not the least idea how to spin straw into gold, and she became more and more distressed until at last she began to weep. Then all at once the door sprang open, and in stepped a little man who said, "Good evening, Mistress Miller. What are you weeping so for?"

"Alas," answered the maiden, "I've got to spin gold out of straw, and don't know how to do it."

Then the little man said, "What will you give me if I spin it for you?"

"My necklace," said the maid.

The little man took the necklace, sat down before the spinning wheel, and whir—whir—whir, in a trice the reel was full. Then he fixed another reel, and whir—whir—whir, thrice round, and that too was full. And so it went on until morning, when all the straw was spun and all the reels were full of gold.

Immediately at sunrise the King came, and when he saw the gold he was astonished and much pleased, but his mind became only the more avaricious. So he had the miller's daughter taken to another chamber full of straw, larger than the former one, and he ordered her to spin it also in one night, if she valued her life.

The maiden was at her wit's end and began to weep. Then again the door sprang open, and the little man appeared and said, "What will you give me if I spin the straw into gold for you?"

"The ring off my finger," answered the maiden.

The little man took the ring, began to whir again at the wheel, and by morning had spun all the straw into gold.

The King was delighted at sight of the masses of gold, but was not even yet satisfied. So he had the miller's daughter taken to a still larger chamber full of straw, and said, "This must you spin tonight into gold, but if you succeed you shall become my Queen." "Even if she is only a miller's daughter," thought he, "I shan't find a richer woman in the whole world."

When the girl was alone the little man came again and said for the third time, "What will you give me if I spin the straw for you this time?"

"I have nothing more to give," answered the girl.

"Well, promise me your first child if you become Queen."

"Who knows what may happen?" thought the miller's daughter, but she did not see any other way of getting out of the difficulty. So she promised the little man what he demanded, and in return he spun the straw into gold once more.

When the King came in the morning and found everything as he had wished, he celebrated his marriage with her, and the miller's daughter became Queen.

About a year afterwards a beautiful child was born, but the Queen had forgotten all about the little man. However, he suddenly entered her chamber and said, "Now, give me what you promised."

The Queen was terrified, and offered the little man all the wealth of the kingdom if he would let her keep the child. But the little man said, "No, I would rather have some living thing than all the treasures of the world."

Then the Queen began to moan and weep to such an extent that the little man felt sorry for her. "I will give you three days," said he, "and if within that time you discover my name you shall keep the child."

Then during the night the Queen called to mind all the names that she had ever heard, and sent a messenger all over the country to inquire far and wide what other names there were.

When the little man appeared the next day, she began with Caspar, Melchior, Balthazar, and mentioned all the names which she knew, one after the other. But at every one the little man said, "No. No. That's not my name."

The second day she had inquiries made all round the

neighborhood for the names of people living there, and suggested to the little man all the most unusual and strange names. "Perhaps your name is Cowribs, or Spindleshanks, or Spiderlegs?"

But again he answered, "No. That's not my name."

On the third day the messenger came back and said, "I haven't been able to find any new names, but as I came round the corner of a wood on a lofty mountain, where the fox says good night to the hare, I saw a little house, and in front of the house a fire was burning. And around the fire a most ridiculous little man was leaping. He was hopping on one leg and singing:

> 'Today I bake; tomorrow I brew my beer;
> The next day I will bring the Queen's child here.
> Ah! lucky 'tis that not a soul doth know
> That Rumpelstiltskin is my name. Ho! Ho!' "

You can imagine how delighted the Queen was when she heard the name! And soon afterwards when the little man came in and asked, "Now, Your Majesty, what is my name?" at first she asked, "Is your name Tom?"

"No."

"Is it Dick?"

"No."

"Is it, by chance, Rumpelstiltskin?"

"The devil told you that! The devil told you that!" shrieked the little man. And in his rage he stamped his right foot into the ground so deep that he sank up to his waist.

Then in his rage he seized his left leg with both hands and tore himself asunder in the middle.

Rapunzel

ex THERE was once a man and his wife who had long wished in vain for a child, and at last they had reason to hope that heaven would grant their wish. There was a little window at the back of their house, which overlooked a beautiful garden full of lovely flowers and shrubs. It was, however, surrounded by a high wall, and nobody dared to enter it, because it belonged to a powerful witch who was feared by everybody.

One day the woman, standing at this window and looking into the garden, saw a bed planted with beautiful rampion. It looked so fresh and green that she longed to eat some of it. This longing increased every day; and as she knew it could never be satisfied, she began to look pale and miserable and to pine away. Then her husband was alarmed and said, "What ails you, my dear wife?"

"Alas!" she answered. "If I cannot get any of the rampion to eat from the garden behind our house, I shall die."

Her husband, who loved her, thought, "Before you let your wife die you must fetch her some of that rampion, cost what it may." So in the twilight he climbed over the wall into the witch's garden, hastily picked a handful of rampion, and took it back to his wife. She immediately prepared it and ate it very eagerly. It was so very, very nice that the next day her longing for it increased three-fold. She could have no peace unless her husband fetched her some more. So in the twilight he set out again, but when he got over the wall he was terrified to see the witch before him.

"How dare you come into my garden like a thief and steal my rampion?" she said, with angry looks. "It shall be the worse for you!"

"Alas!" he answered. "Be merciful to me. I am only here from necessity. My wife sees your rampion from the window, and she has such a longing for it that she would die if she could not get some of it."

The anger of the witch abated and she said to him, "If it is as you say, I will allow you to take away with you as much rampion as you like, but on one condition. You must give me the child which your wife is about to bring into the world. I will care for it like a mother, and all will be well with it."

In his fear the man consented to everything. And when the baby was born, the witch appeared, gave it the name of Rapunzel (rampion), and took it away with her.

Rapunzel was the most beautiful child under the sun. When she was twelve years old, the witch shut her up in a tower which stood in a wood. It had neither staircase nor doors, but only a little window quite high up in the wall.

When the witch wanted to enter the tower, she stood at the foot of it and cried:

"Rapunzel, Rapunzel, let down your hair!" Rapunzel had splendid long hair, as fine as spun gold. As soon as she heard the voice of the witch, she unfastened her plaits and twisted them round a hook by the window. They fell twenty ells downwards, and the witch climbed up by them.

It happened a couple of years later that the King's son rode through the forest and came close to the tower. From thence he heard a song so lovely that he stopped to listen. It was Rapunzel who in her loneliness made her sweet voice resound to pass away the time. The King's son wanted to join her, and he sought for the door of the tower but there was none to find.

He rode home, but the song had touched his heart so deeply that he went into the forest every day to listen to it Once when he was hidden behind a tree he saw a witch come to the tower and call out:

"Rapunzel, Rapunzel, let down your hair!"

Then Rapunzel lowered her plaits of hair and the witch climbed up to her.

"If that is the ladder by which one ascends," he thought, "I will try my luck myself." And the next day, when it began to grow dark, he went to the tower and cried:

"Rapunzel, Rapunzel, let down your hair!"

The hair fell down and the King's son climbed up it.

At first Rapunzel was terrified, for she had never set eyes on a man before. But the King's son talked to her kindly, and told her that his heart had been so deeply touched by her song that he had no peace and was obliged to see her. Then Rapunzel lost her fear. And when he asked if she would have him for her husband, and she saw that he was young and handsome, she thought, "He will love me better than old Mother Gothel." So she said, "Yes," and laid her hand in his. She said, "I will gladly go with you, but I do not know how I am to get down from this tower. When you come, will you bring a skein of silk with you every time? I will twist it into a ladder, and when it is long enough I will descend by it, and you can take me away with you on your horse."

She arranged with him that he should come and see

her every evening, for the old witch came in the daytime. The witch discovered nothing till suddenly Rapunzel said to her, "Tell me, Mother Gothel, how can it be that you are so much heavier to draw up than the young prince who will be here before long?"

"Oh, you wicked child, what do you say? I thought I had separated you from all the world, and yet you have deceived me." In her rage she seized Rapunzel's beautiful

hair, twisted it twice round her left hand, snatched up a pair of shears, and cut off the plaits, which fell to the ground. She was so merciless that she took poor Rapunzel away into a wilderness, where she forced her to live in the greatest grief and misery.

In the evening of the day on which she had banished Rapunzel, the witch fastened the plaits which she had cut off to the hook by the window. And when the Prince came and called: "Rapunzel, Rapunzel, let down your hair!" she lowered the hair. The Prince climbed up, but there he found, not his beloved Rapunzel, but the witch, who looked at him with angry and wicked eyes.

"Ah!" she cried mockingly, "you have come to fetch your ladylove, but the pretty bird is no longer in her nest. And she can sing no more, for the cat has seized her and it will scratch your own eyes out too. Rapunzel is lost to you. You will never see her again."

The Prince was beside himself with grief, and in his despair he sprang out of the window. He was not killed, but his eyes were scratched out by the thorns among which he fell. He wandered about blind in the wood and had nothing but roots and berries to eat. He did nothing but weep and lament over the loss of his beloved wife Rapunzel. In this way he wandered about for some years, till at last he reached the wilderness where Rapunzel had been living in great poverty. He heard a voice which seemed very familiar to him and he went towards it. Rapunzel knew him at once and fell weeping upon his neck. Two of her tears fell upon his eyes, and they immediately grew quite clear and he could see as well as ever.

He took her to his kingdom, where he was received with joy, and they lived long and happily together.

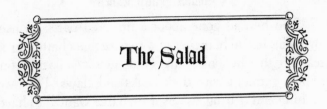

The Salad

THERE was once a merry young huntsman who went into the forest to hunt. He was gay and lighthearted, and whistled a tune upon a leaf as he went along.

Suddenly an ugly old crone spoke to him and said, "Good morning, dear huntsman. You are merry and happy enough, while I am hungry and thirsty. Pray give me an alms."

The huntsman pitied the poor old woman, put his hand in his pocket, and made her a present according to his means.

Then he wanted to go on, but the old woman held him back and said, "Hark ye, dear huntsman, I will make you a present because of your good heart. Go on your way and you will come to a tree on which nine birds are sitting. They will have a cloak in their claws, over which they are fighting. Take aim with your gun and shoot into the middle of them. They will drop the cloak and one of the birds will fall down dead. Take the cloak with you. It is a wishing cloak. When you throw it round your shoulders you only have to wish yourself at a place to be there at once. Take the heart out of the dead bird and swallow it whole. Then you will find a gold coin under your pillow every single morning when you wake."

The huntsman thanked the wise woman and thought, "She promises fine things. If only they turn out as well!"

When he had gone about a hundred paces he heard above him, in the branches of a tree, such a chattering and screaming that he looked up. There he saw a flock of birds tearing a garment with their beaks and claws. They were snatching and tearing at it as if each one wanted to have it for himself.

"Well," said the huntsman, "this is extraordinary. It is exactly what the old woman said."

He put his gun to his shoulder, took aim, and fired right into the middle of them, making the feathers fly about. The birds took flight with a great noise, all except one, which fell dead, and the cloak dropped at his feet.

He did as the old woman had told him: he cut the heart out of the bird and swallowed it whole. Then he took the cloak home with him. When he woke in the morning, he remembered the old woman's promise, and looked under his pillow to see if all was true. There, sure enough, lay the golden coin shining before him. The next morning he found another, and found the same every morning when he got up. He collected quite a heap of gold and at last he thought, "What is the good of all my gold if I stay at home here? I will go and look about me in the world." So he took leave of his parents, shouldered his gun, and started off into the world.

It so happened that one day he came to a thick forest, and when he got through it he saw a fine castle lying in the plain beyond. He saw an old woman standing in one of the windows looking out, with a beautiful golden-haired maiden beside her.

But the old woman was a witch and she said to the maiden, "Here comes someone out of the forest. He has a wonderful treasure inside him. We must try to get it from him, my darling. It will suit us better than him. He has a bird's heart about him, and therefore he finds a gold coin every morning under his pillow when he wakes."

She told the girl how he had got it and at last said, "If you don't get it from him it will be the worse for you."

When the huntsman got nearer, he saw the maiden and said, "I have been wandering about a long time. I will go into this castle and rest. I have plenty of money."

But the real reason was that he had caught sight of the pretty picture at the window. He went in and he was kindly received and hospitably treated. Before long, he was so enamored of the witch maiden that he thought of nothing else and cared for nothing but pleasing her.

The old woman said to the maiden, "Now we must get the bird's heart. He will never miss it."

They concocted a potion, and when it was ready they put it into a goblet. And the maiden took it to him and said, "Now, my beloved, you must drink to me."

He took the cup and drank the potion, and when he was overpowered by it the bird's heart came out of his mouth. The maiden took it away secretly and swallowed it herself, for the old woman wanted to have it.

From this time on, the huntsman found no more gold under his pillow, but the coin was always under the maiden's instead. The old woman used to fetch it away every morning. He was so much in love that he thought of nothing but enjoying himself in the maiden's company.

Then the old woman said, "We have got the bird's heart but we must have his wishing cloak too."

The maiden said, "Let us leave him that. We have taken away his wealth."

The old woman was very angry and said, "A cloak like that is a very wonderful thing and not often to be got. Have it I must and will." So the maiden obeyed the witch's orders, placed herself at the window, and looked sadly out at the distant range of hills.

The huntsman said, "Why are you so sad?"

"Alas, my love," was her answer, "over there are the garnet mountains, where the precious stones are found. I long for them so much that I grow sad whenever I think of them. But who could ever get them? The birds which fly, perhaps. No mortal could ever reach them."

"If that is all your trouble," said the huntsman, "I can soon lift that load from your heart."

Then he drew her under his cloak and in a moment they were both sitting on the mountain. The precious stones were glittering around them. Their hearts rejoiced at the sight of them and they soon gathered together some of the finest and largest.

Now the witch had so managed that the huntsman began to feel his eyes grow very heavy. Then he said to the maiden, "We will sit down to rest a while. I am so tired I can hardly stand."

So they sat down and he laid his head on her lap and was soon fast asleep. As soon as he was asleep, the maiden slipped the cloak from his shoulders and put it on her own, loaded herself with the precious garnets, and wished herself at home. When the huntsman had had his sleep out, he woke up and saw that his beloved had betrayed him and left him alone on the wild mountain.

"Oh, what treachery is in the world!" he exclaimed, as he sat down in grief. He did not know what to do.

Now the mountain belonged to some wild and savage giants who lived on it, and before long he saw three of them striding along. He quickly lay down again and pretended to be fast asleep.

The first one, as he came along, stumbled against him and said, "What kind of earthworm is this?"

The second said, "Tread on him and kill him."

But the third said, "It isn't worth the trouble. Let him alone! He can't live here, and when he climbs higher up the mountain the clouds will roll down and carry him off."

Then they passed on and as soon as they were gone, the huntsman, who had heard all they said, got up and climbed to the top of the mountain. After he had sat there for a time, a cloud floated over him and carried him away. At first he was swept through the air, but then he was gently lowered and deposited within a large walled garden, upon a soft bed of lettuce and other herbs.

He looked around him and said, "If only I had something to eat! I am so hungry, and it will be difficult to get away from here. I see neither apples nor pears nor any other fruit—nothing but salad and herbs."

At last, however, he thought, "At the worst, I can eat some of this salad. It does not taste very good, but it will at least be refreshing."

He picked out a fine head of lettuce and began eating it. But he had hardly swallowed a little piece when he began to feel very odd and quite changed. He felt four legs growing, a big head, and two long ears, and he saw to his horror that he was changed into an ass.

As he still felt as hungry as ever and the juicy salad was now very much to his taste, he went on eating greedily. At last he reached another kind of salad, which he had hardly tasted when he felt a new change taking place, and found himself back in his human shape. After this he lay down and slept off his fatigue.

When he woke next morning he broke off a head of the bad salad and a head of the good and thought, "These will help me to regain my own and also to punish the traitors."

He put the salad into his wallet, climbed over the wall, and went off to find the castle of his beloved.

After wandering about for a few days, he was fortunate enough to find it. Then he stained his face and disguised himself so that his own mother would not have known him, and went to the castle to ask for shelter.

"I am so tired," he said. "I cannot go any further."

The witch said, "Who are you, countryman, and what do you want?"

He answered, "I am a messenger from the King. He sent me to find the rarest salad which grows under the sun. I have been lucky enough to find it and I carry it with me. But the sun is so burning that I am afraid the tender plant will be withered, and I don't know if I shall be able to take it any further."

When the old witch heard about the rare salad, she felt a great desire to have some and said, "Good country-man, let me try the wonderful salad."

"By all means," he answered. "I have two heads with me and you shall have one." So saying, he opened his sack and handed her the bad one.

The witch had no suspicions, and her mouth so watered for the new dish that she went to the kitchen her-self to prepare it. When it was ready, she could not wait till it was put upon the table, but put a few leaves into her mouth at once. Hardly had she swallowed them when she lost her human shape, and she ran out into the courtyard as an old she-ass.

Then the kitchen maid came in and saw the salad standing ready, and was about to put it on the table. But on the way the fancy to taste it seized her, according to her usual habit, and she ate a few leaves. The power of the salad at once became apparent, because she also turned into an ass and ran out into the yard to join the old witch, while the dish of salad fell to the ground.

In the meantime the messenger was sitting with the

beautiful maiden, and as no one appeared with the salad, she also was seized with a desire to taste it. She said, "I don't know what has become of the salad."

But the huntsman thought, "The plant must have done its work," and said, "I will go into the kitchen and see."

As soon as he got downstairs he saw the two asses running about and the salad lying on the ground.

"This is all right," he said. "Two of them are done for." Then he picked up the leaves, put them on a dish, and took them to the maiden.

"I am bringing the precious food to you myself," said he, "so that you will not have to wait any longer."

She ate some, and like the others was immediately changed into an ass, and ran out to them in the yard.

When the huntsman had washed his face so that the creatures might know him, he went into the courtyard and said, "Now you shall be paid for your treachery."

He tied them all together with a rope and drove them along till he came to a mill. He tapped at the window, and the miller put his head out and asked what he wanted.

"I have three bad animals here," he said, "that I want to get rid of. If you will take them and feed them and treat them as I wish, I will pay you what you like to ask."

"How do you want them treated?" said the miller.

The huntsman said he wanted the old she-ass (the witch) to be well beaten three times a day and fed once. The younger one, which was the maid, beaten once and fed three times. The youngest of all, who was the beautiful maiden, was to be fed three times and not beaten at all. He could not find it in his heart to have her beaten. Then he went back to the castle and found everything he wanted.

A few days later the miller came and told him that

the old ass which was to be beaten three times and fed
once was dead. "The other two," he said, "which are to be
fed three times, are not dead, but they are pining away and
won't last long."

The huntsman's heart was stirred with pity and he told
the miller to bring them back to him. When they came he
gave them some of the other salad to eat, so that they took
their human shapes again. The beautiful maiden fell on
her knees before him, and said, "Oh, my beloved, forgive
me all the wrong I have done you. My mother forced me
to do it. It was against my own will, for I love you dearly.
Your wishing cloak is hanging in the cupboard, and you
shall have the bird's heart back too."

But he said, "Keep it. It will be all the same, as I will
take you to be my own true wife."

Their marriage was soon after celebrated and they
lived happily together till they died.

The Bremen Town Musicians

A CERTAIN man had an ass which for many years carried sacks to the mill without tiring. At last, however, its strength was worn out and it was no longer of any use for work. Accordingly its master began to ponder as to how best to cut down its keep. But the ass, seeing mischief in the air, ran away and started on the road to Bremen. There he thought he could become a town musician.

When he had been traveling a short time, he fell in with a hound, who was lying panting on the road as though he had run himself off his legs.

"Well, why are you panting so, Growler?" said the ass.

"Ah," said the hound, "just because I am old, and every day I get weaker. And also, because I can no longer keep up with the pack, my master wanted to kill me, so I took my departure. But now how am I to earn my bread?"

"Do you know what?" said the ass. "I am going to Bremen and shall there become a town musician. Come with me and take your part in the music. I shall play the lute, and you shall beat the kettledrum."

The hound agreed and they went on.

A short time afterwards they came upon a cat sitting in the road, with a face as long as a wet week.

"Well, why are you so cross, Whiskers?" the ass asked him.

"Who can be cheerful when he is out at elbows?" said the cat. "I am getting on in years and my teeth are blunted, and I prefer to sit by the stove and purr instead of hunting round after mice. Just because of this my mistress wanted to drown me. I made myself scarce, but now I don't know where to turn."

"Come with us to Bremen," said the ass. "You are a great hand at serenading, so you can become a town musician."

The cat consented and joined them.

Next the fugitives passed by a yard where a barnyard fowl was sitting on the door, crowing with all its might.

"You crow so loud you pierce one through and through," said the ass. "What is the matter?"

"Why, didn't I prophesy fine weather for Lady Day, when Our Lady washes the Christ Child's little garment and wants to dry it? But notwithstanding this, because Sunday visitors are coming tomorrow, the mistress has no pity, and she has ordered the cook to make me into soup. So I shall have my neck wrung tonight. Now I am crowing with all my might while I have the chance."

"Come along, Red-comb," said the ass. "You had much better come with us. We are going to Bremen and you will find a much better fate there. You have a good voice, and when we make music together there will be quality in it."

The cock allowed himself to be persuaded and they all four went off together. They could not, however, reach the town in one day, and by evening they arrived at a wood, where they determined to spend the night. The ass and the hound lay down under a big tree. The cat and the cock settled themselves in the branches, the cock flying right up to the top, which was the safest place for him. Before going to sleep he looked round once more in every direction. Suddenly he called out to his comrades that there must be a house not far off, for he saw a light.

"Very well," said the ass. "Let us set out and make our way to it, for the entertainment here is very bad."

The hound thought some bones or meat would suit him too, so they set out in the direction of the light. They soon saw it shining more clearly and getting bigger and bigger, till they reached a brightly lighted robbers' den. The ass, being the tallest, looked in the window.

"What do you see, old Jackass?" asked the cock.

"What do I see?" answered the ass. "Why, a table spread with delicious food and drink, and robbers seated at it enjoying themselves."

"That would just suit us," said the cock.

"Yes, if we were only there," answered the ass.

Then the animals took counsel as to how to set about driving the robbers out. At last they hit upon a plan.

The ass was to take up his position with his forefeet on the window sill, the hound was to jump on his back, the cat to climb up onto the hound, and last of all the cock was to up and perch on the cat's head. When they were thus arranged, at a given signal they all began to perform their music. The ass brayed, the hound barked, the cat mewed, and the cock crowed. Then they dashed through the window, shivering the panes. The robbers jumped up at the terrible noise. They thought nothing less than that the devil was coming in upon them and fled into the wood in the greatest alarm. Then the four animals sat down to table and helped themselves according to taste, and they ate as though they had been starving for weeks. When they had finished, they extinguished the light and looked for sleeping places, each one to suit his nature and taste.

The ass lay down on a pile of straw, the hound behind the door, the cat on the hearth near the warm ashes, and the cock flew up to the rafters. As they were tired from the long journey, they soon went to sleep.

When midnight was past, and the robbers saw from a distance that the light was no longer burning and that all seemed quiet, the chief said, "We ought not to have been scared by a false alarm." And he ordered one of the robbers to go and examine the house.

Finding all quiet, the messenger went into the kitchen to kindle a light. And taking the cat's glowing, fiery eyes for live coals, he held a match close to them so as to light it. But the cat would stand no nonsense—it flew at his face, spat, and scratched. He was terribly frightened and ran away. He tried to get out the back door, but the hound, who was lying there, jumped up and bit his leg. As he ran across the pile of straw in front of the house, the ass gave him a good sound kick with his hind legs; while the cock, who had awakened at the uproar quite fresh and gay, cried out from his perch, "Cock-a-doodle-doo."

Thereupon the robber ran back as fast as he could to his chief and said, "There is a gruesome witch in the house who breathed on me and scratched me with her long fingers. Behind the door there stands a man with a knife, who stabbed me, while in the yard lies a black monster who hit me with a club. And upon the roof the judge is seated, and he called out, 'Bring the rogue here!' So I hurried away as fast as I could."

Thenceforward the robbers did not venture again to the house, which pleased the four Bremen musicians so much that they never wished to leave it again.

The Raven

THERE was once a queen who had a little daughter still in arms. One day the child was naughty and would not be quiet, whatever her mother might say.

Then she grew impatient, and as the ravens were flying round the castle, she opened the window and said, "I wish you were a raven, that you might fly away, and then I should have peace."

She had hardly said the words when the child was changed into a raven and flew out of the window. She flew straight into a dark wood, and her parents did not know what had become of her. One day a man was passing through this wood and heard the raven calling.

When he was near enough, the raven said, "I am a princess by birth, and I am bewitched, but you can deliver me from the spell."

"What must I do?" asked the man.

"Go further into the wood," she said, "and you will come to a house with an old woman in it. She will offer you food and drink, but you must not take any. If you eat or drink what she offers you, you will fall into a deep sleep, and then you will never be able to deliver me. There is a great heap of tanbark in the garden behind the house. You must stand on it and wait for me. I will come for three days in a coach drawn by four horses which on the first day will be white. On the second day the horses will be chestnut, and on the last day black. If you are not awake, I shall not be delivered."

The man promised to do everything that she asked, but the raven said, "Alas, I know that you will not deliver me! You will take what the woman offers you, and I shall never be freed from the spell."

He promised once more not to touch either the food or the drink, but when he reached the house the old woman said to him, "Poor man, how tired you are! Come and refresh yourself. Eat and drink."

"No," said the man, "I will neither eat nor drink."

But she persisted and said, "Well, if you won't eat, take a sip out of the glass. One sip is nothing." Then he yielded and took a little sip.

About two o'clock he went down into the garden and stood on the tan-heap to wait for the raven. All at once he became so tired that he could not keep on his feet, and he lay down for a moment, not meaning to go to sleep. But he had hardly stretched himself out before his eyelids closed, and he fell fast asleep. He slept so soundly that nothing in the world could have awakened him.

At two o'clock the raven came, drawn by her four white horses. She was already very sad, for she said, "I know he is asleep." She alighted from the carriage, went to him, shook him, and called him, but he did not wake.

Next day at dinnertime the old woman came again and brought him food and drink, but again he refused to touch it. But she left him no peace, till at last she induced him to take a sip from the glass.

Towards two o'clock he again went into the garden and stood on the tan-heap, meaning to wait for the raven.

But he suddenly became so tired that he sank down and fell into a deep sleep.

When the raven drove up with her chestnut horses, she was very mournful and said, "I know he is asleep." She went to him but he was fast asleep, and would not wake.

Next day the old woman said, "What is the meaning of this? If you don't eat or drink you will die."

He said, "I must not, and I will not, either eat or drink." She put the dish of food and the glass of wine before him, and when the scent of the wine reached him he could withstand it no longer and swallowed a good draught.

When the time came he went into the garden and stood on the tan-heap and waited for the raven. But he was more tired than ever, and lay down and slept like a log.

At two o'clock the raven came, drawn by four black horses. The coach and everything about it was black. She herself was in the deepest mourning and said, "Alas! I know he is asleep." She shook him and called him, but she could not wake him.

Finding her efforts in vain, she placed a loaf beside him, a piece of meat, and a bottle of wine. Then she took a golden ring on which her name was engraved, and put it on his finger. Last, she laid a letter by him, saying that the bread, the meat, and the wine were inexhaustible. She also said, "I see that you cannot deliver me here, but if you still wish to do so, come to the Golden Castle of Stromberg. I know that it is still in your power."

Then she seated herself in her coach again and drove to the Golden Castle of Stromberg.

When the man woke and found that he had been asleep, his heart grew heavy and he said, "She certainly must have passed, and I have not delivered her."

Then his eyes fell on the things lying by him and he read the letter which told him all that had occurred. So he got up and went away to find the Golden Castle of Stromberg, but he had no idea where to find it.

When he had wandered about for a long time he came to a dark wood whence he could not find his way out. After walking about in it for a fortnight, he lay down one night under a bush to sleep, for he was very tired. But he heard such lamentations and howling that he could not go to sleep. Then he saw a light glimmering in the distance and went towards it. When he reached it, he found that it came from a house which looked very tiny because a huge giant was standing at the door. He thought, "If I go in and the giant sees me, I shan't escape with my life." But at last he ventured to go forward.

When the giant saw him, he said, "It's a good thing you have appeared, for I have had nothing to eat for an age. I will just swallow you for my supper."

"I had much rather that you did not," said the man. "I do not really like to be eaten. But if you only want something to eat, I have plenty here to satisfy you."

"If you are speaking the truth," said the giant, "you may be quite easy. I was only going to eat you because I had nothing else."

Then they went in and sat down at the table, and the man produced the bread, the meat, and the wine, which were all inexhaustible. "This just suits me fine," said the giant, and he ate as much as ever he could.

The man said to him, "Can you tell me where to find the Golden Castle of Stromberg?"

The giant said, "I will look at my map. Every town, village, and house is marked upon it."

He fetched the map, but the castle was not to be found.

"It doesn't matter," he said. "I have bigger maps upstairs in my chest. We will look for it there."

At last on a very old map they found the Golden Castle of Stromberg, but it was many thousands of miles away.

"How am I ever to get there?" asked the man.

The giant said, "I have a couple of hours to spare, and I can carry you rather near it. But then I must come back home to look after my wife and child."

Then the giant transported him to within a hundred leagues of the castle and said, "You will be able to find your way easily from here alone." Then he went back, and the man went on till at last he came to the Golden Castle.

It stood on a mountain of glass, and the bewitched maiden drove round and round it every day in her coach. He was delighted to see her again and wanted to go to her at once, but when he tried to climb the mountain, he found it was so slippery that he slid back at every step.

When he found he could not reach her, he grew very sad and said to himself, "I will stay down here below and wait for her."

So he built himself a little hut and lived in it for a whole year, and every day he could see the Princess above, driving round and round the castle, but he could never get to her.

Then one day he saw three robbers fighting, and called out to them, "God be with you!"

They stopped at the sound of his voice, but seeing nothing they began to fight again.

Then he cried again, "God be with you!"

They stopped and looked about, but seeing no one, went on fighting.

At two o'clock the raven came, drawn by
her four white horses.

Then he cried for the third time, "God be with you!"

Again they stopped and looked about, but as there was no one visible they fell to fighting more savagely than ever.

He said to himself, "I must see what it is all about."

He went up and asked them why they were fighting. One of them said he had found a stick which made any door fly open which it touched. The second said he had found a cloak which made him invisible when he wore it. The third said he had caught a horse which could go anywhere, even up the mountain of glass. They could not decide whether these things should be common property or whether they should divide them.

Then said the man, "I will give you something in exchange for them if you like. I have no money, but I have something more valuable. First, however, I must test your things to see if you are speaking the truth."

They let him get onto the horse, put on the cloak, and take the stick in his hand. When he had got them all, he was nowhere to be seen.

Then he gave them each a sound drubbing and said, "Now you have your deserts, you rascals! You may be satisfied with that."

Then he rode up the glass mountain, and when he reached the castle he found the gate was shut. He touched it with his stick and it flew open.

He entered and went straight up the stairs into the gallery, where the maiden sat with a golden cup of wine before her. She, however, could not see him because he had the cloak on. Then he took the ring she had given him and dropped it into the cup, where it fell with a clink.

She cried, "That is my ring! The man who is to deliver me must be here."

They searched for him all over the castle but could not find him, for he had gone outside, taken off the cloak, and mounted his horse. When the people came to the gate and saw him, they raised cries of joy.

Then he dismounted and took the Princess in his arms. She kissed him, and said, "Now you have delivered me, and tomorrow we will celebrate our marriage."

Cinderella

THE wife of a rich man fell ill, and when she felt that she was nearing her end she called her only daughter to her bedside and said, "Dear child, continue devout and good. Then God will always help you, and I will look down upon you from heaven and watch over you."

Thereupon she closed her eyes and breathed her last.

The maiden went to her mother's grave every day and wept, and she continued to be devout and good. When the winter came, the snow spread a white covering on the grave. And when the sun of spring had unveiled it again, the husband took another wife. The new wife brought home with her two daughters who were fair and beautiful to look upon, but base and black at heart.

Then began a sad time for the unfortunate stepchild.

"Is this stupid goose to sit with us in the parlor?" they said. "Whoever wants to eat bread must earn it. Go and sit with the kitchenmaid."

They took away her pretty clothes and made her put on an old gray frock, and gave her wooden clogs.

"Just look at the proud princess! How well she's dressed," they laughed, as they led her to the kitchen.

There the girl was obliged to do hard work from morning till night, to get up at daybreak, carry water, light the fire, cook, and wash. Not content with that, the sisters inflicted on her every vexation they could think of. They made fun of her, and tossed the peas and lentils among the ashes, so that she had to sit down and pick them out again. In the evening, when she was worn out with work, she had no bed to go to but had to lie on the hearth among the cinders. And because, on account of that, she always looked dusty and dirty, they called her Cinderella.

It happened one day that the father had a mind to go to the fair. So he asked both his stepdaughters what he should bring home for them.

"Fine clothes," said one.

"Pearls and jewels," said the other.

"But you, Cinderella," said he, "what will you have?"

"Father, break off for me the first twig which brushes against your hat on your way home."

Well, for his two stepdaughters he brought beautiful clothes, pearls, and jewels. And on his way home, as he was riding through a green copse, a hazel twig grazed against him and knocked his hat off. Then he broke off the branch and took it with him.

When he got home he gave his stepdaughters what they had asked for, and to Cinderella he gave the twig from the hazel tree.

Cinderella thanked him, and went to her mother's grave and planted the twig upon it. She wept so much that her tears fell and watered it, and it took root and became a fine tree.

Cinderella went to the grave three times every day. She wept and prayed there, and every time she went a little white bird came and perched upon the tree. And when she uttered a wish, the little bird threw down to her what she had wished for.

Now it happened that the King proclaimed a festival which was to last three days, and to which all the beautiful maidens in the country were invited, in order that his son might choose a bride.

When the two stepdaughters heard that they were also to be present, they were in high spirits.

They called Cinderella and said, "Brush our hair and clean our shoes and fasten our buckles, for we are going to the feast at the King's palace."

Cinderella obeyed but wept, for she also would gladly have gone to the ball with them, and she begged her stepmother to give her leave to go.

"You, Cinderella?" she said. "Why, you are covered with dust and dirt. You go to the festival? You have no clothes or shoes, and yet you want to go to the ball."

As she went on asking, however, her stepmother said, "Well, I have thrown a dishful of lentils into the cinders. If you have picked them all out in two hours you shall go."

The girl went through the back door into the garden and cried, "Ye gentle doves, ye turtledoves, and all ye little birds under heaven, come and help me—

"The good into a dish to throw,
The bad into your crops can go."

Then two white doves came in by the kitchen window and were followed by the turtledoves, and finally all the little birds under heaven flocked in chirping and settled down among the ashes. And the doves gave a nod with their little heads, peck, peck, peck. And then the rest began also, peck, peck, peck, and collected all the good beans into the dish. Scarcely had an hour passed before they had finished and had all flown out again.

Then the girl brought the dish to her stepmother, and was delighted to think that now she would be able to go to the feast with them.

But she said, "No, Cinderella, you have no clothes and cannot dance. You will only be laughed at."

But when she began to cry, the stepmother said, "If you can pick out two whole dishes of lentils from the ashes in an hour, you shall go with us." And she thought, "She will never be able to do that."

When her stepmother had thrown the dishes of lentils among the ashes, the girl went out through the back door and cried, "Ye gentle doves, ye turtledoves, and all ye little birds under heaven, come and help me—

> "The good into a dish to throw,
> The bad into your crops can go."

Then two white doves came in by the kitchen window, and were followed by the turtledoves and all the other little birds under heaven. And in less than an hour the lentils had been picked up, and they had all flown away.

Then the girl carried the dish to her stepmother and was delighted to think that she would now be able to go to the ball.

But she said, "It's not a bit of good. You can't go with us, for you've got no clothes and you can't dance. We should be quite ashamed of you."

Thereupon she turned her back upon her and hurried off with her two proud daughters.

After everyone had left the house, Cinderella went out to her mother's grave under the hazel tree, and cried:

> "Shiver and shake, dear little tree,
> Gold and silver shower on me."

Then the bird threw down to her a gold and silver robe and a pair of slippers embroidered with silk and silver. With all speed she put on the robe and went to the feast. But her stepsisters and their mother did not recognize her. They supposed that she was some foreign princess, so beautiful did she appear in her golden dress. They never gave a thought to Cinderella, but imagined that she was sitting at home in the dirt, picking the lentils out of the cinders.

The Prince came up to the stranger, took her by the hand, and danced with her. In fact he would not dance with anyone else and never let go of her hand. If anyone

came up to ask her to dance, he said, "This is my partner."

She danced until nightfall and then wanted to go home, but the Prince said, "I will go with you and escort you."

He wanted to see to whom the beautiful maiden belonged. But she slipped out of his way and sprang into the pigeon house.

Then the Prince waited till her father came, and told him that the unknown maiden had vanished into the pigeon house.

The old man thought, "Could it be Cinderella?" And he had an ax brought to him so that he might break down the pigeon house, but there was no one inside.

When they went home, there lay Cinderella in her dirty clothes among the cinders, and a dismal oil lamp was burning in the chimney corner, for Cinderella had quietly jumped out of the pigeon house and had run back to the hazel tree. There she had taken off her beautiful clothes and laid them on the grave, and the bird had taken them away again. Then she had settled herself among the ashes on the hearth in her old gray frock.

On the second day, when the festival was renewed and her parents and stepsisters had started forth again, Cinderella went to the hazel tree and said:

"Shiver and shake, dear little tree,
Gold and silver shower on me."

Then the bird threw down a still more gorgeous robe than on the previous day. And when she appeared at the festival in this robe, everyone was astounded by her beauty.

The King's son had waited till she came and at once took her hand, and she danced with no one but him.

When others came forward and invited her to dance, he said, "This is my partner."

At nightfall she wished to leave; but the Prince went after her, hoping to see into what house she went, but she sprang out into the garden behind the house. There stood a fine big tree on which the most delicious pears hung. She climbed up among the branches as nimbly as a squirrel, and the Prince could not make out what had become of her.

But he waited till her father came and then said to him, "The unknown maiden has slipped away from me, and I think that she has jumped into the pear tree."

The father thought, "Can it be Cinderella?" And he had the ax brought to cut down the tree, but there was no one in it. When they went home and looked into the kitchen, there lay Cinderella among the cinders as usual, for she had jumped down on the other side of the tree, taken back the beautiful clothes to the bird on the hazel tree, and put on her old gray frock.

On the third day, when her parents and sisters had started, Cinderella went again to her mother's grave and said:

> *"Shiver and shake, dear little tree,*
> *Gold and silver shower on me."*

Then the bird threw down a dress which was so magnificent that no one had ever seen the like before, and the slippers were entirely of gold. When she appeared at the festival in this attire, they were all speechless with astonishment. The Prince danced only with her, and if anyone else asked her to dance he said, "This is my partner."

When night fell and she wanted to leave, the Prince was more desirous than ever to accompany her, but she darted away from him so quickly that he could not keep up with her. But the Prince had used a stratagem, and had caused the steps to be covered with cobbler's wax. The consequence was, that as the maiden sprang down them, her left slipper remained sticking there. The Prince took it up. It was small and dainty and made entirely of gold.

The next morning he went with it to Cinderella's father and said to him, "No other shall become my wife but she whose foot this golden slipper fits."

The two sisters were delighted at that, for they both had beautiful feet. The eldest went into the room intending to try on the slipper, and her mother stood beside her. But her great toe prevented her getting it on. Her foot was too long.

Then her mother handed her a knife and said, "Cut off the toe. When you are Queen you won't have to walk any more."

The girl cut off her toe, forced her foot into the slipper, stifled her pain, and went out to the Prince. Then he took her up on his horse as his bride and rode away with her.

However, they had to pass the grave on the way, and there sat the two doves on the hazel tree and cried:

> "Prithee, look back, prithee, look back,
> There's blood on the track.
> The shoe is too small;
> At home the true bride is waiting thy call."

Then he looked at her foot and saw how the blood was streaming from it. So he turned his horse round and carried the false bride back to her home, and said that she was not the right one.

Then the second sister must try the shoe. She went

into the room and succeeded in getting her toes into the shoe, but her heel was too big.

Then her mother handed her a knife and said, "Cut a bit off your heel. When you are Queen you won't have to walk any more."

The maiden cut a bit off her heel, forced her foot into the shoe, stifled her pain, and went out to the Prince. Then he took her up on his horse as his bride and rode off with her. As they passed the grave, the two doves were sitting on the hazel tree, crying:

> "Prithee, look back, prithee, look back,
> There's blood on the track.
> The shoe is too small;
> At home the true bride is waiting thy call."

He looked down at her foot and saw that it was streaming with blood and that there were dark red spots on her stockings. Then he turned his horse and brought the false bride back to her home.

"This is not the right one either," he said. "Have you no other daughter?"

"No," said the man. "There is only a daughter of my late wife's, a puny, stunted drudge, but she cannot possibly be the bride."

The Prince said that she must be sent for.

But the mother answered, "Oh no. She is much too dirty. She mustn't be seen on any account."

He was absolutely determined, however, to have his way, and they were obliged to summon Cinderella.

When she had washed her hands and face, she went up and curtsied to the Prince, who handed her the golden slipper. Then she sat down on a bench, pulled off her wooden clog, and put on the slipper, which fitted to a nicety. And when she stood up and the Prince looked into her face, he recognized the beautiful maiden that he had danced with and cried, "This is the true bride!"

The stepmother and the two sisters were dismayed and turned white with rage. But he took Cinderella on his horse and rode off with her.

As they rode past the hazel tree the two doves cried:

> "Prithee, look back, prithee, look back,
> No blood's on the track.
> The shoe's not too small;
> You carry the true bride home to your hall."

And when they had said this they both came flying down and settled on Cinderella's shoulders, one on the right and one on the left, and they remained perched there.

When the wedding was going to take place, the two false sisters came and wanted to curry favor with her and take part in her good fortune. As the bridal party was going to the church, the elder was on the right side, the younger on the left, and the doves picked out one of the eyes of each of them.

Afterwards when they were coming out of the church, the elder was on the left, the younger on the right, and the doves picked out the other eye of each of them. And so for their wickedness and falseness they were punished with blindness for the rest of their days.

Snow-White and the Seven Dwarfs

ONCE upon a time in the middle of winter, when the snowflakes were falling like feathers from the sky, a queen sat at her window working, and her embroidery frame was of ebony. And as she worked, gazing at times out on the snow, she pricked her finger, and there fell from it three drops of blood on the snow. And when she saw how bright and red it looked, she said to herself, "Oh, that I had a child as white as snow, as red as blood, and as black as the wood of the embroidery frame!"

Not very long afterwards she had a daughter, with a skin as white as snow, lips as red as blood, and hair as black as ebony, and she was named Snow-White. And when she was born the Queen died.

After a year had gone by, the King took another wife, a beautiful woman, but proud and overbearing, and she could not bear to be surpassed in beauty by anyone. She had a magic looking glass, and she used to stand before it and look in it and say:

> "Looking glass upon the wall,
> Who is fairest of us all?"

And the looking glass would answer:

> "You are fairest of them all."

And she was contented, for she knew that the looking glass spoke the truth.

Now Snow-White was growing prettier and prettier, and when she was seven years old she was as beautiful as day, far more so than the Queen herself. So one day when the Queen went to her mirror and said:

> *"Looking glass upon the wall,*
> *Who is fairest of us all?"*

It answered:

> *"Queen, you are full fair, 'tis true,*
> *But Snow-White fairer is than you."*

This gave the Queen a great shock, and she became yellow and green with envy, and from that hour her heart turned against Snow-White and she hated her. And envy and pride like ill weeds grew higher in her heart every day until she had no peace day or night.

At last she sent for a huntsman and said, "Take the child out into the woods, so that I may set eyes on her no more. You must put her to death and bring me her heart for a token."

The huntsman consented and led her away. But when he drew his cutlass to pierce Snow-White's innocent heart, she began to weep and to say, "Oh, dear huntsman, do not take my life. I will go away into the wildwood and never come home again."

And as she was so lovely the huntsman had pity on her and said, "Away with you then, poor child."

He thought the wild animals would be sure to devour her, and it was as if a stone had been rolled away from his heart when he was spared putting her to death.

Just at that moment a young wild boar came running by, so he caught and killed it. And taking out its heart, he brought it to the Queen for a token. And it was salted and cooked and the wicked woman ate it up, thinking that there was an end of Snow-White.

Now when the poor child found herself quite alone in the wild woods, she felt full of terror, even of the very leaves on the trees, and she did not know what to do for fright. Then she began to run over the sharp stones and through the thorn bushes, and the wild beasts ran about her but they did her no harm. She ran as long as her feet would carry her. And when the evening drew near she came to a little house and she went inside to rest. Everything there was very small, but as pretty and clean as possible. There stood a little table, ready laid. It was covered with a white cloth and seven little plates, and seven knives and forks, and drinking cups. By the wall stood seven little beds side by side, covered with clean white quilts.

Snow-White, being very hungry and thirsty, ate from each plate a little porridge and bread, and drank out of each little cup a drop of wine, so as not to finish up any one portion. After that she felt so tired that she lay down in turn on each of the beds, but none of them seemed to suit her. One was too long, another too short; but at last the seventh was quite right, and so she lay down upon it, committed herself to heaven, and fell asleep.

When it was quite dark, the masters of the house came home. They were seven dwarfs whose work it was to dig underground among the mountains. When they had lighted their seven candles and it was quite light in the little house, they saw that someone must have been in, as everything was not in the same order in which they left it.

The first said, "Who has been sitting in my little chair?"

The second said, "Who has been eating from my little plate?"

The third said, "Who has been taking from my little loaf?"

The fourth said, "Who has been tasting my porridge?"

The fifth said, "Who has been using my little fork?"

The sixth said, "Who has been cutting with my little knife?"

The seventh said, "Who has been drinking from my little cup?"

Then the first one, looking round, saw a hollow in his bed and cried, "Who has been lying on my bed?"

And the others came running and cried, "Someone has been on our beds too!"

But when the seventh looked at his bed, he saw little Snow-White lying there asleep. Then he told the others, who came running up, crying out in their astonishment and holding up their seven little candles to throw a light upon Snow-White.

"Goodness gracious!" they cried. "What beautiful child is this?" And they were so full of joy to see her that they did not wake her, but let her sleep on. And the seventh dwarf slept with his comrades, an hour at a time with each, until the night had passed.

When it was morning, and Snow-White awoke and saw the seven dwarfs, she was very frightened. But they seemed quite friendly and asked her what her name was, and she told them. Then they asked her how she came to be in their house. And she related to them how her step-mother had wished her to be put to death, and how the huntsman had spared her life, and how she had run the whole day long until at last she had found their little house.

Then the dwarfs said, "If you will keep our house for us, and cook, and wash, and make the beds, and sew and knit, and keep everything tidy and clean, you may stay with us, and you shall lack nothing."

"With all my heart," said Snow-White. And so she stayed and kept the house in good order. In the morning the dwarfs went to the mountain to dig for gold. In the evening they came home, and their supper had to be ready for them.

All the day long the maiden was left alone, and the good little dwarfs warned her, saying, "Beware of your stepmother! She will soon know you are here. Let no one into the house."

Now the Queen, having eaten Snow-White's heart, as she supposed, felt quite sure that now she was the first and fairest, and so she came to her mirror and said:

> *"Looking glass upon the wall,*
> *Who is fairest of us all?"*

And the glass answered:

> *"Queen, thou art of beauty rare,*
> *But Snow-White living in the glen*
> *With the seven little men*
> *Is a thousand times more fair."*

Then she was very angry, for the glass always spoke the truth, and she knew that the huntsman must have deceived her and that Snow-White must still be living. And she thought and thought how she could manage to make an end of her, for as long as she was not the fairest in the land, envy left her no rest. At last she thought of a plan. She painted her face and dressed herself like an old peddler woman, so that no one would have known her. In this disguise she went across the seven mountains, until she came to the house of the seven little dwarfs.

And she knocked at the door and cried, "Fine wares to sell! Fine wares to sell!"

Snow-White peeped out of the window and cried, "Good day, good woman, what have you to sell?"

"Good wares, fine wares," answered she. "Laces of all colors." And she held up a piece that was woven of many-colored silk.

"I need not be afraid of letting in this good woman," thought Snow-White, and she unbarred the door and bought the pretty lace.

"What a figure you are, child!" said the old woman. "Come and let me lace your bodice properly for once."

Snow-White, suspecting nothing, stood up before her and let her lace her with the new lace. But the old woman laced so quickly and tightly that it took Snow-White's breath away, and she fell down as dead.

"Now you are no longer the fairest," said the old woman as she hastened away.

Not long after that, towards evening, the seven dwarfs came home, and they were terrified to see their dear Snow-White lying on the ground without life or motion. They raised her up, and when they saw how tightly the lace was drawn, they cut it in two. Then she began to draw breath, and little by little she returned to life.

When the dwarfs heard what had happened they said, "The old peddler woman was no other than the wicked

Queen. You must beware of letting anyone in when we are not here!"

And when the wicked woman got home she went to her glass and said:

> *"Looking glass against the wall,*
> *Who is fairest of us all?"*

And it answered as before:

> *"Queen, thou art of beauty rare,*
> *But Snow-White living in the glen*
> *With the seven little men*
> *Is a thousand times more fair."*

When she heard that, she was so struck with surprise that all the blood left her heart, for she knew that Snow-White must still be living.

"But now," said she, "I will think of something that will be her ruin." And by witchcraft she made a poisoned comb. Then she dressed herself up to look like another and different sort of old woman.

So she went across the seven mountains and came to the house of the seven dwarfs, and knocked at the door and cried, "Good wares to sell! good wares to sell!"

Snow-White looked out and said, "Go away, I must not let anybody in."

"But you are not forbidden to look," said the old woman, taking out the poisoned comb and holding it up. It pleased the poor child so much that she was tempted to open the door. And when the bargain was made the old woman said, "Now for once your hair shall be properly combed."

Poor Snow-White, thinking no harm, let the old woman do as she would, but no sooner was the comb put in her hair than the poison began to work, and the poor girl fell down senseless.

"Now, you paragon of beauty," said the wicked woman, "this is the end of you!" And she went off.

By good luck it was now near evening and the seven little dwarfs came home. When they saw Snow-White lying on the ground as dead, they thought directly that it was the stepmother's doing. They looked about and found the poisoned comb, and no sooner had they drawn it out of her hair than Snow-White came to herself and related all that had passed. Then they warned her once more to be on her guard, and never again to let anyone in at the door.

And the Queen went home and stood before the looking glass and said:

> *"Looking glass against the wall,*
> *Who is fairest of us all?"*

And the looking glass answered as before:

> *"Queen, thou art of beauty rare,*
> *But Snow-White living in the glen*
> *With the seven little men*
> *Is a thousand times more fair."*

When she heard the looking glass speak thus she trembled and shook with anger.

"Snow-White shall die," cried she, "though it should cost me my own life!"

And then she went to a secret lonely chamber where no one was likely to come, and there she made a poisonous apple. It was beautiful to look upon, being white with red cheeks, so that anyone who should see it must long for it, but whoever ate even a little bit of it must die. When the apple was ready, she painted her face and clothed herself like a peasant woman, and went across the seven mountains to where the seven dwarfs lived.

And when she knocked at the door Snow-White put her head out of the window and said, "I dare not let anybody in. The seven dwarfs told me not to."

"All right," answered the woman. "I can easily get rid of my apples elsewhere. There, I will give you one."

"No," answered Snow-White. "I dare not take anything."

"Are you afraid of poison?" said the woman. "Look here, I will cut the apple in two pieces. You shall have the red side. I will have the white one."

The apple was so cunningly made that all of the poison was in the rosy half of it. Snow-White longed for the beautiful apple. And as she saw the peasant woman eating a piece of it she could no longer refrain, but stretched out her hand and took the poisoned half. But no sooner had she taken a morsel of it into her mouth than she fell to the earth as dead.

And the Queen, casting on her a terrible glance, laughed aloud and cried, "As white as snow, as red as blood, as black as ebony! This time the dwarfs will not be able to bring you to life again."

When she went home and asked the looking glass·

> *"Looking glass against the wall,*
> *Who is fairest of us all?"*

—at last it answered, "You are the fairest now of all."

Then her envious heart had peace, as much as an envious heart can have.

The dwarfs, when they came home in the evening, found Snow-White lying on the ground, and there came no breath out of her mouth, and she was dead. They lifted her up, sought if anything poisonous was to be found, cut her laces, combed her hair, washed her with water and wine, but all was of no avail. The poor child was dead, and remained dead. Then they laid her on a bier, and all seven of them sat around it, and wept and lamented three whole days. And then they would have buried her, except that she still looked as if she were living, with her beautiful blooming cheeks. So they said, "We cannot hide her away in the black ground."

And they had made a coffin of clear glass, that could be looked into from all sides. They laid her in it and wrote upon it in golden letters her name, and that she was a king's daughter. Then they set the coffin out upon the mountain and one of them always remained by it to watch. And the birds came too and mourned for Snow-White: first an owl, then a raven, and last, a dove.

Now for a long while Snow-White lay in the coffin and never changed, but looked as if she were asleep, for she was still as white as snow, as red as blood, and her hair was as black as ebony. It happened, however, that one day a king's son rode through the wood and up to the dwarfs' house, which was near it. He saw on the mountain the coffin, and beautiful Snow-White within it, and he read what was written in golden letters upon it.

Then he said to the dwarfs, "Let me have the coffin, and I will give you whatever you like to ask for it."

But the dwarfs told him that they could not part with it for all the gold in the world.

But he said, "I beseech you to give it to me, for I cannot live without looking upon Snow-White. If you consent, I will bring you to great honor and care for you as if you were my brethren."

When he pleaded, the good little dwarfs had pity upon him and gave him the coffin, and the King's son called his servants and bid them carry it away on their shoulders. Now it happened that as they were going along they stumbled over a bush, and with the shaking the bit of poisoned apple flew out of her throat. It was not long before she opened her eyes, threw up the cover of the coffin, and sat up, alive and well. "Oh dear, where am I?" cried she.

The King's son answered, full of joy, "You are near me." And relating all that had happened, he said, "I would rather have you than anything in the world. Come with me to my father's castle and you shall be my bride."

And Snow-White was kind and went with him, and their wedding was held with pomp and great splendor.

But Snow-White's wicked stepmother was also bidden to the feast. And when she had dressed herself in beautiful clothes she went to her looking glass and said:

> "Looking glass upon the wall,
> Who is fairest of us all?"

The looking glass answered:

"O Queen, although you are of beauty rare,
The young bride is a thousand times more fair."

Then she railed and cursed, and was beside herself with disappointment and anger. First she thought she would not go to the wedding, but then she felt she should have no peace until she went and saw the bride. And when she saw her she knew her for Snow-White, and could not stir from the place for anger and terror. For they had ready red-hot iron shoes, in which she had to dance until she fell down dead.

The Elves and the Shoemaker

THERE was once a shoemaker who through no fault of his own had become so poor that at last he had only leather enough left for one pair of shoes. At evening he cut out the shoes which he intended to begin upon the next morning, and since he had a good conscience, he lay down quietly, said his prayers, and fell asleep.

In the morning, when he had said his prayers and was preparing to sit down to work, he found the pair of shoes standing finished on his table. He was amazed and could not understand it in the least.

He took the shoes in his hand to examine them more closely. They were so neatly sewn that not a stitch was out of place, and were as good as the work of a master hand.

Soon afterwards a purchaser came in and, as he was much pleased with the shoes, he paid more than the ordinary price for them, so that the shoemaker was able to buy leather for two pairs of shoes with the money.

He cut them out in the evening, and the next day with fresh courage was about to go to work. But he had no need to, for when he got up the shoes were finished, and buyers were not lacking. These gave him so much money that he was able to buy leather for four pairs of shoes.

Early next morning he found the four pairs finished, and so it went on. What he cut out at evening was finished

in the morning, so that he was soon again in comfortable circumstances and became a well-to-do man.

Now it happened one evening not long before Christmas, when he had cut out some shoes as usual, that he said to his wife, "How would it be if we were to sit up tonight to see who it is that lends us such a helping hand?"

The wife agreed and lighted a candle, and they hid themselves in the corner of the room behind the clothes which were hanging there. At midnight came two little naked men who sat down at the shoemaker's table, took up the cut-out work, and began with their tiny fingers to stitch, sew, and hammer so neatly and quickly that the shoemaker could not believe his eyes. They did not stop till everything was quite finished and stood complete on the table. Then they ran swiftly away.

The next day the wife said, "The little men have made us rich, and we ought to show our gratitude. They were running about with nothing on, and must freeze with cold. Now I will make them little shirts, coats, waistcoats, and hose, and will even knit them a pair of stockings. And you shall make them each a pair of shoes."

The husband agreed. And at evening, when they had everything ready, they laid out the presents on the table and hid themselves to see how the little men would behave.

At midnight they came skipping in and were about to set to work. But instead of the leather ready cut out, they found the charming little clothes.

At first they were surprised, then excessively delighted. With the greatest speed they put on and smoothed down the pretty clothes, singing:

> "Now we're boys so fine and neat,
> Why cobble more for others' feet?"

Then they hopped and danced about, and leapt over chairs and tables and out the door. Henceforward they came back no more, but the shoemaker fared well as long as he lived, and had good luck in all his undertakings.

The Water of Life

THERE was once a king who was so ill that it was thought impossible his life could be saved. He had three sons, and they were all in great distress on his account, and they went into the castle gardens and wept at the thought that he must die. An old man came up to them and asked the cause of their grief. They told him that their father was dying, and nothing could save him.

The old man said, "There is only one remedy which I know. It is the Water of Life. If he drinks of it he will recover, but it is very difficult to find."

The eldest son said, "I will soon find it." And he went to the sick man to ask permission to go in search of the Water of Life, as that was the only thing to cure him.

"No," said the King. "The danger is too great. I would rather die." But he persisted so long that at last the King gave his permission.

The Prince thought, "If I bring this water I shall be the favorite, and I shall inherit the kingdom."

So he set off, and when he had ridden some distance he came upon a dwarf standing in the road, who cried, "Whither away so fast?"

"Stupid little fellow," said the Prince proudly, "what business is it of yours?" And he rode on.

The little man was very angry and made an evil vow.

Soon afterwards, the Prince came to a gorge in the mountains, and the farther he rode the narrower it became, till he could go no farther. His horse could neither go forward nor turn round for him to dismount. So there he sat, jammed in.

The sick King waited a long time for him, but he never came back. Then the second son said, "Father, let me go and find the Water of Life." He was thinking, "If my brother is dead I shall have the kingdom."

The King at first refused to let him go but at last he gave his consent. So the Prince started on the same road as his brother and met the same dwarf, who stopped him and asked where he was going in such a hurry.

"Little snippet, what does it matter to you?" he said, and rode away without looking back.

But the dwarf cast a spell over him, and he, too, got into a narrow gorge like his brother, where he could neither go backwards nor forwards. That is what happens to the haughty.

As the second son also stayed away, the youngest one offered to go and fetch the Water of Life, and at last the King was obliged to let him go.

When he also met the dwarf, and the dwarf asked him where he was hurrying to, he stopped and said, "I am searching for the Water of Life, because my father is dying."

"Do you know where it is to be found?"

"No," said the Prince.

"As you have spoken pleasantly to me, and not been haughty like your false brothers, I will help you and tell you how to find the Water of Life. It flows from a fountain in the courtyard of an enchanted castle. But you will never.

get in unless I give you an iron rod and two loaves of bread. With the rod strike three times on the iron gate of the castle and it will spring open. Inside you will find two lions with wide-open jaws, but if you throw a loaf to each they will be quiet. Then you must make haste to fetch the Water of Life before it strikes twelve, or the gates of the castle will close and you will be shut in."

The Prince thanked him, took the rod and the loaves, and set off. When he reached the castle all was just as the dwarf had said. At the third knock the gate flew open, and when he had pacified the lions with the loaves, he walked into the castle. In the great hall he found several enchanted princes, and he took the rings from their fingers. He also took a sword and a loaf which were lying by them.

On passing into the next room he found a beautiful maiden, who rejoiced at his coming. She embraced him and said that he had saved her, and should have the whole of her kingdom, and if he would come back in a year she would marry him. She also told him where to find the fountain with the enchanted water, but she said he must make haste to get out of the castle before the clock struck twelve.

Then he went on and came to a room where there was a beautiful bed freshly made, and as he was very tired he thought he would take a little rest. So he lay down and fell asleep. When he woke it was striking a quarter to twelve. He sprang up in a fright, and ran to the fountain and took some of the water in a cup which was lying near, and then hurried away. The clock struck just as he reached the iron gate, and it banged so quickly that it took off a bit of his heel.

He rejoiced at having got some of the Water of Life,

and hastened on his homeward journey. He again passed the dwarf, who said when he saw the sword and the loaf, "Those things will be of much service to you. You will be able to strike down whole armies with the sword, and the loaf will never come to an end."

The Prince did not want to go home without his brothers and he said, "Good dwarf, can you not tell me where my brothers are? They went in search of the Water of Life before I did, but they never came back."

"They are both stuck fast in a narrow mountain gorge. I cast a spell over them because of their pride."

Then the Prince begged so hard that they might be released that at last the dwarf yielded. But he warned him against them and said, "Beware of them! They have bad hearts."

He was delighted to see his brothers when they came back, and told them all that had happened to him: how he had found the Water of Life and brought a gobletful with him; how he had released a beautiful princess, who would wait a year for him and then marry him, and he would then become a great prince.

Then they rode away together and came to a land where famine and war were raging. The King thought he would be utterly ruined, so great was the destitution.

The Prince went to him and gave him the loaf, and with it he fed and satisfied his whole kingdom. The Prince also gave him his sword, and he smote the whole army of his enemies with it, and then he was able to live in peace and quiet. Then the Prince took back his sword and his loaf, and the three brothers rode on.

But later they had to pass through two more countries where war and famine were raging, and each time the

They emptied the water of life from his goblet.

Prince gave his sword and his loaf to the King and in this way he saved three kingdoms.

After that they took a ship and crossed the sea. During the passage the two elder brothers said to each other, "Our youngest brother found the Water of Life, and we did not. So our father will give him the kingdom which we ought to have, and he will take away our fortune from us."

This thought made them very vindictive and they made up their minds to get rid of him. They waited till he was asleep, and then they emptied the Water of Life from his goblet and took it themselves, and filled up his cup with salt sea water.

As soon as they got home the youngest Prince took his goblet to the King so that he might drink of the water which was to make him well. But after drinking only a few drops of the sea water he became more ill than ever. As he was bewailing himself, his two elder sons came to him and accused the youngest of trying to poison him, and said that they had the real Water of Life, and gave him some. No sooner had he drunk it than he felt better, and he soon became as strong and well as he had been in his youth.

Then the two went to the youngest brother and mocked him, saying, "It was you who found the Water of Life. You had all the trouble, while we have the reward. You should have been wiser and kept your eyes open. We stole it from you while you were asleep on the ship. When the end of the year comes, one of us will go and bring away the beautiful Princess. But don't dare to betray us. Our father will certainly not believe you, and if you say a single word you will surely lose your life. Your one and only chance is to keep silence."

The old King was very angry with his youngest son,

thinking that he had tried to take his life. So he had the court assembled to give judgment upon him, and it was decided that he must be secretly got out of the way.

One day when the Prince was going out hunting, thinking no evil, the King's huntsman was ordered to go with him. Seeing the huntsman look sad, the Prince said to him, "My good huntsman, what is the matter with you?"

The huntsman answered, "I can't bear to tell you, and yet I must."

The Prince said, "Say it out. Whatever it is I will forgive you."

"Alas!" said the huntsman, "I am to shoot you dead. It is the King's command."

The Prince was horror-stricken and said, "Dear huntsman, do not kill me. Give me my life. Let me have your dress, and you shall have my royal robes."

The huntsman said, "I will gladly do so. I could never have shot you." So they changed clothes and the huntsman went home, but the Prince wandered away into the forest.

After a time three wagonloads of gold and precious stones came to the King for his youngest son. They were sent by the kings who had been saved by the Prince's sword and his miraculous loaf, and who now wished to show their gratitude.

Then the old King thought, "What if my son really was innocent?" And he said to his people, "If only he were still alive! How sorry I am that I ordered him to be killed."

"He is still alive," said the huntsman. "I could not find it in my heart to carry out your commands." And he told the King what had taken place.

A load fell from the King's heart on hearing the good news, and he sent out a proclamation to all parts of his kingdom that his son was to come home, where he would be received with great favor.

In the meantime, the Princess had caused a road to be made of pure shining gold leading to her castle, and told her people that whoever came riding straight along it would be the true bridegroom, and they were to admit him. But anyone who came either on one side of the road or the other would not be the right one, and he was not to be let in.

When the year had almost passed, the eldest Prince thought that he would hurry to the Princess, and by giving himself out as her deliverer would gain a wife and a king-dom as well. So he rode away, and when he saw the beau-tiful golden road he thought it would be a thousand pities to ride upon it, so he turned aside and rode to the right of it. But when he reached the gate the people told him that he was not the true bridegroom, and he had to go away.

Soon after the second Prince came, and when he saw the golden road he thought it would be a thousand pities for his horse to tread upon it, so he turned aside and rode up on the left of it. But when he reached the gate he was also told that he was not the true bridegroom, and like his brother was turned away.

When the year had quite come to an end, the third Prince came out of the wood to ride to his beloved, and through her to forget all his past sorrows. So on he went, thinking only of her and wishing to be with her, and he never even saw the golden road. His horse cantered right along the middle of it, and when he reached the gate it was flung open and the Princess received him joyfully, and called him her deliverer and the lord of her kingdom. Their marriage was celebrated without delay and with much rejoicing. When it was over, she told him that his father had called him back and forgiven him. So he went to him and told him everything: how his brothers had deceived him, and how they had forced him to keep silence. The old King wanted to punish them, but they had taken a ship and sailed away over the sea, and they never came back as long as they lived.

The Gallant Tailor

ONE summer morning a little tailor was sitting at his bench near the window, working cheerfully with all his might, when an old woman came down the street.

She was crying, "Good jelly to sell! Good jelly to sell!"

The cry sounded pleasant in the little tailor's ears, so he put his head out of the window and called out, "Here, my good woman! Come here, if you want a customer."

So the poor woman climbed the steps with her heavy basket, and was obliged to unpack and display all her pots to the tailor. He looked at every one of them and, lifting all the lids, applied his nose to each.

At last he said, "The jelly seems pretty good. You may weigh me out four half ounces, or I don't mind having a quarter of a pound."

The woman, who had expected to find a good customer, gave him what he asked for but went off angry and grumbling.

"This jelly is the very thing for me!" cried the little tailor. "It will give me strength and cunning." And he took down the bread from the cupboard, cut a big slice off the loaf and spread the jelly on it, laid it near him, and went on stitching more gallantly than ever. All the while the scent of the sweet jelly was spreading throughout the room, where there were quantities of flies. They were attracted by it and flew down to eat of it.

"Now then, who invited you here?" said the tailor, and drove the unbidden guests away. But the flies, not understanding his language, were not to be got rid of like that, and returned in larger numbers than before. Then the tailor, unable to stand it any longer, took from his chimney corner a ragged cloth.

"Now, I'll let you have it!" he said, and beat it among them unmercifully. When he ceased and counted the slain, he found seven lying dead before him.

"This is indeed something," he said, wondering at his own bravery. "The whole town shall know about this."

So he hastened to cut out a belt, and he stitched it and put on it in large capitals: "Seven at one blow!"

"The town, did I say?" said the little tailor. "The whole world shall know it!" And his heart quivered with joy, like a lamb's tail.

The tailor fastened the belt round him and began to

think of going out into the world, for his workshop seemed too small for his valor. So he looked about in all the house for something that would be useful to take with him, but he found nothing but an old cheese, which he put in his pocket. Outside the door he noticed that a bird had got caught in the bushes, so he took that and put it in his pocket with the cheese. Then he set out gallantly on his way, and as he was light and active he felt no fatigue.

The way led over a mountain, and when he reached the topmost peak he saw a terrible giant sitting there, and looking about him at his ease.

The tailor went bravely up to him, called out to him, and said, "Good day, comrade! There you sit looking over the wide world. I am on the way thither to seek my fortune. Have you a fancy to go with me?"

The giant looked at the tailor contemptuously and said, "You vagabond! You miserable little creature!"

"That may be," answered the little tailor, and undoing his coat he showed the giant his belt. "You can read there whether I am a man or not."

The giant read, "Seven at one blow!" And thinking it meant men that the tailor had killed, he at once felt more respect for the little fellow. But as he wanted to prove him, he took up a stone and squeezed it so hard that water came out of it.

"Now you can do that," said the giant, "that is, if you have the strength for it."

"That's not much!" said the little tailor. "I call that play." And he put his hand in his pocket and took out the cheese and squeezed it till the whey ran out of it.

"Well," said he, "what do you think of that?"

The giant did not know what to say, for he could not

have believed it of the little man. Then the giant took a stone and threw it so high that it was nearly out of sight.

"Now, little fellow, suppose you do that!"

"Well thrown!" said the tailor. "But the stone fell back to earth again. I will throw you one that will never come back." So he felt in his pocket, took out the bird, and threw it into the air. And the bird, when it found itself at liberty, took wing, flew off, and returned no more.

"What do you think of that, comrade?" asked the tailor.

"There is no doubt that you can throw," said the giant. "Now we will see if you can carry."

He led the little tailor to a mighty oak tree which had been felled and was lying on the ground, and said, "Now, if you are strong enough, help me to carry this tree out of the wood."

"Willingly," answered the little man. "You take the trunk on your shoulders and I will take the branches with all their foliage. That is by far the biggest end."

So the giant took the trunk on his shoulders, and the tailor seated himself on a branch. And the giant, who could not see what he was doing, had the whole tree to carry, and the little man on it as well. And the little man was very cheerful and merry and whistled the tune, *"There were three tailors riding by,"* as if carrying the tree were mere child's play.

The giant, when he had struggled on under his heavy load a part of the way, was tired out and cried, "Look here, I must let go the tree!"

The tailor jumped off quickly. Then, taking hold of the tree with both arms as if he were carrying it, he said to the giant, "You see you can't carry the tree, though you are such a big fellow!"

They went on together a little farther and presently they came to a cherry tree. And the giant took hold of the topmost branches, where the ripest fruit hung, and pulling them downward gave them to the tailor to hold, bidding him eat. But the little tailor was much too weak to hold the tree, and as the giant let go, the tree sprang back and the tailor was thrown up into the air.

And when he dropped down again without any damage, the giant said to him, "How is this? Haven't you strength enough to hold such a weak sprig as that?"

"It is not strength that is lacking," answered the little tailor. "How should it to one who has slain seven at one blow? I just jumped over the tree because the hunters are shooting down there in the bushes. Why don't you jump it too, if you can."

The giant made the attempt and, not being able to vault the tree, he remained hanging in the branches, so that once more the little tailor got the better of him.

Then said the giant, "As you are such a gallant fellow, suppose you come with me to our den and stay the night."

The tailor was quite willing and followed him. When they reached the den, there sat some other giants by the fire and all gladly welcomed him.

The little tailor looked round and thought, "There is more elbow room here than in my workshop."

The giant showed him a bed and told him he had better lie down on it and go to sleep. The bed, however, was too big for the tailor, so he did not stay in it but crept into a corner to sleep. As soon as it was midnight the giant got up, took a great staff of iron and beat the bed through with one stroke, and supposed he had made an end of that grasshopper of a tailor. Very early in the morning the giants went into the wood and forgot all about the little tailor, and when they saw him coming after them alive and merry, they were terribly frightened. And thinking he was going to kill them, they ran away in all haste.

So the little tailor marched on, always following his nose. And after he had gone a great way he entered the courtyard belonging to a king's palace, and there he felt so overpowered with fatigue that he lay down and fell asleep. In the meanwhile came various people, who looked at him curiously and read on his belt, "Seven at one blow!"

"Oh," said they, "why should this great lord come here in time of peace? What a mighty champion he must be!"

Then they went and told the King about him. They thought that if war should break out what a worthy and useful man he would be, and he ought not to be allowed to depart at any price. The King then summoned his council and sent one of his courtiers to the little tailor to beg him, so soon as he should wake up, to consent to serve in the King's army. So the messenger stood and waited at the sleeper's side until he began to stretch his limbs and to open his eyes, and then he carried his answer back.

"That was the reason for which I came," the little tailor had said. "I am ready to enter the King's service."

So he was received into it very honorably, and a separate dwelling was set apart for him.

But the rest of the soldiers were very much set against the little tailor, and wished him a thousand miles away.

"What shall be done about it?" they said among themselves. "If we pick a quarrel and fight with him, then seven of us will fall at each blow. That will be of no good to us."

So they came to a resolution, and went all together to the King to ask for their discharge.

"We never intended," said they, "to serve with a man who kills seven at a blow."

The King felt sorry to lose all his faithful servants because of one man. He wished that he had never seen him, and would willingly get rid of him if he might. But he did not dare to dismiss the little tailor for fear he should kill all the King's people and place himself upon the throne. He thought a long while about it, and at last made up his mind what to do.

He sent for the little tailor and told him that as he was so great a warrior he had a proposal to make to him. He told him that in a wood in his dominions dwelt two giants who did great damage by robbery, murder, and fire, and that no man dared go near them for fear of his life. But that if the tailor should overcome and slay both these giants the King would give him his only daughter in marriage and half his kingdom as dowry, and that a hundred horsemen should go with him to give him assistance.

"That would be a fine thing for a man like me," thought the little tailor. "A beautiful princess and half a kingdom are not to be had every day."

So he said to the King, "Oh yes, I can soon overcome the giants, and yet I have no need of the hundred horsemen. He who can kill seven at one blow has no need to be afraid of two."

So the little tailor set out and the hundred horsemen followed him.

When he came to the border of the wood he said to his escort, "Stay here while I go to attack the giants."

Then he sprang into the wood and looked about him right and left. After a while he caught sight of the two giants. They were lying down under a tree asleep, and snoring so that all the branches shook. The little tailor, all alert, filled both his pockets with stones and climbed up into the tree, and made his way to an overhanging bough so that he could seat himself just above the sleepers. And from there he let one stone after another fall on the chest of one of the giants.

For a long time the giant was quite unaware of this, but at last he waked up and pushed his comrade and said, "What are you hitting me for?"

"Are you dreaming?" said the other. "I am not touching you." And they composed themselves again to sleep, and the tailor let fall a stone on the other giant.

"What can that be?" cried he. "What are you casting at me?"

"I am casting nothing at you," answered the first, grumbling.

They disputed about it for a while, but as they were tired they gave it up at last, and their eyes closed once more. Then the little tailor began his game anew. He picked out a heavier stone and threw it down with force upon the first giant's chest.

"This is too much!" cried he, and sprang up like a madman and struck his companion such a blow that the tree shook above them. The other paid him back with ready coin, and they fought with such fury that they tore up trees by their roots to use for weapons against each other, so that at last both of them lay dead upon the ground. And now the little tailor got down.

"What a lucky thing," he said, "that the tree I was sitting in did not get torn up, too! Or else I should have had to jump like a squirrel from one tree to another."

Then he drew his sword and gave each of the giants a few hacks in the breast, and went back to the horsemen and said, "The deed is done. I have made an end of both of them, though it went hard with me. In the struggle they rooted up trees to defend themselves, but it was of no use. They had to do with a man who can kill seven at one blow."

"Then are you not wounded?" asked the horsemen.

"Nothing of the sort!" answered the tailor. "They have not injured a hair."

The horsemen still would not believe it and rode into the wood to see, and there they found the giants wallowing in their blood, and all about them the uprooted trees.

The little tailor then claimed the promised boon, but the King repented of his offer and again sought how to rid himself of the hero.

"Before you can possess my daughter and the half of my kingdom," said he to the tailor, "you must perform another heroic act. In the wood lives a unicorn who does great damage. You must capture him."

"A unicorn does not strike more terror into me than two giants. Seven at one blow! That is my way," was the tailor's answer.

So taking a rope and an ax with him, he went out into the wood and told those who were ordered to attend him to wait outside. He had not far to seek. The unicorn soon came out and sprang at him, as if he would make an end of him without delay.

"Softly, softly!" said the tailor. "Most haste, worst speed." And he remained standing until the animal came quite near; then he slipped quietly behind a tree. The unicorn ran with all his might against the tree and stuck his horn so deep into the trunk that he could not get it out again, and so was captured.

"Now I have you," said the tailor, coming out from behind the tree. And putting the rope around the unicorn's neck, he took the ax and cut free the horn; and when all his party was assembled he led forth the animal and brought it to the King.

The King did not yet wish to give him the promised reward and set him a third task to do. Before the wedding could take place the tailor was to secure a wild boar which had done a great deal of damage in the wood.

The huntsmen were to accompany him and help him.

"All right," said the tailor. "This is child's play."

But he did not take the huntsmen into the wood, and they were all the better pleased, for the wild boar had many a time before received them in such a way that they had no fancy to disturb him.

When the boar caught sight of the tailor he ran at him with foaming mouth and gleaming tusks to bear him to the ground, but the nimble hero rushed into a chapel which chanced to be near and jumped quickly out of a window on the other side. The boar ran after him, and when he got inside the little tailor shut the door after him, and there he was imprisoned, for the creature was too big and unwieldy to jump out of the window too.

Then the tailor called the huntsmen that they might see the prisoner with their own eyes. And then he betook himself to the King, who now, whether he liked it or not, was obliged to fulfill his promise and give him his daughter and the half of his kingdom. But if he had known that the great warrior was only a little tailor he would have taken it still more to heart.

So the wedding was celebrated with great splendor and little joy, and the tailor was made into a king.

One night the young Queen heard her husband talking in his sleep and saying, "Boy, make me that waistcoat and patch me those breeches, or I will wrap my yardstick about your shoulders!"

And as she perceived of what low birth her husband was, she went to her father the next morning and told him all, and begged him to set her free from a man who was nothing better than a tailor.

The King bade her be comforted, saying, "Tonight leave your bedroom door open. My guards shall stand outside, and when he is asleep they shall come in and bind him and carry him off to a ship that will take him to the other side of the world."

So the wife felt consoled, but the King's water bearer, who had been listening all the while, went to the little tailor and disclosed to him the whole plan.

"I shall put a stop to all this," said he.

At night he lay down as usual in bed, and when his wife thought that he was asleep she got up, opened the door, and lay down again. The little tailor, who only made believe to be asleep, began to murmur plainly.

"Boy, make me that waistcoat and patch me those breeches, or I will wrap my yardstick about your shoulders! I have slain seven at one blow, killed two giants, caught a unicorn, and taken a wild boar. And shall I be afraid of those who are standing outside my room door?"

And when they heard the tailor say this, a great fear seized the guards. They fled away as if they had been wild hares and none would venture to attack him.

And so the little tailor all his lifetime remained a king.

The Golden Goose

THERE was once a man who had three sons, the youngest of whom was called Simpleton. He was scorned and despised by the others and kept in the background.

The eldest son was going into the forest to cut wood, and before he started his mother gave him a nice sweet cake and a bottle of wine to take with him so that he might not suffer from hunger or thirst.

In the wood he met a little old gray man, who bade him good day and said, "Give me a bit of the cake in your pocket, and let me have a drop of your wine. I am so hungry and thirsty."

But the clever son said, "If I give you my cake and wine, I shan't have enough for myself. Be off with you!"

He left the little man standing there and went on his way. But he had not been long at work, cutting down a tree, before he made a false stroke. He dug the ax into his own arm and he was obliged to go home to have it bound.

Now this was no accident. It was brought about by the little gray man.

The second son now had to go into the forest to cut wood, and like the eldest, his mother gave him a sweet cake and a bottle of wine. In the same way the little gray man met him and asked for a piece of his cake and a drop of his wine. But the second son made the same sensible answer, "If I give you any, I shall have the less for myself. Be off and out of my way!" And he went on.

His punishment, however, was not long delayed. After a few blows at the tree, he hit his own leg and had to be carried home.

Then Simpleton said, "Let me go to cut the wood, father."

But his father said, "Your brothers have only come to harm by it. You had better leave it alone. You know nothing about it." But Simpleton begged so hard to be allowed to go that at last his father said, "Well, off you go then. You will be wiser when you have hurt yourself."

His mother gave him a cake which was mixed only with water and baked in the ashes, and a bottle of sour beer. When he reached the forest, like the others he met the little gray man.

"Give me a bit of the cake in your pocket and a drop of your wine. I am so hungry and thirsty," said the little man.

Simpleton answered, "I only have a cake baked in the ashes, and some sour beer. But if you like such fare, we will sit down and eat it together."

So they sat down. But when Simpleton pulled out his cake it was a nice sweet cake, and his sour beer was turned into good wine. So they ate and drank, and the little man said, "As you have such a good heart and are willing to share your goods, I will give you good luck. There stands an old tree. Cut it down and you will find something at the roots."

So saying, he disappeared without giving Simpleton any further directions.

Simpleton cut down the tree, and when it fell, lo and behold! a goose was sitting among the roots, and its feathers were of pure gold. He picked it up and took it with him to an inn where he meant to stay the night. The landlord had three daughters, who saw the goose and were very curious as to what kind of bird it could be, and wanted to get one of its golden feathers.

The eldest thought, "There will soon be some opportunity for me to pull out one of the feathers." And when Simpleton went outside, she took hold of its wing to pluck out a feather, but her hand stuck fast and she could not get away.

Soon afterwards, the second sister came up, meaning also to pluck out one of the golden feathers. But she had hardly touched her sister when she herself was held fast.

Finally the third one came with the same intention, but the others screamed out, "Keep away! For goodness' sake, keep away!"

But she, not knowing why she was to keep away, thought, "Why should I not be there if they are there?"

So she ran up. But as soon as she touched her sisters she had to stay hanging on to them, and they all had to pass the night like this.

In the morning, Simpleton took up the goose under his arm without noticing the three girls hanging on behind. They had to keep running behind, dodging his legs right and left.

In the middle of the fields they met the parson, who when he saw the procession cried out, "For shame, you bold girls! Why do you run after the lad like that? Do you call that proper behavior?"

Then he took hold of the hand of the youngest girl to pull her away. But no sooner had he touched her than he felt himself held fast, and he too had to run behind.

Soon afterwards the sexton came up and, seeing his master the parson treading on the heels of the three girls, cried out in amazement, "Hallo, your reverence! Where are you going so fast? Don't forget that we have a christening!" So saying, he plucked the parson by the sleeve and soon found that he could not get away.

As this party of five, one behind the other, tramped on, two peasants came along the road, carrying their hoes. The parson called them and asked them to set the sexton and himself free, but as soon as ever they touched the sexton they were held fast. So now there were seven people running behind Simpleton and his goose.

By and by they reached a town where a king ruled whose only daughter was so solemn that nothing and nobody could make her laugh. So the King had proclaimed that whoever could make her laugh should marry her.

When Simpleton heard this he took his goose, with all his following, before her, and when she saw these seven people running one behind another, she burst into fits of laughter and seemed as if she could never stop.

Thereupon Simpleton asked her in marriage. But the King did not like him for a son-in-law and made all sorts of conditions. First, he said Simpleton must bring him a man who could drink up a cellarful of wine.

Then Simpleton at once thought of the little gray man who might be able to help him, and he went out to the forest to look for him. On the very spot where the tree that he had cut down had stood, he saw a man sitting with a very sad face.

Simpleton asked him what was the matter and he answered, "I am so thirsty, and I can't quench my thirst. I hate cold water, and I have already emptied a cask of wine. But what is a drop like that on a burning stone?"

"Well, there I can help you," said Simpleton. "Come with me and you shall soon have enough to drink and to spare."

He led him to the King's cellar, and the man started upon the great casks. And he drank and drank till his sides ached, and by the end of the day the cellar was empty.

Then again Simpleton demanded his bride. But the King was annoyed that a wretched fellow called "Simpleton" should have his daughter and he made new conditions. He was now to find a man who could eat up a mountain of bread.

Simpleton did not reflect long, but went straight to the forest. And there in the selfsame place sat a man tightening a strap round his body and making a very miserable face.

He said, "I have eaten up a whole ovenful of rolls. But what is the good of that when anyone is as hungry as I am? I am never satisfied. I have to tighten my belt every day if I am not to die of hunger."

Simpleton was delighted and said, "Get up and come with me. You shall have enough to eat."

And he took him to the court, where the King had caused all the flour in the kingdom to be brought together and a huge mountain of bread to be baked. The man from the forest sat down before it and began to eat, and at the end of the day the whole mountain had disappeared.

Now for the third time Simpleton asked for his bride.

But again the King tried to find an excuse, and demanded a ship which could sail on land as well as at sea.

"As soon as you sail up in it, you shall have my daughter," he said.

Simpleton went straight to the forest, and there sat the little gray man to whom he had given his cake. The little man said, "I have eaten and drunk for you, and now I will give you the ship, too. I do it all because you were merciful to me."

Then he gave him the ship which could sail on land as well as at sea, and when the King saw it he could no longer withhold his daughter. The marriage was celebrated, and at the King's death Simpleton inherited the kingdom, and lived long and happily with his wife.

The Blue Light

ↄ THERE was once a soldier who had served his king well and faithfully for many years, but on account of his many wounds he could serve no longer. The King said, "You can go home now. I have no further need for you, and I can only pay those who serve me."

The soldier did not know what to do for a living, and he went sadly away. He walked all day till he reached a wood, and there in the distance he saw a light. On approaching it, he found a house inhabited by a witch.

"Pray give me shelter for the night and something to eat and drink," he said, "or I shall perish."

"Oh ho!" she said. "Who gives anything to a runaway soldier, I should like to know? But I will be merciful and take you in if you will do something for me."

"What is it?" asked the soldier.

"I want you to dig up my garden tomorrow."

The soldier agreed to this and the next day he worked as hard as he could, but he could not finish before evening.

"I see," said the witch, "that you can do no more this evening. I will keep you one night more, and tomorrow you shall split up some logs for firewood."

The soldier took the whole day over this task, and in the evening the witch proposed that he should again stay another night.

"You shall only have a very light task tomorrow," she said. "There is an old dry well behind my house. My light, which burns blue and never goes out, has fallen into it and I want you to bring it back."

Next day the witch led him to the well, and let him down in a basket. He found the light and made a sign to be pulled up, but when he was near the top, the witch put out her hand and wanted to take it from him.

But seeing her evil designs he said, "No. I will not give you the light till I have both feet safe on dry land again."

The witch flew into a passion, let him fall back into the well again, and went away. The poor soldier fell on the damp ground without being injured, and the blue light burnt as brightly as ever. But what was the good of that? He saw that he could not escape death.

He sat for some time feeling very sad. Then, happening to put his hand into his pocket, he found his pipe still half full. "This will be my last pleasure," he thought, as he lighted it at the blue light and began to smoke.

When the cloud of smoke he made cleared off a little, a tiny black man appeared before him and asked, "What orders, master?"

"What do you mean?" the soldier asked in amazement.

"I must do anything that you command," said the little man.

"Oh, if that is so," said the soldier, "get me out of this well first."

The little man took him by the hand and led him through an underground passage, but the soldier did not forget to take the blue light with him. On the way he showed the soldier all the treasures the witch had amassed there, and the soldier took as much gold as he could carry.

When they reached the top he said to the little man, "Now go and bind the witch and take her before the judge."

Before long the witch came by, riding at a furious pace on a tomcat and screaming at the top of her voice.

The little man soon after appeared and said, "Everything is done as you commanded and the witch hangs on the gallows. What further orders have you, master?"

"Nothing at this moment," answered the soldier. "You can go home. Only be at hand when I call."

"You only have to light your pipe at the blue light and I will be there," said the little man, and then he vanished.

The soldier went back to the town that he had left and ordered some new clothes. Then he went to the best inn and told the landlord to give him the best rooms.

When he had taken possession, he summoned the little black man and said, "I served my king faithfully, but he sent me away to die of hunger. Now I will have my revenge."

"What do you wish me to do?" asked the little man.

"Late at night when the Princess is sleeping in her bed, bring her asleep to me and I will make her do menial service for me."

"It is an easy enough thing for me to do," said the little man. "But it will be a bad business for you if it happens."

As the clock struck twelve the door sprang open and the little man bore the maiden in.

"Ah ha! There you are," cried the soldier. "Set about your work at once. Fetch the broom and sweep the floor."

When she had finished he sat down and ordered her to take off his boots. Then he threw them at her and made her pick them up and clean them. She did everything he ordered without resistance, silently and with half-shut eyes.

At the first cockcrow, the little man carried her away to the royal palace and put her back in bed. In the morning when the Princess got up, she went to her father and told him that she had had an extraordinary dream.

"I was carried through the streets at lightning speed and taken to the room of a soldier, whom I had to serve as a maid and do all kinds of menial work. I had to sweep the room and clean his boots. Of course it was only a dream, and yet I am as tired this morning as if I had done it all."

"The dream could not have been true," said the King, "but I will give you a piece of advice. Fill your pocket with peas, and cut a little hole in it. If you are carried away again, and they will drop out and leave a trail on the road."

When the King said this, the little man was standing by, invisible, and heard it all.

That night, when he again carried off the Princess, the peas certainly fell out of her pocket, but they were useless to trace her by, for the cunning little man had scattered peas all over the streets. Again the Princess had to perform her menial duties till cockcrow.

The next morning the King sent out people who were to find the trail. But they were unable to do so, because in every street the poor children were picking up peas and saying, "It must have rained peas in the night."

"We must devise a better plan," said the King. "Keep your shoes on when you go to bed, and before you come away from the place where you are taken, hide one of them. I shall be sure to find it."

The little man heard this plan also, and when the soldier told him to bring the Princess again, he advised him to put it off. He said he knew no further means against their craftiness, and if the shoe was found it would be very dangerous for his master.

"Do what I tell you," answered the soldier. And for the third time the Princess was brought and made to work like a servant. But before leaving, she hid one of her shoes under the bed.

Next morning the King ordered the whole town to be searched for his daughter's shoe, and it was soon found in the soldier's room. He himself, at the request of the little man, had gone outside the gates, but before long he was seized and thrown into prison. In his flight he had forgotten his greatest treasures, the blue light and his gold. He had but one ducat in his pocket. As he stood loaded with chains at his window in the prison, he saw one of his comrades going by.

He tapped on the pane, and said, "Be so good as to fetch me the little bundle I left behind at the inn and I will give you a ducat."

His comrade hurried off and brought him the bundle. As soon as the soldier was alone, he lighted his pipe and summoned the little man.

"Don't be afraid," he said to his master. "Go where they take you and let what will happen. Only take the blue light with you."

Next day a trial was held and, although the soldier had done no harm, the judge sentenced him to death. When he was led out to execution he asked a last favor of the King.

"What is your wish?" asked the King.

"That I may smoke a last pipe."

"You may smoke three," answered the King. "But don't imagine that I will therefore grant you your life."

Then the soldier drew out his pipe and lighted it at the blue light.

As soon as a few rings of smoke arose, the little man appeared with a little cudgel in his hand and said, "What is my master's command?"

"Strike the false judge and his minions to the ground. And do not spare the King either for all his cruelty to me."

Then the little man flew about like lightning—zig-zag, hither and thither! And whomever he touched with his cudgel fell to the ground and dared not move. The King was now seized with alarm. And begging on his knees that his life might be spared, he rendered up his kingdom and gave his daughter to the soldier to be his wife.

The Straw, the Coal, and the Bean

ONCE there was a poor old woman who lived in a village. She had collected a bundle of beans and was going to cook them. So she prepared a fire on her hearth, and to make it burn up quickly she lighted it with a handful of straw. When she threw the beans into the pot, one escaped her unnoticed and slipped onto the floor, where it lay by a straw. Soon afterwards a glowing coal jumped out of the fire and joined the others.

Then the straw began and said, "Little friends, how did you come here?"

The coal answered, "I have happily escaped the fire, and if I had not done so by force of will, my death would certainly have been a most cruel one. I should have been burnt to a cinder."

The bean said, "I also have escaped so far with a whole skin. But if the old woman had put me into the pot, I should have been pitilessly boiled down to broth like my comrades."

"Would a better fate have befallen me, then?" asked the straw. "The old woman packed all my brothers into the fire and smoke. Sixty of them were all done for at once. Fortunately I slipped through her fingers."

"What are we to do now, though?" asked the coal.

"My opinion is," said the bean, "that, as we have escaped death, we must all keep together like good comrades. And so that we may run no further risks, we had better quit the country."

This proposal pleased both the others, and they set out together. Before long they came to a little stream where there was neither path nor bridge, and they did not know how to get over.

The straw at last had an idea and said, "I will throw myself over and then you can walk across upon me like a bridge."

So the straw stretched himself across from one side to the other, and the coal, which was of a fiery nature, tripped gaily over the newly built bridge. But when it got to the middle and heard the water rushing below, it was frightened and remained speechless, not daring to go any further. The straw, beginning to burn, broke in two and fell into the stream. The coal, falling with it, fizzled out in the water. The bean, who had cautiously remained on the bank, could not help laughing over the whole business, and having begun could not stop, but laughed till she split her sides. Now all would have been up with her had not, fortunately, a wandering tailor been taking a rest by the stream. As he had a sympathetic heart, he brought out a needle and thread and stitched her up again, but as he used black thread all beans have a black seam to this day.

Fundevogel

THERE was once a forester who went into the woods to hunt, and he heard a cry like that of a little child. He followed the sound and at last came to a big tree where a tiny child was sitting high up on one of the top branches. The mother had gone to sleep under the tree, and a bird of prey, seeing the child on her lap, had flown down and carried it off in its beak to the top of the tree.

The forester climbed the tree and brought down the child, thinking to himself, "I will take it home, and bring it up with my own little Lina."

So he took it home, and the two children were brought up together. The foundling was called Fundevogel, because it had been found by a bird. Fundevogel and Lina were so fond of each other that they could not bear to be out of each other's sight.

Now the forester had an old cook, who one evening took two pails and began carrying water. She did not go once but many times, backwards and forwards to the well.

Lina saw this and said, "Dear me, Sanna, why are you carrying so much water?"

"If you will not tell anyone, I will tell you why."

Lina said no, she would not tell anyone.

So then the cook said, "Tomorrow morning early, when the forester goes out hunting, I am going to boil the

When the three men came up they found nothing
but a church with a chandelier in it.

water. And when it bubbles in the kettle, I am going to throw Fundevogel into it and boil him."

Next morning the forester got up very early and went out hunting, leaving the children still in bed.

Then said Lina to Fundevogel, "Never forsake me, and I will never forsake you."

And Fundevogel answered, "I will never forsake you."

Then Lina said, "I must tell you now. Old Sanna brought in so many pails of water last night that I asked her what she was doing. She said if I would not tell anybody she would tell me what it was for. So I promised not to tell anybody, and she said that in the morning, when our father had gone out hunting, she would fill the kettle, and when it was boiling she would throw you into it and boil you. Now we must get up quickly, dress ourselves, and run away."

So the children got up, dressed quickly, and hurriedly left the house.

When the water boiled, the cook went to their bedroom to fetch Fundevogel to throw him into it. But when she entered the room and went to the bed, both the children were gone. She was terribly frightened and said to herself, "Whatever am I to say to the forester when he comes home and finds the children gone? We must hurry after them and get them back." So the cook dispatched three menservants to catch up with the children and bring them back.

The children were sitting near a wood, and when they saw the three men a great way off, Lina said to Fundevogel, "Do not forsake me, and I will never forsake you."

And Fundevogel answered, "I will never forsake you as long as I live."

Then Lina said, "You must turn into a rosebush, and I will be a rosebud upon it."

When the three men reached the wood, they found nothing but a rosebush with one rosebud on it. No children were to be seen. They said to each other, "There is nothing to be done here."

So they went home and told the cook that they had seen nothing whatever but a rosebush with only one rosebud on it.

The old cook scolded them and said, "You boobies, you ought to have hacked the rosebush to pieces, broken off the bud, and brought it home to me. Off with you at once and do it." So they had to start off again on their search.

But the children saw them a long way off and Lina said to Fundevogel, "Do not forsake me, and I will never forsake you."

Fundevogel promised, "I will never forsake you as long as I live."

Then said Lina, "You must become a church, and I will be the chandelier in it."

Now when the three men came up they found nothing but a church with a chandelier in it. And they said to each other, "What are we to do here? We had better go home again."

When they reached the house, the cook asked if they had not found anything. They said, "Nothing but a church with a chandelier in it."

"You fools!" screamed the cook. "Why did you not destroy the church and bring me the chandelier?" Then the old cook put her best foot foremost and started herself with the three men in pursuit of the children.

But the children saw the three men in the distance, and the old cook waddling behind them. Then said Lina, "Fundevogel, do not forsake me, and I will never forsake you."

Again he promised, "I will never forsake you as long as I live."

Lina said, "You must become a pond, and I will be the duck swimming upon it."

When the cook reached the pond, she lay down beside it to drink it up, but the duck swam quickly forward, seized her head with his bill, and dragged her under water. So the old witch was drowned.

Then the children went home together as happy as possible, and if they are not dead yet, then they are still alive.

Karl Katz

IN the midst of the Hartz forests there is a high mountain of which the neighbors tell all sorts of stories: how the goblins and fairies dance on it by night, and how the old Emperor Redbeard holds his court there and sits on his marble throne, with his long beard sweeping on the ground.

A great many years ago there lived in a village at the foot of this mountain, one Karl Katz. Now Karl was a goatherd, and every morning he drove his flock to feed upon the green spots that are here and there found on the mountainside. In the evening he sometimes thought it too late to drive his charges home, so then he would shut them up in a spot in the woods, where the old ruined walls of some castle that had long ago been deserted were left standing. They were high enough to form a fold, in which he could count his goats and let them rest for the night.

One evening he found that the prettiest goat of his flock had vanished soon after they were driven into this fold. He searched everywhere for it in vain but, to his surprise and delight, when he counted his flock in the morning what should he see but his lost goat! Again and again the same thing happened.

At last he thought he would watch still more narrowly.

And having looked carefully over the old walls, he found a narrow doorway through which it seemed that his favorite made her way. Karl followed and found a path leading downwards through a cleft in the rocks. On he went, scrambling as well as he could, down the side of the rock and at last came to the mouth of a cave, where he lost sight of his goat. Just then he saw that his faithful dog was not with him. He whistled but no dog was there. He was therefore forced to go into the cave and try to find his goat by himself.

He groped his way for a while and at last came to a place where a little light found its way in. And there he wondered not a little to find his goat employing itself, very much at its ease in the cavern, in eating corn which kept dropping from some place over its head. He went up and looked about him to see where all this corn, that rattled about his ears like a hailstorm, could come from, but all overhead was dark and he could find no clew to this strange business.

At last, as he stood listening, he thought he heard the neighing and stamping of horses. He listened again; it was plainly so. And after a while he was sure that horses were feeding above him and that the corn fell from their mangers. What could these horses be, which were thus kept in the clefts of rocks where none but the goat's foot ever trod? There must be people of some sort or other living here, and who could they be? Was it safe to trust himself in such company? Karl pondered awhile but his wonder only grew greater and greater, when of a sudden he heard his own name, "Karl Katz!" echo through the cavern. He turned round, but could see nothing. "Karl Katz!" again sounded sharply in his ears. And soon out came a little dwarfish page with a high-peaked hat and a scarlet cloak, from a dark corner at one end of the cave.

The dwarf nodded and beckoned him to follow. Karl thought he should first like to know a little about who it was that thus sought his company. He asked, but the dwarf shook his head, answering not a word, and again beckoned him to follow. He did so, and winding his way through ruins he soon heard rolling overhead what sounded like peals of thunder echoing among the rocks. The noise grew louder and louder as he went on, and at last he came to a courtyard surrounded by old ivy-grown walls. The spot seemed to be the bosom of a little valley. Above rose on every hand high masses of rock. Wide-branching trees threw their arms overhead so that nothing but a glimmering twilight made its way through. And here on the cool smooth-shaven turf Karl saw twelve strange old figures amusing themselves very sedately with a game of ninepins.

Their dress did not seem altogether strange to Karl, for in the church of the town whither he went every week to market there was an old monument, with figures of queer old knights upon it, dressed in the very same fashion. Not a word fell from any of their lips. They moved about soberly and gravely, each taking his turn at the game; but the oldest of them ordered Karl Katz, by dumb signs, to busy himself in setting up the pins as they knocked them down. At first his knees trembled, and he hardly dared snatch a stolen sidelong glance at the long beards and old-fashioned dresses of the worthy knights. But he soon saw that as each knight played out his game he went to his seat and there took a hearty draught at a flagon, which the dwarf kept filled and which sent up the smell of the richest old wine.

Little by little Karl got bolder, and at last he plucked up his heart so far as to beg the dwarf, by signs, to let him too take his turn at the flagon. The dwarf gave it him with a grave bow, and Karl thought he never had tasted anything half so good before. This gave him new strength for his work, and as often as he flagged at all he turned to the same kind friend for help in his need.

Which was tired first, he or the knights, Karl never could tell, or whether the wine got the better of his head. What he knew was that sleep at last overpowered him, and that when he awoke he found himself stretched out upon the old spot within the walls where he had folded his flock, and saw that the bright sun was high up in the heavens. The same green turf was spread beneath, and the same tottering ivy-clad walls surrounded him. He rubbed his eyes and called his dog, but neither dog nor goat was to be seen. And when he looked about him again, the grass seemed to be longer under his feet than it was yesterday. And trees hung over his head, which he had either never seen before or had quite forgotten. Shaking his head and hardly knowing whether he was in his right mind, he got up and stretched himself. Somehow or other his joints felt stiffer than they were. "It serves me right," said he. "This comes of sleeping out of one's own bed." Little by little he recollected his evening's sport and licked his lips as he thought of the charming wine he had taken so much of. "But who," thought he, "can those people be that come to this odd place to play ninepins?"

His first step was to look for the doorway through which he had followed his goat, but to his astonishment not the least trace of an opening of any sort was to be seen. There stood the wall, without chink or crack big enough for a rat to pass through. Again he paused and scratched his head. His hat was full of holes. "Why, it was new last Shrovetide!" said he. By chance his eyes fell next on his shoes, which were almost new when he last left home. But now they looked so old that they were likely to fall to pieces before he could get home. All his clothes seemed in the same sad plight. The more he looked, the more he pondered, and the more he was at a loss to know what could have happened to him.

At length he turned round and left the old walls to look for his flock. Slow and out of heart he wound his way among the mountain steeps, through paths where his flocks were wont to wander. Still not a goat was to be seen. Again he whistled and called his dog, but no dog came. Below him in the plain lay the village where his home was, so at length he took the downward path and set out with a heavy heart and a faltering step in search of his flock.

"Surely," said he, "I shall soon meet some neighbor who can tell me where my goats are." But the people who met him as he drew near to the village were all unknown to him. They were not even dressed as his neighbors were, and they seemed as if they hardly spoke the same tongue. When he eagerly asked each, as he came up, after his goats, they only stared at him and stroked their chins. At last he did the same too—and what was his wonder to find that his beard was grown at least a foot long!

"The world," said he to himself, "is surely turned upside down. If not, I must be bewitched." Yet he knew the mountain, as he turned round again and looked back on its woody heights. And he knew the houses and cottages also, with their little gardens, as he entered the village. All were where he had always known them to be. And he heard some children, too (as a traveler that passed by was asking his way), call the village by the very same name he had always known it to bear.

Again he shook his head and went straight through the village to his own cottage. Alas, it looked sadly out of repair. The windows were broken, the door off its hinges, and in the courtyard lay an unknown child in a ragged dress, playing with a rough, toothless old dog, whom he thought he ought to know, but who snarled and barked in his face when he called to him. He went in at the open doorway, but he found all so dreary and empty that he staggered out again like a drunken man, and called his wife and children loudly by their names. But no one heard —at least no one answered him.

A crowd of women and children soon flocked around

the strange-looking man with the long gray beard, and all broke upon him at once with the questions, "Who are you?" "Who is it that you want?" It seemed to him so odd to ask other people, at his own door, about his wife and children that, in order to get rid of the gaping crowd, he named the first man that came into his head.

"Hans the blacksmith," said he. Most held their tongues and stared, but at last an old woman said, "He went these seven years ago to a place that you will not reach today."

"Fritz the tailor, then."

"Heaven rest his soul!" said an old beldam upon crutches. "He has lain these ten years in a house that he'll never leave."

Karl Katz looked at the old woman again and shuddered, as he knew her to be one of the old gossips, but saw she had a strangely altered face. All wish to ask further questions was gone, but at last a young woman made her way through the gaping throng. She had a baby in one arm and a little girl of about three years old clinging to her other hand. All three looked the very image of his own wife.

"What is your name?" he asked wildly.

"Liese," said she.

"And your father's?"

"Karl Katz, heaven bless him!" said she. "But poor man, he is lost and gone. It is now full twenty years since we sought for him day and night on the mountain. His dog and his flock came back, but he never was heard of any more. I was then seven years old."

Poor Karl could restrain himself no longer. "I am Karl Katz and no other," said he, as he took the child from his daughter's arms and kissed it over and over again.

All stood gaping, hardly knowing what to say or think, when old Stropken the schoolmaster hobbled by and took a long and close look at him. "Karl Katz! Karl Katz!" said he slowly. "Why it *is* Karl Katz sure enough. There is my own mark upon him. There is the scar over his right eye that I gave him myself one day with my oak stick."

Then several others also cried out, "Yes, it is! It is Karl Katz. Welcome, neighbor, welcome home!"

"But where," said or thought all, "can an honest steady fellow like you have been these twenty years?"

And now the whole village had flocked around. The children laughed, the dogs barked, and all were glad to see neighbor Karl home alive and well. As to where he had been for the twenty years, that was a part of the story at which Karl shrugged up his shoulders. For he never could very well explain it, and he seemed to think the less that was said about it the better. But it was plain enough that what dwelt most in his memory was the noble wine that had tickled his mouth while the knights played their game of ninepins.

The Table, the Ass, and the Stick

THERE was once a tailor who had three sons and one goat. And as the goat nourished them all with her milk, she was obliged to have good food, and so she was led every day down to the willows by the waterside. And this business the sons did in turn. One day the eldest took the goat to the churchyard, where the best sprouts are, that she might eat her fill and gambol about.

In the evening, when it was time to go home, he said, "Well, goat, have you had enough?"

The goat answered:

> "I am so full,
> I cannot pull
> Another blade of grass—ba! baa!"

"Then come home," said the youth, and he fastened a string to her, led her to her stall, and fastened her up.

"Now," said the old tailor, "has the goat had her proper food?"

"Oh," answered the son, "she is so full, she no more can pull."

But the father, wishing to see for himself, went out to the stall, stroked his dear goat, and said, "My dear goat, are you full?"

And the goat answered:

"How can I be full?
There was nothing to pull,
Though I looked all about me—ba! baa!"

"What is this that I hear?" cried the tailor. And he ran and called out to the youth, "Oh, you liar, to say that the goat was full, and she has been hungry all the time!" And in his wrath he took up his yardstick and drove his son out of the house with many blows.

The next day came the turn of the second son, and he found a fine place in the garden hedge where there were good green sprouts, and the goat ate them all up.

In the evening, when he came to lead her home, he said, "Well, goat, have you had enough?"

And the goat answered:

"I am so full,
I cannot pull
Another blade of grass—ba! baa!"

"Then come home," said the youth, and led her home and tied her up.

"Now," said the old tailor, "has the goat had her proper food?"

"Oh," answered the son, "she is so full, she no more can pull."

The tailor, not feeling satisfied, went out to the stall and said, "My dear goat, are you really full?"

And the goat answered:

> *"How can I be full?*
> *There was nothing to pull,*
> *Though I looked all about me—ba! baa!"*

"The good-for-nothing rascal," cried the tailor, "to let the dear creature go hungry!" And running back, he chased the youth with his yardstick out of the house.

Then came the turn of the third son, who, meaning to make all sure, found some shrubs with the finest sprouts possible and left the goat to eat them.

In the evening, when he came to lead her home, he said, "Well, goat, are you full?"

And the goat answered:

> *"I am so full,*
> *I cannot pull*
> *Another blade of grass—ba! baa!"*

"Then come home," said the youth. And he took her to her stall and fastened her up.

"Now," said the old tailor, "has the goat had her proper food?"

"Oh," answered the son, "she is so full, she no more can pull."

But the tailor, not trusting his word, went to the goat and said, "My dear goat, are you really full?"

The malicious animal answered:

> *"How can I be full?*
> *There was nothing to pull,*
> *Though I looked all about me—ba! baa!"*

"Oh, the wretches!" cried the tailor. "The one as good-for-nothing and careless as the other. I will no longer have such fools about me." And rushing back, in his wrath he laid about him with his yardstick and belabored his son's back so unmercifully that he ran away out of the house.

So the old tailor was left alone with the goat. The next day he went out to the stall and let out the goat, saying, "Come, my dear creature, I will take you myself to the willows."

So he led her by the string and brought her to the green hedges and pastures where there was plenty of food to her taste, and said to her, "Now for once you can eat to your heart's content."

He left her there till the evening. Then he returned and said, "Well, goat, are you full?"

She answered:

> *"I am so full,*
> *I could not pull*
> *Another blade of grass—ba! baa!"*

"Then come home," said the tailor. And leading her to her stall, he fastened her up.

Before he left her he turned once more, saying, "Now then, for once you are full."

But the goat actually cried:

"*How can I be full?
There was nothing to pull,
Though I looked all about me—ba! baa!*"

When the tailor heard that he marveled, and saw at once that his three sons had been sent away without reason.

"Wait a minute," cried he, "you ungrateful creature! It is not enough merely to drive you away—I will teach you to show your face again among honorable tailors."

So in haste he went and fetched his razor, and seizing the goat he shaved her head as smooth as the palm of his hand. And as the yardstick was too honorable a weapon, he took the whip and fetched her such a crack that with many a jump and spring she ran away.

The tailor felt very sad as he sat alone in his house. He would willingly have had his sons back again, but no one knew where they had gone, so he could not send for them.

The eldest son, when he was driven from home, apprenticed himself to a joiner and applied himself diligently to his trade. And when the time came for him to travel, his master gave him a little table, nothing much to look at and made of common wood, but it had one great quality. When anyone set it down and said, "Table, be covered!" all at once the good little table had a clean cloth on it, and a plate and knife and fork, and dishes with roast and boiled meat, and a large glass of red wine sparkling so as to cheer the heart. The young apprentice thought he was set up for life and went merrily out into the world, and he never cared whether an inn were good or bad or whether he could get anything to eat there or not. When he was hungry, it did not matter where he was, whether in the fields, in the woods, or in a meadow, he set down his table and said, "Be covered!" And there he was provided with everything that heart could wish. At last it occurred to him that he would go back to his father, whose wrath might by this time have subsided, and perhaps because of the wonderful table he might receive him again gladly. It happened that one evening during his journey home he came to an inn that was quite full of guests, who bade him welcome and asked him to sit down with them and eat, as otherwise he would have found some difficulty in getting anything.

"No," answered the young joiner, "I could not think of depriving you. You had much better be my guests."

Then they laughed and thought he must be joking. But he brought his little wooden table and put it in the middle of the room and said, "Table, be covered!" Immediately it was set with food much better than the landlord had been able to provide, and the good smell of it greeted the noses of the guests very agreeably.

"Fall to, good friends!" said the joiner. And the guests, when they saw how it was, needed no second asking, but taking up knife and fork fell to valiantly. And what seemed most wonderful was that when a dish was empty, immediately a full one stood in its place.

All the while the landlord stood in a corner and watched all that went on. He did not know what to say about it but he thought, "Such cooking as that would make my inn prosper."

The joiner and his companions kept it up very merrily until late at night. At last they went to sleep, and the young joiner, going to bed, left his wishing table standing against the wall. The landlord, however, could not sleep for thinking of the table. And he remembered that there was in his lumber room an old table very like it, so he fetched it, took away the joiner's table, and left the other in its place. The next morning the joiner paid his reckoning, took up the table, not dreaming that he was carrying off the wrong one, and went on his way. About noon he reached home, and his father received him with great joy.

"Now, my dear son, what have you learned?" said he to him.

"I have learned to be a joiner, father," he answered.

"That is a good trade," returned the father. "But what have you brought back with you from your travels?"

"The best thing I've got, father, is this table," said he.

The tailor looked at it on all sides and said, "You have certainly produced no masterpiece. It is a shabby old table."

"But it is a very wonderful one," answered the son. "When I set it down and tell it to be covered, at once the finest meats are standing on it, and wine so good that it

cheers the heart. Let us invite all the friends and neighbors that they may feast and enjoy themselves, for the
table will provide enough for all."

When the company was all assembled, he put his table
in the middle of the room and said, "Table, be covered!"

But the table never stirred, and remained just as empty
as any other table that does not understand talking. When
the poor joiner saw that the table remained unfurnished,
he felt ashamed to stand there like a fool. The company
laughed at him freely, and were obliged to return unfilled
and uncheered to their houses. The father gathered his
pieces together and returned to his tailoring, and the son
went to work under another master.

The second son had bound himself apprentice to a
miller. And when his time was up, his master said to him,
"As you have behaved yourself so well, I will give you an
ass of a remarkable kind. He will draw no cart and carry no
sack."

"What is the good of him then?" asked the young apprentice.

"He spits out gold," answered the miller. "If you put a
cloth before him and say, 'Bricklebrit,' out come gold
pieces."

"That is a capital thing!" said the apprentice, and thanking his master he went out into the world.

Whenever he wanted gold he had only to say, "Bricklebrit" to his ass, and there was a shower of gold pieces. And
so he had no cares as he traveled about. Wherever he went
he lived on the best, and the dearer the better, as his purse
was always full. And when he had been looking about the
world a long time, he thought he would go and seek out
his father, who would perhaps forget his anger and re-

ceive him kindly because of his gold-ass. And it happened that he came to lodge in the same inn where his brother's table had been exchanged.

He was leading his ass, and the landlord was about to take the ass from him to tie it up, but the young apprentice said, "Don't trouble yourself, old fellow. I will take him into the stable myself and tie him up, and then I shall know where to find him."

The landlord thought this was very strange, and he never supposed that a man who was accustomed to look after his ass himself could have much to spend. But when the stranger, feeling in his pocket, took out two gold pieces and told him to get him something good for supper, the landlord ran and fetched the best that could be got.

After supper the guest called for the reckoning, and the landlord, wanting to get all the profit he could, said that it would amount to two gold pieces more. The apprentice felt in his pocket, but his gold had come to an end.

"Wait a moment, landlord," said he. "I will go and fetch some money." And he went out of the room, carrying the tablecloth with him.

The landlord could not tell what to make of it, and, curious to know his proceedings, slipped after him. And as the guest shut the stable door, he peeped in through a knothole. Then he saw how the stranger spread the cloth before the ass, saying, "Bricklebrit," and directly the ass spat out gold, which rained upon the ground.

"Dear me!" said the landlord. "That is an easy way of getting ducats. A purse of money like that is no bad thing."

After that the guest paid his reckoning and went to bed. But the landlord slipped down to the stable in the middle of the night, led the gold-ass away, and tied up another ass in his place. Early the next morning the apprentice set forth with his ass, never doubting that it was the right one. By noon he came to his father's house, who rejoiced to see him again and received him gladly.

"What trade have you taken up, my son?" asked the father.

"I am a miller, dear father," answered he.

"What have you brought home from your travels?" continued the father.

"Nothing but an ass," answered the son.

"We have plenty of asses here," said the father. "You had much better have brought me a nice goat!"

"Yes," answered the son, "but this is no common ass. When I say, 'Bricklebrit,' the good creature spits out a whole clothful of gold pieces. Let me call all the neighbors together. I will make rich people of them all."

"That will be fine!" said the tailor. "Then I need labor no more at my needle." And he rushed out himself and called the neighbors together. As soon as they were all assembled, the miller called out to them to make room, and brought in the ass and spread his cloth before him.

"Now, pay attention!" said he, and he cried, "Bricklebrit!" But no gold pieces came, and that showed that the animal was no more scientific than any other ass.

So the poor miller made a long face when he saw that he had been taken in, and begged pardon of the neighbors, who all went home as poor as they had come. And there was nothing for it but that the old man must take to his needle again and that the young one should take service with a miller.

The third brother had bound himself apprentice to a turner. And as turning is a very ingenious handicraft, it took him a long time to learn it. His brother told him in a letter how badly things had gone with them, and how on the last night of their travels the landlord deprived them of their treasures. When the young turner had learned his trade and was ready to travel, his master, to reward him for his good conduct, gave him a sack and told him that there was a stick inside it.

"I can hang up the sack, and it may be very useful to me," said the young man. "But what is the good of the stick?"

"I will tell you," answered the master. "If anyone does you any harm, and you say, 'Stick, out of the sack!' the stick will jump out upon them and will belabor them so soundly that they shall not be able to move or to leave the place for a week. And it will not stop until you say, 'Stick, into the sack!' "

The apprentice thanked him and took up the sack and started on his travels, and when anyone attacked him he would say, "Stick, out of the sack!" And directly out jumped the stick and dealt a shower of blows on the coat or jerkin, and the back beneath, which quickly ended the affair. One evening the young turner reached the inn where his two brothers had been taken in. He laid his knapsack on the table and began to describe all the wonderful things he had seen in the world.

"Yes," said he, "you may talk of your self-spreading table, your gold-supplying ass, and so forth. Very good things, I do not deny, but they are nothing in comparison with the treasure that I have acquired and carry with me in that sack!"

Then the landlord opened his ears.

"What in the world can it be?" thought he. "Very likely

the sack is full of precious stones. And I have a perfect right to it, for all good things come in threes."

When bedtime came, the guest stretched himself on a bench and put his sack under his head for a pillow. And the landlord, when he thought the young man was sound asleep, came, stooped down, pulled gently at the sack so as to remove it cautiously, and put another in its place. The turner had only been waiting for this to happen. And just as the landlord was giving a last courageous pull, he cried, "Stick, out of the sack!" Out flew the stick directly and laid to heartily on the landlord's back. And in vain he begged for mercy! The louder he cried, the harder the stick beat time on his back, until he fell exhausted to the ground.

Then the turner said, "If you do not give me the table and the ass directly, this game shall begin all over again."

"Oh dear!" cried the landlord, quite overcome. "I will

gladly give it all back again if you will only make this terrible goblin go back into the sack."

Then said the young man, "I will be generous instead of just. But beware!" Then he cried, "Stick, into the sack!" and left him in peace.

The next morning the turner set out with the table and the ass on his way home to his father. The tailor was very glad indeed to see him again and asked him what he had learned abroad.

"My dear father," answered he, "I am become a turner."

"A very ingenious handicraft," said the father. "And what have you brought with you from your travels?"

"A very valuable thing, dear father," answered the son. "A stick in a sack!"

"What?" cried the father. "A stick! The thing is not worth so much trouble when you can cut one from any tree."

"But it is not a common stick, dear father," said the young man. "When I say, 'Stick, out of the sack!' out jumps the stick upon anyone who means harm to me, and makes him dance, and does not leave off till he is beaten to the earth and asks pardon. Just look here! With this stick I have recovered the table and the ass which the thieving landlord took from my two brothers. Now let them both be sent for, and bid all the neighbors too, and they shall eat and drink to their hearts' content, and I will fill their pockets with gold."

The old tailor could not quite believe in such a thing, but he called his sons and all the neighbors together.

Then the turner brought in the ass, opened a cloth before him, and said to his brother, "Now, my dear brother, speak to him."

And the miller said, "Bricklebrit!" And immediately the cloth was covered with gold pieces, until they had all got more than they could carry away. (I tell you this because it is a pity you were not there.)

Then the turner set down the table and said, "Now, my dear brother, speak to it."

The joiner said "Table, be covered!" And directly it was covered and set forth plentifully with the richest dishes. Then they held such a feast as had never taken place in the tailor's house before, and the whole company remained through the night, merry and content.

After that the tailor locked up in a cupboard his needle and thread, his yardstick and goose, and lived ever after with his three sons in great joy and splendor.

But what became of the goat, the unlucky cause of the tailor's sons being driven out? I will tell you. She felt so ashamed of her bald head that she ran into a fox's hole and hid herself. When the fox came home he caught sight of two great eyes staring at him out of the darkness, and was very frightened and ran away.

A bear met him, and seeing that he looked very dis-

turbed asked him, "What is the matter, brother fox, that you should look like that?"

"Oh dear," answered the fox, "a horrible beast is sitting in my hole, and he stared at me with fiery eyes."

"We will soon drive him out," said the bear, and went to the hole and looked in. But when he caught sight of the fiery eyes he likewise felt great terror seize him, and not wishing to have anything to do with so grisly a beast, he made off.

He was soon met by a bee, who remarked that he had not a very courageous air and said to him, "Bear, you have a very depressed countenance. What has become of your high spirit?"

"You may well ask," answered the bear. "In the fox's hole there sits a grisly beast with fiery eyes, and we cannot drive him out."

The bee answered, "I know you despise me, bear. I am a poor feeble little creature, but I think I can help you."

So she flew into the fox's hole and, settling on the goat's smooth-shaven head, stung her so severely that she jumped up crying, "Ba-baa!" and ran out like mad into the world. And to this hour no one knows where she ran.

Red Riding Hood

ONCE upon a time there was a sweet little maiden who was loved by all who knew her, but she was especially dear to her grandmother, who did not know how to make enough of the child. Once she gave her a little red velvet cloak. It was so becoming and she liked it so much that she would never wear anything else, and so she got the name of Red Riding Hood.

One day her mother said to her, "Come here, Red Riding Hood! Take this cake and bottle of wine to grandmother. She is weak and ill, and they will do her good. Go quickly, before it gets hot. Don't loiter by the way, nor run, or you will fall and break the bottle, and there will be no wine for grandmother. When you get there, don't forget to say 'Good morning' prettily, without staring about you."

"I will do just as you tell me," Red Riding Hood promised her mother.

Her grandmother lived away in the wood, a good half hour from the village. When she got to the wood she met a wolf, but Red Riding Hood did not know what a wicked animal he was, so she was not a bit afraid of him.

"Good morning, Red Riding Hood," he said.

"Good morning, wolf," she answered.

"Whither away so early, Red Riding Hood?"

"To grandmother's."

"What have you got in your basket?"

"Cake and wine. We baked yesterday, so I'm taking a cake to her. She wants something to make her well."

"Where does she live, Red Riding Hood?"

"A good quarter of an hour farther into the wood. Her house stands under three big oak trees, near a hedge of nut trees which you must know," said Red Riding Hood.

The wolf thought, "This tender little creature will be a plump morsel! She will be nicer than the old woman. I must be cunning and snap them both up."

He walked along with Red Riding Hood for a while. Then he said, "Look at the pretty flowers, Red Riding Hood. Why don't you look about you? I don't believe you even hear the birds sing. You are as solemn as if you were going to school. All else is so gay out here in the woods."

Red Riding Hood raised her eyes, and when she saw the sunlight dancing through the trees, and all the bright flowers, she thought, "I'm sure grandmother would be pleased if I took her a bunch of fresh flowers. It is still quite early. I shall have plenty of time to pick them."

So she left the path and wandered off among the trees to pick the flowers. Each time she picked one, she always saw another prettier one farther on. So she went deeper and deeper into the forest.

In the meantime the wolf went straight off to the grandmother's cottage and knocked at the door.

"Who is there?"

"Red Riding Hood, bringing you a cake and some wine. Open the door!"

"Lift the latch," called out the old woman. "I am too weak to get up."

The wolf lifted the latch and the door sprang open. He went straight in and up to the bed without saying a word, and ate up the poor old woman. Then he put on her nightdress and cap, got into bed and drew the curtains.

Red Riding Hood picked flowers till she could carry no more, and then she remembered her grandmother again. She was astonished when she got to the house to find the door open, and when she entered the room everything seemed so strange. She felt quite frightened but she did not know why. "Generally I like coming to see grandmother so much," she thought. "Good morning, grandmother," she cried. But she received no answer.

Then she went up to the bed and drew the curtain back. There lay her grandmother, but she had drawn her cap down over her face and she looked very odd.

"Oh grandmother, what big ears you have," she said.

"The better to hear you with, my dear."

"Grandmother, what big eyes you have."

"The better to see you with, my dear."

"What big hands you have, grandmother."

"The better to catch hold of you with, my dear."

"But grandmother, what big teeth you have."

"The better to eat you with, my dear."

Hardly had the wolf said this than he made a spring out of bed and swallowed poor little Red Riding Hood. When the wolf had satisfied himself he went back to bed, and he was soon snoring loudly.

A huntsman went past the house and thought, "How loudly the old lady is snoring. I must see if there is anything the matter with her."

So he went into the house and up to the bed, where he found the wolf fast asleep. "Do I find you here, you old sinner!" he said. "Long enough have I sought you!"

He raised his gun to shoot, when it just occurred to him that perhaps the wolf had eaten up the old lady, and that she might still be saved. So he took a knife and began cutting open the sleeping wolf. At the first cut he saw the little red cloak, and after a few more slashes, the little girl sprang out and cried, "Oh, how frightened I was! It was so dark inside the wolf." Next the old grandmother came out, alive but hardly able to breathe.

Red Riding Hood brought some big stones with which they filled the wolf. He woke up and tried to spring away, but the stones dragged him back and he fell down dead.

They were all quite happy now. The huntsman skinned the wolf and took the skin home. The grandmother ate the cake and drank the wine which Red Riding Hood had brought, and she soon felt quite strong. Red Riding Hood thought to herself, "I will never again wander off into the forest as long as I live, when my mother forbids it."

The King of the
Golden Mountain

THERE was once a merchant who had two children, a boy and a girl. They were both small and not old enough to run about. He had also two richly laden ships at sea, and just as he was expecting to make a great deal of money by the merchandise, news came that they had both been lost. So now instead of being a rich man he was quite poor, and had nothing left but one field near the town. To turn his thoughts from his misfortune, he went out into this field. And as he was walking up and down, a little black mannikin suddenly appeared before him and asked why he was so sad.

The merchant said, "I would tell you at once if you could help me."

"Who knows?" answered the little mannikin. "Perhaps I could help you."

Then the merchant told him that all his wealth had been lost in a wreck, and that now he had nothing left but this field.

"Don't worry yourself," said the mannikin. "If you will promise to bring me in twelve years' time the first thing which rubs against your legs when you go home, you shall have as much gold as you want."

The merchant thought, "What could it be but my dog?" He never thought of his boy, but said yes, and gave the mannikin his bond signed and sealed and went home.

When he reached the house his little son, delighted to hold on to the benches and totter towards his father, seized him by the leg to steady himself.

The merchant was horror-stricken, for his vow came into his head, and now he knew what he had promised to give away. But as he still found no gold in his chests, he thought it must only have been a joke of the mannikin's. A month later he went up into the loft to gather together some old tin to sell it, and there he found a great heap of gold on the floor. So he was soon up in the world again. He bought and sold, became a richer merchant than ever, and was altogether contented.

In the meantime the boy had grown up and he was both clever and wise. But the nearer the end of the twelve years came, the more sorrowful the merchant grew. You could even see his misery in his face. One day his son asked him what was the matter but his father would not tell him. The boy, however, persisted so long that at last he told him that he had promised, without knowing what he was doing, to give him up at the end of twelve years to a little black mannikin, in return for a quantity of gold. He had given his hand and seal on it, and the time was now near for him to go.

Then his son said, "Father, don't be frightened! It will be all right. The little mannikin has no power over me."

When the time came, the son asked a blessing of the priest, and he and his father went to the field together, and the son made a circle within which they took their places.

When the little black mannikin appeared he said to the father, "Have you brought what you promised me?"

The man was silent but his son said, "What do you want?"

"My business is with your father,
and not with you."

The mannikin said, "My business is with your father and not with you."

The son answered, "You deceived and cheated my father. Give me back his bond."

"Oh no!" said the little man. "I won't give up my rights."

They talked to each other for a long time, and at last they decided that, as the son no longer belonged to his father and declined to belong to his foe, he should get into a boat on a flowing stream, and his father should himself push it off, thus giving him up to the stream.

So the youth took leave of his father, got into the boat, and his father pushed it off. Then, thinking that his son was lost to him forever, he went home and sorrowed for him. The little boat, however, did not sink. It drifted quietly down the stream, and the youth sat in it in perfect safety. It drifted for a long time till at last it stuck fast on an unknown shore.

The youth landed and, seeing a beautiful castle near, walked towards it. As he passed through the door, however, a spell fell upon him. He went through all the rooms, but found them empty till he came to the very last one, where a serpent lay coiling and uncoiling itself.

The serpent was really an enchanted maiden, who was delighted when she saw the youth and said, "Have you come at last, my preserver? I have been waiting twelve years for you. This whole kingdom is bewitched and you must break the spell."

"How am I to do that?" he asked.

She said, "Tonight twelve black men hung with chains will appear, and they will ask what you are doing here. But do not speak a word, whatever they do or say to you. They will torment you, strike, and pinch you, but don't say a word. At twelve o'clock they will have to go away. On the second night twelve more will come, and on the third twenty-four. These will cut off your head. But at twelve o'clock their power goes, and if you have borne it and not spoken a word, I shall be saved. Then I will come to you and bring a little flask containing the Water of Life, with which I will sprinkle you. And you will be brought to life again as sound and well as ever you were."

Then he said, "I will gladly save you."

Everything happened just as she had said. The black men could not force a word out of him. And on the third night the serpent became a beautiful princess, who brought the Water of Life as she had promised, and restored the youth to life. Then she fell on his neck and kissed him, and there were great rejoicings all over the castle.

Their marriage was celebrated and he became King of the Golden Mountain.

They lived happily together, and in course of time a beautiful boy was born to them.

When eight years had passed, the King's heart grew tender within him as he thought of his father, and he wanted to go home to see him. But the Queen did not want him to go.

She said, "I know it will be to my misfortune." He gave her no peace, however, till she agreed to let him go.

On his departure she gave him a wishing ring and said, "Take this ring and put it on your finger, and you will at once be at the place where you wish to be. Only you must promise never to use it to wish me away from here to be with you at your father's."

He made the promise and put the ring on his finger. He then wished himself before the town where his father lived, and at the same moment found himself at the gate. But the sentry would not let him in because his clothes, though of rich material, were of such strange cut. So he went up a mountain where a shepherd lived, and exchanging clothing with him, put on his old smock and passed into the town unnoticed.

When he reached his father he began making himself known. But his father, never thinking that it was his son, said that it was true he had once had a son, but he had long been dead. But he added, seeing that he was a poor shepherd, he would give him a plate of food.

The supposed shepherd said to his parents, "I am indeed your son. Is there no mark on my body by which you may know me?"

His mother said, "Yes, our son had a strawberry mark under his right arm."

He pushed up his shirt sleeve and there was the strawberry mark, so they no longer doubted that he was their son. He told them that he was the King of the Golden Mountain, his wife was a princess, and they had a little son seven years old.

"That can't be true," said his father. "You are a fine sort of King to come home in a tattered shepherd's smock."

His son grew angry and, without stopping to reflect, turned his ring round and wished his wife and son to appear. In a moment they both stood before him, but his wife did nothing but weep and lament, and said that he had broken his promise and so had made her very unhappy.

He said, "I have acted incautiously, but from no bad motive." And he tried to soothe her.

She appeared to be calmed, but really she nourished evil intentions towards him in her heart.

Shortly afterwards he took her outside the town to the field and showed her the stream down which he had drifted in the little boat. Then he said, "I am tired. I want to rest a little."

So she sat down, and he rested his head upon her lap and soon fell fast asleep. As soon as he was asleep, she drew the ring from his finger and drew herself gently away from him, leaving only her slipper behind. Last of all, taking her child in her arms, she wished herself back in her own kingdom. When he woke up, he found himself quite deserted. Wife and child were gone, the ring had disappeared from his finger, and only her slipper remained as a token.

"I can certainly never go home to my parents," he said. "They would say I was a sorcerer. I must go away and walk till I reach my own kingdom again."

So he went away, and at last he came to a mountain where three giants were quarreling about the division of their father's property. When they saw him passing, they called to him and said, "Little people have sharp wits," and asked him to divide their inheritance for them.

It consisted first, of a sword, with which in one's hand, if one said, "All heads off, mine alone remain!" every head fell to the ground. Second, of a mantle which rendered anyone putting it on invisible. Third, of a pair of boots which transported the wearer to whatever place he wished.

He said, "Give me the three articles so that I may see if they are all in good condition."

So they gave him the mantle and he at once became invisible. He took his own shape again and said, "The mantle is good. Now give me the sword."

But they said, "No, we can't give you the sword. If you were to say, 'All heads off, mine alone remain!' all our heads would fall, and yours would be the only one left."

At last, however, they gave it to him on condition that he was to try it on a tree. He did as they wished, and the sword went through the tree trunk as if it had been a straw.

Then he wanted the boots but they said, "No, we won't give them away. If you were to put them on and wish yourself on the top of the mountain, we should be left standing here without anything."

"No," said he, "I won't do that."

So they gave him the boots too. But when he had all three he could think of nothing but his wife and child, and he said to himself, "Oh, if only I were on the Golden Mountain again!" And immediately he disappeared from the sight of the giants, and that was the end of their inheritance.

When he approached his castle he heard sounds of music—fiddles and flutes—and shouts of joy. People told him that his wife was celebrating her marriage with another husband.

He was filled with rage and said, "The false creature! She deceived me and deserted me when I was asleep."

He put on his mantle and went to the castle, invisible to all. Then he went into the hall, where a great feast was spread with the richest foods and the costliest wines, and the guests were joking and laughing while they ate and drank. The Queen sat on her throne in their midst in gorgeous clothing, with the crown on her head.

He placed himself behind her, and no one saw him. Whenever the Queen put a piece of meat on her plate, he took it away and ate it, and when her glass was filled he took it away and drank it. Her plate and her glass were constantly refilled, but she never had anything, for it disappeared at once. At last she grew frightened, got up, and went to her room in tears, but he followed her there too.

She said to herself, "Am I still in the power of the demon? Did my preserver never come?"

He struck her in the face and said, "Did your preserver never come? He is with you now, deceiver that you are. Did I deserve such treatment at your hands?"

Then he made himself visible, and went into the hall and cried, "The wedding is stopped. The real king has come."

The kings, princes, and nobles who were present laughed him to scorn. But he only said, "Will you go, or will you not?"

They tried to seize him but he drew his sword and said, "All heads off, mine alone remain!"

Then all their heads fell to the ground, and he remained sole king and lord of the Golden Mountain.

The Robber Bridegroom

THERE was once a miller who had a beautiful daughter. When she grew up, he wanted to have her married and settled. He thought, "If a suitable bridegroom comes and asks for my daughter, I will give her to him."

Soon afterwards a suitor came who appeared to be rich, and as the miller knew nothing against him he promised his daughter to him. The maiden, however, did not like him as a bride ought to like her bridegroom, nor had she any faith in him. Whenever she looked at him or thought about him, a shudder came over her.

One day he said to her, "You are my betrothed, and yet you have never been to see me."

The maiden answered, "I don't even know where your house is."

Then the bridegroom said, "My house is in the depths of the forest."

She made excuses and said she could not find the way.

The bridegroom answered, "Next Sunday you must come and see me without fail. I have invited some other guests, and so that you may be able to find the way I will strew some ashes to guide you."

When Sunday came and the maiden was about to start, she was frightened, though she did not know why. So that she should be sure of finding her way back she filled her pockets with peas and lentils. At the entrance to the forest she found the track of ashes and followed it, but every step or two she scattered a few peas right and left.

She walked nearly the whole day, right into the midst of the forest, where it was almost dark. Here she saw a solitary house, which she did not like: it was so dark and dismal. She went in but found nobody, and there was dead silence. Suddenly a voice cried:

"Turn back, turn back, thou bonnie bride,
Nor in this house of death abide."

The maiden looked up and saw that the voice came from a bird in a cage hanging on the wall. Once more it made the same cry:

"Turn back, turn back, thou bonnie bride,
Nor in this house of death abide."

The beautiful bride went from room to room, all over the house, but they were all empty. Not a soul was to be seen. At last she reached the cellar and there she found an old, old woman with a shaking head.

"Can you tell me if my bridegroom lives here?"

"Alas, poor child!" answered the old woman. "Little dost thou know where thou art. Thou art in a murderers' den. Thou thoughtest thou wast about to be married, but death will be thy marriage. See here, I have had to fill this kettle with water, and when they have thee in their power they will kill thee without mercy, and cook and eat thee, for they are eaters of human flesh. Unless I take pity on thee and save thee, thou art lost." Then the old woman led her behind a great cask where she could not be seen. "Be as quiet as a mouse," she said. "Don't stir, or all will be lost. Tonight when the murderers are asleep, we will flee. I have long waited for an opportunity."

Hardly had she said this when the riotous crew came home. They dragged another maiden with them, but as they were quite drunk they paid no attention to her shrieks and lamentations. They gave her wine to drink, three glasses full—red, white, and yellow. After she had drunk them she fell down dead. The poor bride hidden behind the cask was terrified. She trembled and shivered, for she saw plainly to what fate she was destined.

One of the men noticed a gold ring on the little finger

of the murdered girl. And as he could not pull it off he took an ax and chopped the finger off, but it sprang into the air and fell into the lap of the bride behind the cask. The man took a light to look for it, but he could not find it. One of the others said, "Have you looked behind the big cask?"

But the old woman called out, "Come and eat, and leave the search till tomorrow. The finger won't run away."

The murderer said, "The old woman is right," and they gave up the search and sat down to supper. But the old woman dropped a sleeping draught into their wine, so they soon lay down, went to sleep, and snored lustily.

When the bride heard them snoring she came out from behind the cask, but she was obliged to step over the sleepers as they lay in rows upon the floor. She was dreadfully afraid of touching them, but God helped her and she got through without mishap. The old woman went with her and opened the door, and they hurried away as quickly as they could from this vile den.

All the ashes had been blown away by the wind, but the peas and lentils had taken root and shot up, and showed them the way in the moonlight.

They walked the whole night and reached the mill in the morning. The maiden told her father all that she had been through.

When the day which had been fixed for the wedding came, the bridegroom appeared and the miller invited all his friends and relations. As they sat at table, each one was asked to tell some story. The bride was very silent, but when it came to her turn the bridegroom said, "Come, my love, have you nothing to say? Pray tell us something."

"I will tell you a dream I have had," she answered. "I was walking alone in a wood and I came to a solitary house where not a soul was to be seen. A cage was hanging on the wall of one of the rooms, and in it was a bird which cried:

> " 'Turn back, turn back, thou bonnie bride,
>   Nor in this house of death abide.'

"It repeated the same words twice. This was only a dream, my love! I walked through all the rooms but they were all empty and dismal. At last I went down to the cellar, and there sat a very old woman, with a shaking head.

"I asked her, 'Does my bridegroom live here?' She answered, 'Alas, you poor child, you are in a murderers' den! Your bridegroom indeed lives here, but he will cut you to pieces, cook you, and eat you.' This was only a dream, my love!

"Then the old woman hid me behind a cask, but hardly had she done so when the murderers came home, dragging a maiden with them. They gave her three kinds of wine to drink—red, white, and yellow—and after drinking them she fell down dead. My love, I was only dreaming this! Then they took her things off and cut her to pieces. My love, I was only dreaming! One of the murderers saw a gold ring on the girl's little finger, and, as he could not pull it off, he chopped off the finger. But the finger bounded into the air and fell behind the cask upon my lap. Here is the finger with the ring!"

At these words she produced the finger and showed it to the company.

When the bridegroom heard these words, he turned as pale as ashes and tried to escape. But the guests seized him and handed him over to justice. And he and all his band were executed for their crimes.

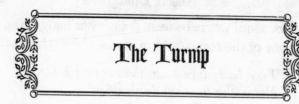

The Turnip

THERE were once two brothers who both served as soldiers, and one was rich and the other was poor.

The poor one, wishing to better himself, discarded his uniform and worked like a peasant. He dug and hoed his little field and sowed turnips. The seed came up, and one of the turnips grew to such an enormous size that it seemed as though it would never stop growing. It might have been called the Queen of Turnips, for its like had never been seen before nor ever will be again. At last it was so big that it filled a cart and needed two oxen to draw it. The peasant could not imagine what would come of it, whether it would bring good luck or bad.

At last he said to himself, "If I sell it what shall I gain? I might eat it, but the little turnips would do as well for that. The best thing will be to take it to the King and offer it to him."

So he loaded a cart, harnessed two oxen, and took it to the court to present it to the King.

"What is this extraordinary object?" asked the King. "I have seen many marvels in my time, but never anything so remarkable as this. What seed did it spring from? Perhaps it belongs to you, especially if you are a child of good luck?"

"Oh no," said the peasant. "Lucky I certainly am not, for I am a poor soldier, who, since he could keep himself no longer, hung up his uniform on a nail and tills the earth. I have a brother who is rich and well known to you, my Lord King. But I, because I have nothing, am forgotten by all the world."

Then the King pitied him and said, "Your poverty shall be at an end, and you shall receive such rich presents from me that your wealth will equal that of your brother."

Thereupon he gave him plenty of gold, lands, fields, and flocks, and enriched him with precious stones so that the other brother's wealth could not be compared with his.

Now when the rich brother heard what his brother with the single turnip had acquired, he envied him and pondered how he might gain a like treasure for himself.

But he wanted to show himself much cleverer, so he took gold and horses and presented them to the King, feeling certain that he would give him a far handsomer gift. For if his brother got so much for a turnip, what would not he get for his beautiful things?

The King took the present, saying that he could give him in return nothing rarer or better than the huge turnip. So the rich brother had to put his brother's turnip into a cart and have it taken home.

Then he did not know on whom to expend his wrath and bitterness, till evil thoughts came to him and he determined to kill his brother. He hired murderers who were to place themselves in ambush, and then he went to his brother and said, "Dear brother, I know of a secret treasure which we will carry off and divide."

The other agreed and went without suspicion, but when they reached the ambush the murderers sprang upon him, bound him, and prepared to hang him on a tree.

While they were about it, they heard in the distance the clatter of hoofs and the sound of singing, which frightened them so much that they stuck their prisoner head-foremost into a sack, slung it up on a branch, and took to flight. But the man up in the sack worked a hole in it, and stuck his head through.

Now the traveler turned out to be nothing more than a student, a young fellow who was riding through the wood, singing cheerily.

When the man up in the sack saw someone down below, he called out, "Good day. You come in the nick of time."

The student looked all around, but could not make out where the voice came from. At last he said, "Who calls?"

A voice from above answered, "Raise your eyes. I am sitting up here in the Sack of Wisdom, and in a short time I have learned so much that the wisdom of the schools is as air compared to mine. Soon I shall be quite perfect and shall come down and be the wisest of all mankind. I understand the stars and signs of the heavens, the blowing of the winds, the sand of the sea, the healing of sickness, and the power of herbs, birds, and stones. If you were once inside, you would feel what wonders flow from the Sack of Knowledge."

When the student heard this he was astonished and said, "Blessed be the hour when I met you, if only I too might get into the sack for a little."

The other answered, as though unwillingly, "I will let you in for a little while for payment and kind words, but you must wait an hour as there is something rather difficult which I must learn first."

But when the student had waited a little, he grew impatient and entreated permission to get in, so great was his thirst for knowledge. Then the man in the sack pretended to give in and said, "In order that I may get out of the sack you must let it down, then you can get in."

So the student let it down, undid the sack and released the prisoner, and said, "Now pull me up as fast as possible." And he tried to get into the sack and stand upright in it.

"Stop," said the other. "That won't do." And he packed him in headfirst, tied it up, and slung up the disciple of wisdom, dangling him in the air. Then he said, "How are you, my dear fellow? You will soon feel wisdom coming upon you and will have a most interesting experience. Sit still till you are wiser."

Thereupon he mounted the student's horse and rode off, but sent someone in an hour to let him down again.

The Seven Ravens

THERE was once a man who had seven sons, but never a daughter, however much he wished for one. At last, however, his wife gave him a daughter. His joy was great, but the child was small and delicate, and on account of its weakness it was to be christened at home.

The father sent one of his sons in haste to the spring to fetch some water. The other six ran with him, and because each of them wanted to be the first to draw the water the pitcher fell into the brook. There they stood and didn't know what to do, and not one of them ventured to go home.

As they did not come back, their father became impatient and said, "Perhaps the young rascals are playing about and have forgotten it altogether."

He became anxious lest his little girl should die unbaptized, and in hot vexation he cried, "I wish those youngsters would all turn into ravens!"

Scarcely were the words uttered when he heard a whirring in the air above his head. And looking upwards, he saw seven coal-black ravens flying away.

The parents could not undo the spell and were very sad about the loss of their seven sons, but they consoled themselves in some measure with their dear little daughter, who soon became strong, and every day more beautiful.

For a long time she was unaware that she had had any brothers, for her parents took care not to mention them to her.

One day, however, by chance she heard some people saying about her, "Oh yes, the girl's pretty enough, but you know she is really to blame for the misfortune to her seven brothers."

Then she became very sad and went to her father and mother and asked if she had ever had any brothers, and what had become of them. The parents could no longer conceal the secret. They said, however, that what had happened was by the decree of heaven, and that her birth was merely the innocent occasion.

But the little girl could not get the matter off her conscience for a single day, and thought that she was bound to release her brothers again. She had no peace or quiet until she had secretly gone forth into the wide world to trace her brothers, wherever they might be, and to free them, let it cost what it might.

She took nothing with her but a little ring as a remembrance of her parents, a loaf of bread against hunger, a pitcher of water against thirst, and a little chair in case of fatigue. She kept going on and on until she came to the end of the world.

Then she came to the sun, but it was hot and terrible, and it devoured little children. She ran hastily away to the moon, but it was too cold, and moreover dismal and dreary. And when the child was looking at it, it said, "I smell, I smell man's flesh!"

Then she quickly made off and came to the stars, and they were kind and good, and everyone sat on his own special seat.

But the morning star stood up and gave her a little bone, and said, "Unless you have this bone, you cannot open the Glass Mountain. And in the Glass Mountain are your brothers."

The girl took the bone and wrapped it up carefully in a little kerchief, and went on again until she came to the Glass Mountain. The gate was closed and she meant to get out the little bone. But when she undid the kerchief it was empty, and she had lost the good star's present.

How, now, was she to set to work? She was determined to rescue her brothers, but she had no key to open the Glass Mountain. The good little sister took a knife and cut off her own tiny finger, fitted it into the keyhole, and succeeded in opening the lock.

When she had entered, she met a dwarf who said, "My child, what are you looking for?"

"I am looking for my brothers, the seven ravens," she answered.

The dwarf said, "My masters, the ravens, are not at home, but if you care to wait until they come, please walk in."

Thereupon the dwarf brought in the ravens' supper. It was on seven little plates and in seven little cups, and the little sister ate a crumb or two from each of the little plates, and took a sip from each of the little cups, but she let the ring she had brought with her fall into the last little cup.

All at once a whirring and a crying were heard in the air, and then the dwarf said, "Now my masters the ravens are coming home."

Then they came in and wanted to eat and drink, and began to look about for their little plates and cups.

But they said one after another: "Hallo! who has been eating off my plate? Who has been drinking out of my cup? There has been some human mouth here."

And when the seventh drank to the bottom of his cup, the ring rolled up against his mouth.

He looked at it and recognized it as a ring belonging to his father and mother, and he said, "God grant that our sister may be here, and that we may be delivered."

As the maiden was standing behind the door listening, she heard the wish and came forward, and then all the ravens got back their human form again.

And they embraced and kissed one another and went joyfully home.

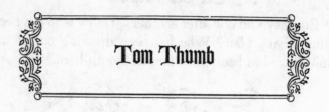

Tom Thumb

A POOR peasant sat one evening by his hearth and poked the fire, while his wife sat opposite spinning. He said, "What a sad thing it is that we have no children. Our home is so quiet, while other folk's houses are noisy and cheerful."

"Yes," answered his wife, and she sighed. "Even if it were an only one, and if it were no bigger than my thumb, I should be quite content. We would love it with all our hearts."

Now some time after this she had a little boy who was strong and healthy, but was no bigger than a thumb. Then they said, "Well, our wish is fulfilled, and small as he is we will love him dearly." And because of his tiny stature they called him Tom Thumb.

They let him want for nothing, yet still the child grew no bigger, but remained the same size as when he was born. Still he looked out on the world with intelligent eyes, and soon showed himself a clever and agile creature who was lucky in all he attempted.

One day when the peasant was preparing to go into the forest to cut wood, he said to himself, "I wish I had someone to bring the cart after me."

"Oh father," said Tom Thumb, "I will soon bring it. You leave it to me. It shall be there at the appointed time."

Then the peasant laughed and said, "How can that be? You are much too small even to hold the reins."

"That doesn't matter, if only mother will harness the horse," answered Tom. "I will sit in his ear and tell him where to go."

"Very well," said the father. "We will try it for once."

When the time came, the mother harnessed the horse, set Tom in his ear, and then the little creature called out "Gee up!" and "Whoa!" in turn, and directed it where to go. It went quite well, just as though it were being driven by its master, and they went the right way to the wood. Now it happened that while the cart was turning a corner, and Tom was calling to the horse, two strange men appeared on the scene.

"My goodness!" said one. "What is this? There goes a cart, and a driver is calling to the horse, but there is nothing to be seen."

"There is something queer about this," said the other. "We will follow the cart and see where it stops."

The cart went on deep into the forest and arrived quite safely at the place where the wood was cut.

When Tom spied his father, he said, "You see, father, here I am with the cart. Now lift me down." The father held the horse with his left hand, and took his little son out of its ear with the right. Then Tom sat down quite happily on a straw. When the two strangers noticed him, they did not know what to say for astonishment.

Then one drew the other aside and said, "Listen, that little creature might make our fortune if we were to show him in the town for money. We will buy him."

So they went up to the peasant and said, "Sell us the little man. He shall be well looked after with us."

"No," said the peasant. "He is the delight of my eyes, and I will not sell him for all the gold in the world."

But Tom Thumb, when he heard the bargain, crept up by the folds of his father's coat, placed himself on his shoulder, and whispered in his ear, "Father, let me go. I will soon come back again."

Then his father gave him to the two men for a fine piece of gold.

"Where will you sit?" they asked him.

"Oh, just put me on the brim of your hat. Then I can walk up and down and observe the neighborhood without falling down."

They did as he wished, and when Tom had said good-by to his father, they went away with him.

They walked on till it was twilight, when the little man said, "You must lift me down."

"Stay where you are," answered the man on whose head he sat.

"No," said Tom, "I will come down. Lift me down immediately."

The man took off his hat and set the little creature in a field by the wayside. He jumped and crept about for a time, here and there among the sods, then slipped suddenly into a mousehole which he had discovered.

"Good evening, gentlemen. Just go on home without me," he called out to them in mockery.

They ran about and poked with sticks into the mousehole, but all in vain. Tom crept further and further back, and as it soon got quite dark, they were forced to go home, full of anger and with empty purses.

When Tom noticed that they were gone, he crept out of his underground hiding place again. "It is dangerous walking in this field in the dark," he said. "One might easily break one's leg or one's neck." Luckily he came to an empty snail shell. "Thank goodness," he said, "I can pass the night in safety here." And he sat down.

Not long after, just when he was about to go to sleep, he heard two men pass by. One said, "How shall we set about stealing the rich parson's gold and silver?"

"I can tell you," interrupted Tom.

"What was that?" said one robber in a fright. "I heard someone speak."

They remained standing and listened.

Then Tom spoke again, "Take me with you and I will help you."

"Where are you?" they asked.

"Just look on the ground and see where the voice comes from," he answered.

At last the thieves found him and lifted him up. "You little urchin, are *you* going to help us?"

"Yes," he said. "I will creep between the iron bars into the pastor's room, and I will hand out to you what you want."

"All right," they said. "We will see what you can do."

When they came to the parsonage, Tom crept into the room but called out immediately with all his strength to the others, "Do you want everything that is here?"

The thieves were frightened and said, "Do speak softly and don't wake anyone."

But Tom pretended not to understand and called out again, "What do you want? Everything?"

The cook, who slept above, heard him and sat up in bed and listened. But the thieves were so frightened that they retreated a little way. At last they summoned up courage again, and thought to themselves, "The little rogue wants to tease us." So they came back and whispered to him, "Now do be serious and hand us out something."

Then Tom called out again as loud as he could, "I will give you everything if you will only hold out your hands."

The maid, who was listening intently, heard him quite distinctly, jumped out of bed, and stumbled to the door. The thieves turned and fled, running as though wild huntsmen were after them. But the maid, seeing nothing, went to get a light. When she came back with it, Tom, without being seen, slipped out into the barn. And the maid, after she had searched every corner and found nothing, went to bed again, thinking she had been dreaming with her eyes and ears open.

Tom Thumb climbed about in the hay and found a splendid place to sleep. There he determined to rest till day came, and then to go home to his parents. But he had other experiences to go through first. This world is full of trouble and sorrow!

The maid got up in the gray dawn to feed the cows. First she went into the barn, where she piled up an armful of hay, the very bundle in which poor Tom was asleep. But he slept so soundly that he knew nothing till he was almost in the mouth of the cow, who was eating him along with the hay.

"Heavens!" he said. "However did I get into this mill?" But he soon saw where he was, and the great thing was to avoid being crushed between the cow's teeth. At last, whether he liked it or not, he had to go down the cow's throat. "They forgot to put windows in this house," he said. "The sun does not shine into it and no light has been provided."

Altogether he was very ill-pleased with his quarters, and worst of all, more and more hay came in at the door, and the space grew narrower and narrower. At last he called out in his fear, as loud as he could, "Don't give me any more food. Don't give me any more food."

The maid was just milking the cow, and when she heard the same voice as in the night, without seeing anyone, she was frightened, and slipped from her stool and spilt the milk. Then in the greatest haste she ran to her master and said, "Oh, your reverence, the cow has spoken!"

"You are mad," he answered, but he went into the stable himself to see what was happening.

Scarcely had he set foot in the cowshed before Tom began again, "Don't bring me any more food."

Then the pastor was terrified too, and thought that the cow must be bewitched. So he ordered it to be killed. It was accordingly slaughtered, but the stomach, in which Tom was hidden, was thrown into the manure heap. Tom had the greatest trouble in working his way out. Just as he stuck out his head, a hungry wolf ran by and snapped up the whole stomach with one bite. But still Tom did not lose courage.

"Perhaps the wolf will listen to reason," he said. So he called out, "Dear wolf, I know where you can find a fine meal."

"Where is it to be had?" asked the wolf.

"Why, in such and such a house," answered Tom. "You must squeeze through the grating of the storeroom window, and there you will find cakes, bacon, and sausages, as many as you can possibly eat." And he went on to describe his father's house.

The wolf did not wait to hear this twice, and at night

forced himself in through the grating and ate to his heart's content. When he was satisfied, he wanted to go away again, but he had grown so fat that he could not get out the same way. Tom had reckoned on this, and began to make a great commotion inside the wolf's body, struggling and screaming with all his might.

"Be quiet!" said the wolf. "You will wake up the people of the house."

"All very fine," answered Tom. "You have eaten your fill, and now I am going to make merry." And he began to scream again with all his might.

At last his father and mother woke up, ran to the room, and looked through the crack of the door. When they saw a wolf they went away, and the husband fetched his ax and the wife a scythe.

"You stay behind," said the man, as they came into the room. "If my blow does not kill him, you must attack him and rip up his body."

When Tom Thumb heard his father's voice, he called out, "Dear father, I am here, inside the wolf's body."

Full of joy, his father cried, "Heaven be praised! Our dear child is found again." And he bade his wife throw aside the scythe that it might not injure Tom.

Then he gathered himself together and struck the wolf a blow on the head, so that it fell down lifeless. Then with knives and shears they ripped up the body and took their little boy out.

"Ah," said his father, "what trouble we have been in about you."

"Yes, father, I have traveled about the world, and I am thankful to breathe fresh air again."

"Wherever have you been?" they asked.

"Down a mousehole, in a cow's stomach, and in a wolf's maw," he answered. "And now I shall stay with you."

"And we will never sell you again for all the riches in the world," they said, kissing and fondling their dear child.

Then they gave him food and drink and had new clothes made for him, as his own had been spoilt in his travels.

The Clever Gretel

THERE was once a cook named Gretel who wore shoes with red knots, and when she went out with them on she used to turn about this way and that way, and then say to herself quite contentedly, "Ah, you are a very pretty girl!" And when she came home she drank a glass of wine for joy. And as the wine made her wish to eat, she used to taste of the best that she had and excuse herself by saying, "The cook ought to know how her cooking tastes."

One day it happened that her master said to her, "Gretel, this evening a guest is coming. So cook me two fowls very nicely."

"I will do it directly, master," replied Gretel. She soon killed the fowls, plucked, dressed, and spitted them, and as evening came on she put them before the fire to roast. They began to turn brown and to cook through, but still the guest had not come. Then Gretel said to the master, "If your guest does not come soon I shall have to take the fowls from the fire, but it will be a great shame not to eat them soon, while they are very juicy."

The master said, "I will run out myself and bring the guest home." And as soon as he had turned his back, Gretel took the spit with its two fowls off the fire, and thought to herself, "Ah, I have stood so long before the fire that I am quite hot and thirsty. Who knows when he will come?

Meanwhile I will run down into the cellar and have a draught."

Gretel ran down the stairs and set down a jug, and saying, "God bless you, Gretel!" she took a good pull at the beer. And when that was down she had another draught.

Then she went up again and placed the fowls before the fire, and turned the spit around quite merrily, first spreading some butter over their skins.

But the roasting fowls smelled so good that Gretel thought, "They had better be tasted now." And so she dipped her finger into the gravy and said, "Ah, how good these fowls are! It is a sin and shame that they should not be eaten at once."

She ran to the window, therefore, to see if her master was yet coming with his guest, but there was nobody, and she turned again to the fowls. "Ah, one wing is burnt!" said she, "I had better eat that." And cutting it off, she ate it. But then she thought, "I had better take the other, too, or master will see that something is wanting."

When she had finished the two wings, she went again to see whether her master was coming, but without success. "Who knows," said she, "whether they will come or not? Perhaps they have stopped along the way. Well, Gretel, be of good courage. The one fowl is begun. Have another drink and then eat it up completely, for when it is eaten you will be at rest. And besides, why should good things be allowed to spoil?"

So thinking, Gretel ran once more into the cellar, took a hearty drink, and then ate up one fowl with great pleasure. As soon as it was down, and the master still had not returned, Gretel looked at the other fowl and said, "Where the one is, the other ought to be also. The two belong with one another. What is right for the one is right for the other. I believe that another draught would not harm me." So saying, she took another hearty drink, and let the second fowl slip down after the other.

Just as she was enjoying the eating, the master came running up and called, "Make haste, Gretel! the guest is coming directly."

"Yes, master," said she. "It will soon be ready."

The master went in to see if the table were properly laid and, taking up the great knife wherewith he was to carve the fowls, he began to sharpen it on the stones. Meantime the guest came and knocked politely at the door.

Gretel ran to see who it was, and when she perceived the guest she held her finger to her mouth to enjoin silence and said, "Hasten quickly away! If my master discovers you here you are lost. He certainly did invite you here to supper, but he has it in his mind to cut off your ears. Just listen how he is sharpening his knife!"

The guest listened to the sound and then hurried down the steps as fast as he could, while Gretel ran screaming to her master and said to him, "You have invited a fine guest!"

"What?" said he. "What do you mean?"

"Why," replied Gretel, "just as I was about to serve them up, your guest took the two fowls off the dish and bolted away with them."

"That is fine manners, certainly!" said the master, grieved for his fine fowls. "He might have left me one of them at least, so that I might have had something to eat." Then he called after his guest to stop, who pretended not to hear him. Then he ran after him, knife in hand, calling out, "Only one! Only one!" meaning that his guest should leave one fowl behind him and not take both. But the latter supposed that his host meant that he would cut off only one ear, and so he ran on as if fire were at his heels, so that he might take both ears home with him.

The Six Servants

A LONG time ago there lived an old queen who was also an enchantress, and her daughter was the most beautiful creature under the sun. But the old woman was forever thinking how to lure men to their death. Every suitor, therefore, who came was compelled, before he could marry the daughter, to perform a task which the old woman set, and which was always so difficult that it could not be accomplished. And then the unfortunate lover received no mercy, but was forced to kneel down and have his head struck off. Many a poor youth had been thus destroyed, for the maiden was very pretty.

Yet a certain king's son was found who made up his mind to brave the danger. He had heard of the beauty of the Princess, and he prayed his father to let him go win her.

"Never!" replied the King. "If you go away, you go to die."

At this answer the son fell sick unto death, and so continued for seven years, for no physician could do him any good. At last when the father saw all hope was gone, he said to his son, "Go now and try your fortune, for I know not how else to restore you."

As soon as the Prince heard these words he jumped from his bed and felt new strength and vigor return to him, and made ready for his journey.

Soon he set off, and as he rode along across a plain he saw at a distance something lying on the ground like a bundle of hay. But as he approached nearer, he discovered that it was a man who had stretched himself on the earth and was as big as a little hill.

The fat man waited till the Prince came up, and then stood up and said to him, "If you need anyone, take me into your service."

"What should I do with such a clumsy man as you?" asked the Prince.

"It would not matter," replied the man, "were I a thousand times as clumsy, if I can render you a service."

"Very well. Perhaps I shall need you," said the Prince. "Come with me." So the fat man accompanied him and soon they met with another man, who was also lying on the ground, with his ear close to the grass.

"What are you doing there?" asked the Prince.

"I am listening," he replied.

"And to what are you listening so attentively?" pursued the Prince.

"I am hearing what is going on in the world around," said the listener. "Nothing escapes my ears. I can even hear the grass growing."

"Tell me, then," said the Prince, "what is happening at the court of the old Queen, who has such a beautiful daughter."

"I hear," replied the listener, "the whistling of the sword which is about to cut off the head of an unsuccessful wooer."

"Follow me. I can use you," said the Prince to the listener. And so the three now journeyed together.

Soon they came to a spot where were lying two feet and

part of two legs, but they could not see the rest of the body till they had walked a great distance farther. Then they came to the body and finally to the head.

"Hallo!" cried the Prince. "What a tall fellow you are!"

"Oh," replied the tall man, "not so much of that! Why, if I stretch my limbs out as far as I can, I am a thousand times as long, and taller than the highest mountain on the earth. But if you will take me, I am ready to serve you."

The Prince said, "Come with me." And as they walked on, they came to a man sitting beside the way who had bandaged up his eyes. "Have you weak eyes?" inquired the Prince. "Can you not look up at the light?"

"No, I have sharp eyes!" said the man. "They are so powerful that I dare not take away the bandage, for whatever I look at splits in two. Yet if I am of use to you, I will go with you."

"I can use you," said the Prince. "Come."

They traveled on and found a man who was lying on the ground in the scorching heat of the sun, and he trembled and shivered so that not a limb in his body stood still.

"What makes you shiver, when the sun shines like this?" asked the Prince.

"Alas, my nature is quite different from all others!" said the cold man. "The hotter it is, the colder I become, and the frost enters into all my bones. And the colder it is, the hotter I feel, so that I cannot touch ice for the heat of my body, nor yet go near the fire for fear I should freeze it."

"You are a strange fellow!" said the Prince. "Come with me. Perhaps I may need you." So they traveled on and saw a man who was standing and stretching his neck to such a length that he could see over all the mountains.

"What are you looking at so eagerly?" said the Prince.

"I have such clear eyes," replied the man, "that I can see over all the forests, fields, valleys, and hills; in fact, quite around the world."

"Come with me," said the Prince. "I am still in need of one like you."

And now the Prince came with his six servants to the city where the old Queen dwelt. When he arrived he would not tell his name, but told the enchantress that if she would give him her daughter, he would do any task she set. She was delighted to have such a handsome young man fall into her net and told him she would set him three tasks, and if he performed them all the Princess should become his wife.

"What is the first?" asked the Prince.

"You must fetch me my ring which I have let fall into the Red Sea," said the Queen.

Then the Prince went home to his servants and said, "The first task is not easy. It is to fetch a ring out of the Red Sea, but let us find a way to do it."

"I will see where it lies," said the man with the clear eyes. And looking down into the water he said, "There it hangs on a pointed stone."

"If I could but see it I would fetch it up," said the tall man.

"Is it there?" said the fat man. And lying down he held his mouth open to the water, and the stream ran into it as if into a pit, till at length the whole sea was as dry as a meadow. The tall man bent down a little and fetched out the ring, and the Prince rejoiced and carried it to the old Queen. She was astonished but confessed it was the ring.

"By luck you have performed the first task," she said. "But now comes the second. Do you see those three hundred oxen grazing on the meadows before my palace? All those you must consume—flesh, bones, and skins, and horns. Then in my cellar lie three hundred casks of wine which must all be drunk empty by you. And if you leave a single hair of any of the oxen or one drop of the wine, you will lose your life."

"May I invite any guests to the banquet?" asked the Prince. "No dinner is worth having alone." The old woman smiled wickedly and told him he might have one guest for company, but no more.

Then the Prince went again to his servants and told them what the task was, and then he invited the fat man to be his guest. He came and quickly ate down the three hundred oxen, flesh and bones, skin and horns, and asked if he was to have only a good breakfast. Then he drank all the wine out of every cask, without so much as requesting a glass, and drained them all to the very dregs. When the meal was over the Prince went to the old woman and told her that the second task was accomplished.

She was full of wonder and said, "No one has ever before done so much, but one task remains." And she thought, "You shall not escape me, and your head will not stay on your shoulders this time!"

She said, "Tonight I will bring my daughter into your room, and you shall place your arms around her. But beware that you do not fall asleep while you sit there, for at twelve o'clock I shall come, and if my daughter is not then in your arms, you are lost."

"The task is easy," the Prince thought. "I shall certainly keep my eyes open."

Still he called his servants together and told them what the old woman had said. "Who knows," said he, "what treachery may be behind this? Foresight is a good thing. You must take care that nobody passes out of the chamber during the night."

When night came the old Queen gave the maiden into the arms of the Prince. Then the tall man coiled himself in a circle about the pair and the fat man placed himself by the door so that no living soul could enter the room. So there the two sat and the maiden spoke not a word, but the moon shone through the window upon her face and the Prince could see her great beauty. He did nothing but look at her, and was full of happiness and love, and his eyes felt no weariness. This lasted till eleven o'clock, and then the old woman cast a charm over them all so that they fell asleep, and at that moment the maiden was carried away. Till a quarter to twelve the three slept soundly, but then the charm lost its strength and they all awoke again.

"Oh, what a terrible misfortune!" cried the Prince as soon as he awoke. "I am lost!"

The faithful servants also began to lament, but the listener said, "Be quiet! I will hear where she is." He listened a moment and then said, "The Princess is sitting three hundred miles from here, on a rock, lamenting her fate. You alone can help us, tall man. If you will stand up you will be there in a couple of strides."

"Certainly!" said the tall man. "But he with the sharp eyes must also go with us to pierce the rock."

Then he hoisted the sharp-eyed man upon his back, and in a moment they were on the enchanted rock. Then the man with the sharp eyes removed his bandage and looked around, and the rock was shattered into a thousand pieces. Then the tall man took the Princess home in an instant, and in the next instant fetched his companion, so that they were all seated as before, and rejoicing.

And when the clock struck twelve, the old enchantress stole into the room, smiling horribly, for she thought her daughter was safe enough on the rock and that the Prince was hers. But when she saw her daughter in the arms of the Prince she was frightened and said, "Here is one that can do more than I can!"

She dared not, however, deny her promise, and the maiden was therefore betrothed to the Prince. But the old woman whispered in her daughter's ear, "It is a shame that you listened to common people and are not permitted to choose a husband to your own liking."

Then the proud heart of the Princess became angry and she thought of revenge. And the next morning she caused three hundred bundles of faggots to be heaped together, and then said to the Prince, "The three tasks were soon performed, but still I will not marry you until someone shall be found who will sit upon the fire of these faggots and endure it."

She thought none of his servants would be burnt for their master, and that out of love for her he would himself sit upon the pile, and she would be freed from him. But the servants said that the cold man had done nothing yet, though the rest had, and so they placed him on the top of the pile of wood. The fire was then kindled and burnt for three days, until all the wood was consumed. But when the flames had ceased, there stood the cold man amidst the ashes, shivering like an aspen leaf and saying, "I have never before suffered such a frost! If it had lasted much longer, I would have frozen."

After this no other excuse could be found and the beautiful Princess had to take the unknown stranger as her husband. But just as they were going to church the old woman said, "I cannot endure the shame!" And she sent her guards after them with orders to bring back her daughter. The listener, however, had kept his ears open and heard the secret talk of the old woman.

"What shall we do?" said he to the fat man. But the latter knew what to do, and spitting behind him a drop or two of the sea water which he had drunk, a great lake was formed, in which the Queen's guards were caught and drowned.

The Queen, when she saw this, sent her horsemen in armor, but the listener heard the rattling of their trappings, and took the bandage off the sharp-eyed man, who looked steadily at the approaching enemy and shivered them all like glass. Then the wedding party passed on undisturbed, and when the two had been blessed in church, the six servants took their leave, saying to their former master, "Your wishes are fulfilled, and you no longer require us. We will therefore journey on and seek our fortunes."

Half a league from the palace of the Prince's father was a village near which a swineherd was tending his pigs. And as the Prince and Princess passed him the Prince said to his wife, "Do you know who I really am? I am no King's son but a swineherd, and this man here with the pigs is my father. We two must get out and help him."

Then he dismounted with her from the carriage and they went together into the inn, and he ordered the host to carry away secretly during the night the royal clothes belonging to his wife. So when morning came, she had nothing to wear, but the innkeeper's wife gave her an old gown and a pair of old slippers, and of these things made a great favor, saying, "If it were not for your husband, I would not give you anything."

The Princess now began really to believe that her husband was a swineherd, and with him she tended the drove, and thought it was a punishment for her pride and haughtiness.

This lasted for eight days, and then she could bear it no longer for her feet were wounded all over. Then two persons came to her and asked if she knew who her husband was.

"Yes, he is a swineherd," she said, "and he is just now

gone to drive a little trade with a few ropes and strings."

"Come with us now, and we will take you to him," said the two strangers. And they took her into the palace, where her husband stood in his royal robes in the great hall.

She did not recognize him, however, till he fell on her neck and said to her, "I have suffered so much for you, that it was only right that you should also suffer for me." And then they celebrated their wedding, and he who told this tale wishes that he, too, had been there.

Frederick and Catherine

THERE was once a man called Frederick who had a wife whose name was Catherine, and they had not long been married.

One day Frederick said, "Kate, I am now going to plow. When I come back I shall be hungry, so let me have something nice cooked, and a good draught of ale."

"Very well," said she. "It shall all be ready."

When dinnertime drew nigh, Catherine took a nice sausage, which was all the meat she had, and put it on the fire to fry. The sausage soon began to look brown and to crackle in the pan, and Catherine stood by with a fork and turned it.

Then she said to herself, "The sausage is almost ready. I may as well go to the cellar for the ale."

So she left the pan on the fire, took a large jug, and went into the cellar and tapped the ale cask. The beer ran into the jug and Catherine stood looking on.

At last it popped into her head, "The dog upstairs is not shut up. He may be running away with the sausage. It's lucky I thought of that."

So up she ran from the cellar, and sure enough the rascally cur had got the sausage in his mouth and was dragging it away on the ground.

Away ran Catherine and away ran the dog across the

field. But he ran faster than she and would not let the sausage go.

"Ah well," said Catherine. "What can't be cured must be endured." So she turned round, and as she had run a good way and was tired, she walked home leisurely to cool herself.

Now all this time the ale was running too, for Catherine had not turned the cock. And when the jug was full the liquor ran upon the floor till the cask was empty. When she got to the cellar stairs she saw what had happened.

"Goodness gracious!" said she. "What shall I do to keep Frederick from finding out about this?"

So she thought for a while, and at last remembered that up in the loft there was a sack of fine flour bought at the last fair, and that if she sprinkled this over the floor it would dry up the ale nicely.

"What a lucky thing," said she, "that we kept that flour! We have now a good use for it. He who saves, has!"

So away she went up to the loft for it, but she managed to set it down on the great jug full of beer and upset it. And thus all the ale that had been saved was set swimming on the floor also.

"Ah well," said she, "when one thing goes, another may as well follow."

Then she strewed the flour all about the cellar, and was quite pleased with her cleverness and said, "How very neat and clean it looks!"

At noon Frederick came home.

"Now, wife," cried he, "what have you for dinner?"

"Oh Frederick!" answered she, "I was cooking you a sausage, but while I went down to draw the ale, the dog ran away with it. And while I ran after him the ale all ran out. And when I went to dry up the ale with the sack of flour that we got at the fair, I upset the jug. But the cellar is now quite dry, and looks so clean!"

"Kate, Kate," said he, "how could you do all this? Why did you leave the sausage to fry and the ale to run, and then spoil all the flour?"

"Why, Frederick," said she, "I did not know I was doing wrong. You should have told me before."

The husband thought to himself, "If my wife manages matters thus, I must look sharp myself." Now he had a good deal of gold in the house, so he said to Catherine, "What pretty yellow buttons these are! I shall put them into a box and bury them in the garden, but take care that you never go near or meddle with them."

"No, Frederick," said she, "that I never will."

As soon as he was gone, there came by some peddlers with earthenware plates and dishes, and they asked her whether she would buy.

"Oh dear me, I should like to buy very much, but I have no money. If you had any use for yellow buttons, I might deal with you."

"Yellow buttons?" said they. "Let us have a look at them."

"Go into the garden and dig where I tell you, and you will find the yellow buttons. I dare not go myself."

So the rogues went, and when they found what these yellow buttons were, they took them all away, and left her plenty of plates and dishes. Then she set them all about the house for a show.

And when Frederick came back, he cried out, "Kate, what have you been doing?"

"Look," said she. "I have bought all these with your

yellow buttons, but I did not touch them myself. The peddlers themselves went and dug them up."

"Wife! wife!" said Frederick. "What a pretty piece of work you have made. Those yellow buttons were all my money. How came you to do such a thing?"

"Why," answered she, "I did not know there was any harm in it. You should have told me."

Catherine stood musing for a while, and at last said to her husband, "Hark ye, Frederick, we will soon get the gold back. Let us run after the thieves."

"Well, we will try," answered he. "But take some butter and cheese with you that we may have something to eat by the way."

"Very well," said she, and they set out. And as Frederick walked the fastest, he left his wife some way behind.

"It does not matter," thought she. "When we turn back, I shall be so much nearer home than he."

Presently she came to the top of a hill, down the side of which there was a road so narrow that the cart wheels had chafed the trees on each side as they passed.

"Ah, see now," said she, "how they have bruised and wounded those poor trees. They will never get well."

So she took pity on them and greased them with her butter so that the wheels might not hurt them so much. While she was doing this kind office, one of her cheeses fell out of the basket and rolled down the hill.

Catherine looked but could not see where it had gone, so she said, "Well, I suppose the other can run down the same way and find you. He has younger legs than I have."

Then she rolled the other cheese after it, and away it went, nobody knows where, down the hill. But she said she supposed that they knew the road and would follow her, and she could not stay there all day waiting for them.

At last she overtook Frederick, who asked her to give him something to eat. Then she gave him the dry bread.

"Where are the butter and cheese?" said he.

"Oh," answered she, "I used the butter to grease those poor trees that the wheels chafed so. And one of the cheeses ran away, so I sent the other after it to find it, and I suppose they are both on the road together somewhere."

"What a goose you are to do such silly things!" said the husband.

"How can you say so?" said she. "I am sure you never told me not to."

Then they ate the dry bread together, and Frederick said, "Kate, I hope you locked the door safe when you came away."

"No," she answered, "you did not tell me to."

"Then go home and do it now before we go any farther," said Frederick. "And bring with you something else to eat. I will wait here for you."

Catherine went, and thought to herself on the way, "Frederick wants something to eat, but I don't think he is very fond of butter and cheese. I'll bring him a bag of fine nuts to eat and a pitcher of vinegar to drink, for I have often seen him take some."

When she reached home, she bolted the back door, but the front door she took off the hinges and said, "Frederick told me to lock the door, but surely it can nowhere be so safe as if I take it with me."

So she took her time by the way, and when she overtook her husband she cried out, "Here, Frederick! Here is the door. Now you may watch it as carefully as you please."

"Alas! alas!" said he. "What a clever wife I have! I sent you to make the house fast, and you take the door away so that everybody may go in and out as they please. However, as you have brought the door, you shall carry it about with you for your pains."

"Very well," answered she, "I'll carry the door, but I'll not carry the nuts and vinegar pitcher also. That would be too much of a load. So I'll just fasten them to the door and it can carry them."

Frederick made no objection to that plan, and they set off into the wood to look for the thieves, but did not find them. And when it grew dark, they climbed up into a tree to spend the night there. Scarcely were they up than who should come by but the very rogues they were looking for. They were indeed great rascals, and belonged to that class of people who find things before they are lost. They were tired, so they sat down and made a fire under the very tree where Frederick and Catherine were. Frederick slipped down on the other side, and picked up some stones. Then he climbed up again and tried to hit the thieves on the head with them.

But they only said, "It must be near morning, for the wind shakes the fir cones down."

Catherine, who had the door on her shoulder, began to be very tired, but she thought it was the nuts upon it that were so heavy.

So she said softly, "Frederick, I must let the nuts go."

"No," answered he, "not now. They will discover us."

"I can't help that. They must go."

"Well, then, throw them down if you must!"

Then away rattled the nuts down among the branches, and one of the thieves cried, "Bless me, it is hailing."

A little while afterwards Catherine thought the door was still very heavy, so she whispered to Frederick, "I must throw the vinegar down."

"Pray don't," answered he. "It will discover us."

"I can't help that," said she. "Go it must."

So she poured all the vinegar down, and the thieves said, "What a heavy dew there is!"

At last Catherine thought, "Can it be the door that is so heavy?" So she said, "Frederick, I must throw the door down."

But he begged and prayed her not to do so, for he was sure it would betray them.

"I am about to let it fall, Frederick," she said.

"Devil take it, then!" said he.

And it fell down with such a clatter upon the thieves that they cried out, "The devil is coming down from the tree!"

And not knowing what was coming, they ran away as fast as they could and left all the gold. So when Frederick and Catherine came down, there they found all their money again and carried it home.

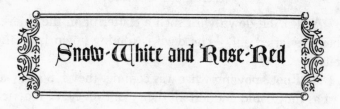

Snow-White and Rose-Red

THERE was once a poor widow who lived alone in her hut with her two children, who were called Snow-White and Rose-Red, because they were like the flowers which bloomed on two rosebushes which grew before the cottage. These two children were as good, happy, industrious, and amiable as any in the world, only Snow-White was more quiet and gentle than Rose-Red.

Rose-Red would run and jump about the meadows, seeking flowers and catching butterflies, while Snow-White sat at home helping her mother to keep house, or reading to her if there were nothing else to do.

The two children loved each other so dearly that they always walked hand in hand when they went out together, and when Snow-White said, "We will never separate from each other," Rose-Red replied, "Not so long as we live!" And their mother said, "What each girl has, she must share with the other."

Often they ran deep into the forest and gathered wild berries, but no beast ever harmed them. For the hare would eat cabbage leaves out of their hands, the fawn grazed by their side, the goats frisked about them in play, and the birds sat perched on the boughs singing as if nobody were near. No accident ever befell them, and if they stayed late in the forest and night came upon them, they used to lie down on the moss and sleep till morning. And because their mother knew they would do so, she felt no concern about them.

Once when they had passed the night in the forest and the dawn of morning awoke them, they saw a beautiful child dressed in shining white dress sitting near their couch. The child rose up and looked at them kindly, but without saying anything went into the forest. And when the children looked round they saw that they had slept close to the edge of a pit, into which they would have certainly fallen had they walked a couple of steps farther in the dark. Their mother told them the figure they had seen was doubtless the good angel who watches over children.

Snow-White and Rose-Red kept their mother's cottage so clean that it was a pleasure to look in it. Every morning in the summertime Rose-Red would put the house in order, and then lay a wreath of flowers at her mother's bed before she woke up, in which she always placed a bud from each rose tree. Every winter in the morning Snow-White would light the fire and put the kettle on to boil, and although the kettle was made of copper it shone like gold, because it was polished so well.

In the evening when the flakes of snow were falling, the mother would say, "Go, Snow-White, and bolt the door." And then they would sit down at the hearth, and the mother would put on her spectacles and read out of a great book, while the two girls sat spinning. By their side lay a little lamb, and on a perch behind them a white dove sat with its head under a wing.

One evening when they were sitting comfortably together, there came a knock at the door, as if someone wished to come in.

"Make haste, Rose-Red," cried her mother. "Make haste and open the door. Perhaps there is some traveler outside who needs shelter."

So Rose-Red went and drew the bolt and opened the door, thinking it was some poor man outside. But instead a great bear poked his head in. Rose-Red cried out and ran back, the little lamb bleated, the dove fluttered on her perch, and Snow-White hid herself behind her mother's bed.

The bear, however, began to speak and said, "Do not be afraid. I will do you no harm. I am half-frozen and only wish to come in and warm myself."

"Poor bear!" cried the mother. "Come in and lie down by the fire, but take care you do not burn your coat." Then she continued, "Come here, Rose-Red and Snow-White. The bear will not harm you. He means well."

So they both came back, and at last the lamb and the dove came near and were no longer afraid of him.

"Come here, children," said the bear, as he entered. "Come and knock the snow off my coat."

So they brought the broom and swept him clean. Then he stretched himself before the fire and growled cheerfully and comfortably, and in a little while the children became friendly enough to play tricks with their unwieldy guest. They tugged at his long shaggy hair, put their feet against his back and rolled him about, and even ventured to hit him with a hazel stick, laughing when he grumbled. The bear bore all their play in good temper, and only when they hit too hard he cried out:

> *"Leave me my life, you children,*
> *Snow-White and Rose-Red,*
> *Or you'll never wed."*

When bedtime came and the others had gone to bed, the mother said to the bear, "You may sleep here by the hearth if you like, and then you will be safe from the cold and the bad weather."

As soon as day came the two children let the bear out again, and he trotted away over the snow, and every evening afterwards he came back at a certain hour. He would lie down on the hearth and allow the children to play with him as much as they liked. And at last they became so used to him that the door was left unbolted till their black friend had arrived.

But as soon as spring returned and everything out of doors was green again, the bear said to Snow-White one morning, "Now I must leave, and I cannot return during the whole summer."

"Where are you going, then, dear bear?" asked Snow-White.

"I must go into the forest and guard my treasures from the evil dwarfs. In winter, when the ground is hard, they are obliged to keep in their holes and cannot break through. But now, since the sun has thawed the earth and warmed it, the dwarfs break through and steal all they can find. And what has once passed into their hands and is hidden by them in their caves is not easily brought to light."

Snow-White, however, was very sad at the departure of the bear, and opened the door so slowly that when he hurried through it he left behind on the latch a piece of his hairy coat. And through the hole which was made in his coat Snow-White thought she saw the glittering of gold, but she was not certain about it. The bear, however, ran hastily away and was soon hidden behind the trees.

Soon afterwards the mother sent the children into the wood to gather sticks. While doing so they came to a tree lying across the path, and near its trunk something was bobbing up and down in the grass, and they could not imagine what it was. When they came nearer they saw a dwarf, with an old wrinkled face and a snow-white beard a yard long. The end of this beard was caught in a split of the tree, and the little man kept jumping about like a dog tied by a chain, for he did not know how to free himself.

He glared at the maidens with his fiery red eyes and cried, "Why do you stand there? Are you going to pass by without offering me any help?"

"What have you done, little man?" asked Rose-Red.

"You foolish goose!" cried the dwarf. "I was going to split the tree, in order to get a little wood for my kitchen. The little food which we get is soon burnt up with great logs. We don't swallow down so much as you greedy people devour! I had just driven the wedge in properly and everything was going well, but the wretched wedge was too smooth and flew out! And the tree closed up so suddenly that I could not draw out my beautiful white beard. So here it sticks, and I cannot get away. Don't laugh there, you silly milk-faced creatures! Ugh! How horrid you are!"

The children tried as hard as they could to pull the dwarf's beard out, but it was caught too tightly. "I will run and get some help," cried Rose-Red at length.

"Oh you crackbrained sheep's head!" snarled the dwarf. "What are you going to call other people for? You are two too many for me now. Can't you think of anything better?"

"Don't be impatient," replied Snow-White. "I have thought of something." And pulling her scissors out of her pocket, she cut off the end of the beard.

As soon as the dwarf found himself at liberty, he snatched up his sack, which lay filled with gold between the roots of the tree, and throwing it over his shoulder he marched off, grumbling to himself, "Stupid people! To cut off a piece of my beautiful beard! Bad luck to you!" Away he went, without once even looking at the children.

Some time afterwards Snow-White and Rose-Red went to catch some fish, and as they came near the pond they saw something like a great grasshopper hopping about on the bank, as if it were going to jump into the water. They ran up and recognized the dwarf.

"What are you doing?" asked Rose-Red. "You will fall into the water."

"I am not quite such a simpleton as that," replied the dwarf. "But don't you see this fish trying to pull me in?"

The little man had been sitting there fishing and unfortunately the wind had entangled his beard with the fishing line. And so when a great fish bit the bait, the weak little fellow was not able to draw it out, and the fish had the upper hand. The dwarf held onto the reeds and rushes which grew near, but to no purpose, for the fish pulled him where it liked and he would soon have been drawn into the pond. Luckily just then the two maidens arrived and tried to release the beard of the dwarf from the fishing line, but they were too closely entangled. So the maiden pulled out her scissors again and cut off another piece of beard.

When the dwarf saw this done he cried out in a great rage, "You donkey! Do you want to disfigure my face? Was it not enough to cut off the end of my beard? Now you have to take away the best part of my fine beard! I dare not show myself again now to my own people. I wish you had run the soles off your boots before you had come here!"

So saying, he took up a bag of pearls which lay among the rushes, and without speaking another word slipped off and disappeared behind a stone.

Not many days after this adventure, it chanced that the mother sent the two maidens to the next town to buy thread, needles and pins, laces and ribbons. Their road led across a field where great pieces of rock lay strewn about. Just over their heads they saw a great bird flying round and round. Every now and then it dropped lower and lower, till at last it flew down behind a rock.

Then they heard a piercing shriek, and running up they saw with fright that the eagle had caught their old acquaintance the dwarf and was trying to carry him off. The gentle children at once laid tight hold of the little man and held him fast till the bird gave up the struggle and flew off.

As soon, then, as the dwarf had recovered from his

fright, he cried out in his shrill voice, "Could you not have held me more gently? You pulled at my fine brown coat so hard that it is all torn and full of holes. What meddling rubbish you are!"

With these words he shouldered a bag filled with precious stones and slipped away to his cave among the rocks.

The maidens were by now used to his ingratitude, and so they walked on to the town and completed their errand. On the way home they crossed the same field and again came suddenly upon the dwarf, who had emptied his bag of precious stones in a clean place, thinking that nobody was near. The sun shone on the bright stones, which glittered with so many colors that the two maidens stood still to admire them.

"What are you standing there gaping for?" asked the dwarf, and his face grew as red as copper with rage. He continued to abuse the poor maidens till a loud growling noise was heard, and a great black bear came lumbering out of the forest. The dwarf jumped up terrified, but he could not reach his cave before the bear overtook him.

Then, terror-stricken, he cried out, "Spare me, my dear Lord Bear! I will give you all my treasures. See these beautiful precious stones which lie here. Only give me my life. What have you to fear from a little weak fellow like me? You would not even feel me with your big teeth. Here, take the two wicked girls! They will make nice morsels for you! They're as fat as young quails! For heaven's sake, eat them!"

The bear, however, did not take the trouble to speak, but gave the wicked dwarf a single blow with his paw, and he did not move again.

The maidens were then going to run away but the bear called after them, "Snow-White and Rose-Red, fear not! Wait and I will go with you."

They recognized his voice and stopped, and when the bear came up to them his rough coat suddenly fell off, and there stood a tall man, dressed entirely in gold.

"I am a king's son," he said, "and was condemned by the wicked dwarf, who stole all my treasures, to wander about in this forest in the form of a bear till his death freed me. Now he has got his well-deserved punishment."

Then they went home, and Snow-White was married to the Prince, and Rose-Red to his brother, with whom they shared the immense treasure which the dwarf had collected. The old mother also lived happily many years with her two children. And the rose trees which had stood before the cottage were now planted before the palace, and every year they bore beautiful red and white roses.

The Four Accomplished Brothers

THERE was once a poor man who had four sons, and when they were grown up he told them that they must now make their own way in the world. "I have nothing to give you," he said, "and so you must each go out among strangers and learn a trade." So the four brothers took their walking staffs and, bidding their father good-by, went out through the gate of the town together. After they had traveled some distance, they came to a point where four crossroads met.

"Here we must part," said the eldest brother. "But in four years we will meet again in this place, and meantime we must seek our fortunes."

Then each brother went his way, and the eldest met a man who inquired of him his business and destination.

"I wish to learn a trade," he replied.

"Then come with me," said the man, "and become a thief."

"No," replied the other. "That is no longer considered an honorable trade, and besides the end of it is that one has to swing from the gallows."

"Oh, you need not fear the gallows," said the thief. "I will teach you so that no one shall ever be able to catch you or find any trace of you."

Then the man let himself be persuaded and became

such an accomplished thief that nothing was safe which he set his mind on having.

Meanwhile the second brother had met a man who asked him the very same questions.

"I do not know yet," he answered.

"Then come with me and become a stargazer," said the man. "There is nothing better than that, for nothing is hidden from you."

He went with him and became so skillful a stargazer that when he was about to part from his master, the latter gave him a telescope and said, "With this you can see all that occurs on earth and in heaven, and nothing can remain hidden from you."

The third brother was taken in hand by a huntsman, and received such excellent instructions in all branches of huntsmanship that he became a famous huntsman. On leaving, his master presented him with a gun which he said would never miss, for whatever he aimed at, it was sure to hit.

The youngest brother had meanwhile met a tailor and was asked if he would not like that trade.

"I am not sure about that," answered he. "I am not sure I would like to sit cross-legged from morning to night, or to send the needle and the goose backwards and forwards the whole day."

"Oh," cried the man, "you are talking about what you do not understand. With me you will learn a different kind of tailoring, which is honorable in its way, besides being easy." So he let the man persuade him, and they went on together, and he learned the tailoring art from its beginning.

When they parted, his master gave him a needle and

said, "With this you can sew together anything, whether it is as tender as an eggshell or as hard as steel, and not even a seam will be visible to anyone afterwards."

When the four years had passed, the four brothers arrived at the same time at the crossroads, and embracing and kissing each other, returned home to their father.

He was pleased and cried out, "Ah! So the wind has blown you back again!"

And thereupon they related all their adventures, and said they had each learned a trade. While they were telling their tales they sat under a great tree, and as soon as they had done, their father said he would now put their accomplishments to the test.

He looked up and then said to his second son, "At the top of this tree, between two boughs, there is a finch's nest. Now tell me how many eggs there are in it."

The stargazer took his glass and looking through it said, "There are five eggs."

"Fetch the eggs down without disturbing the mother bird who is sitting on the eggs," said the father then to his eldest son.

The clever thief climbed up the tree and took the five eggs from underneath the body of the bird without disturbing or frightening her, and brought them to his father.

The father then laid one at each corner of a table, placed the fifth in the middle, and said to the huntsman, "Now with one shot you shall cut them all in halves."

He aimed and at the first trial shot the five eggs as his father had wished. And surely he must have had a good charge of the powder that is made for shooting round a corner!

"Now it is your turn," said the father to his other son.

"You shall sew the eggshells together, and also the young birds which were in them, in such a manner that the shot shall not have injured them."

The tailor drew out his needle and soon did what was wished of him. And when he had finished, the thief had to carry the eggs back into the nest and lay them again under the bird without her being aware of it. He did this and the bird finished hatching her eggs a few days later, and when the young birds crept out they had a red streak round their necks where the tailor had sewn them together.

When his sons had done all these things, the father said to them, "Well, you have certainly used your time well and learned what is very useful. I cannot tell which of you deserves the most praise. That must be left to the next opportunity you have of displaying your talents."

Not long afterwards there arose a great cry of woe in the country because the King's daughter had been carried away by a dragon. Her father was grief-stricken by day and by night, and caused it to be proclaimed that whoever rescued the Princess should have her for his wife.

The four brothers said, "This is the opportunity we await." And they agreed to go forth together and deliver the Princess and show their talents.

"I will soon discover where she is," said the stargazer. Then peeping through his glass he said, "I see her already. She is on a rock in the midst of the sea far away from here, and a dragon is guarding her."

Then he went to the King, and asked for a ship for himself and his brothers, and they sailed over the sea till they came to the rock. The Princess saw them coming, but the dragon was fast asleep with his head in her lap.

"I dare not shoot," said the hunter, "for I should kill the Princess as well as the dragon."

"Then I will try my art," said the thief. And he crept near and stole the Princess out of the power of the dragon, but so quietly and cunningly that the monster noticed nothing, but snored on. Full of joy, they hurried with her into the ship and steered away to the open sea. But the dragon soon awoke, missed the Princess, and came flying through the air in a rage in pursuit of her. Just as he was hovering above the ship and was about to alight, the huntsman took aim, fired, and shot him through the heart.

The dragon fell, but in his fall he crushed the whole ship to pieces, because of his great size and weight. Fortunately, however, they saved a couple of planks, and on these the four brothers and the Princess swam about in the sea. All were now in a great strait, until the tailor with his wonderful needle sewed together the two planks with great stitches, and then collected the remaining pieces of the ship. These he sewed together so cleverly that in a short time the whole vessel was as tight and complete as before, and they sailed home in safety.

As soon as the King saw his dear daughter again he was very glad and said to the four brothers, "One of you shall have my daughter to wife, but you must settle among yourselves which one it is to be."

Thereupon a great quarrel took place between them, for each pressed his own claims. The stargazer said, "If I had not seen the Princess, then your arts would have been of no use. Therefore she is mine!"

But the thief said, "Of what use would your seeing have been if I had not stolen her away from the dragon? The Princess is mine!"

The huntsman said, "But you would have all been torn to pieces by the dragon had not my ball reached his heart. And so she must be mine!"

The tailor said, "If it had not been for my sewing the ship together again you all would have been drowned. No, the Princess is mine!"

Then the King settled the quarrel by saying, "You have all an equal claim. But since you cannot all have the Princess, not one of you shall have her. But instead I will give each of you half a kingdom as a reward."

This decision pleased the brothers, who said, "Yes, it will be better so, for then we shall remain united."

Thereupon each of them received half a kingdom, and they lived happily together with their father to the end of their lives.

The Giant with the Three Golden Hairs

THERE was once upon a time a poor woman whose son was born with a caul, and so it was foretold of him that in his fourteenth year he should marry the King's daughter. As it happened, the King soon after came into the village quite unknown to anyone. And when he asked the people what news there was, they answered, "A few days since a child was born with a caul, which is a sure sign that he will be very lucky. And indeed it has been foretold of him that in his fourteenth year he will marry the King's daughter."

The King had a wicked heart and was disturbed concerning this prophecy. So he went to the parents and said to them in a very friendly manner, "Let me have your child, poor people, and I will take care of him."

At first they refused, but when the stranger offered them much gold, they at last consented and gave him the child, thinking, "It is a luck-child, and therefore everything must go well for it."

The King laid the child in a box and rode away till he came to a deep water. Then he threw the box into it, saying to himself, "From this unsought-for bridegroom have I now freed my daughter."

The box, however, did not sink, but floated along like a boat, and not one drop of water came into it. At last it floated down to a mill two miles from the King's palace, and there at the milldam it came to a halt. The miller's servant boy was by good luck standing there and noticed it, and drew it ashore with a hook, thinking he had found a great treasure. When, however, he opened the box, he saw a beautiful child, alive and merry. He took it to the miller and his wife, who had no children and so adopted it for their own, saying, "God has sent it to us." They took good care of the foundling and it grew up a steady lad.

It happened one day that the King went into the mill for shelter during a thunderstorm, and asked the mill people if the tall boy was their child.

"No," they answered. "He is a foundling who, fourteen years ago, floated into our dam in a box, and the servant boy drew him out of the water."

The King then knew that it was none other than the luck-child he had thrown into the water, and so said to them, "Good people, could not the youth carry a letter to my wife the Queen? If so, I will give him two pieces of gold for a reward."

"As our lord the King commands," they replied, and told the youth to be ready.

Then the King wrote a letter to the Queen, and said, "As soon as this boy arrives with this letter, let him be killed and buried, and all must be done before I return."

The youth set out on his journey with the letter, but he lost his path and at evening came to a great forest. In the darkness he saw a small light, and going up to it he found a cottage, into which he went and saw an old woman sitting alone by the fire. Upon seeing the boy she was terror-stricken and exclaimed, "From whence do you come and whither do you go?"

"I come from the mill," he said, "and I wish to find the Queen, to whom I am taking this letter, but as I have lost my way in this forest, I wish to pass the night here."

"Poor boy!" said the woman. "You have come to a robbers' den, who will murder you when they come home."

"Let whoever will, come," he said. "I am not afraid. I am so weary that I can go no farther." And stretching himself upon a bench, he fell asleep. A little later the robbers came and asked angrily what strange lad was lying there.

"Ah," said the old woman, "it is an innocent boy who has lost his way in the forest, and out of pity I have taken him in. He has with him a letter to the Queen."

The robbers opened the letter and read it, and understood that as soon as the youth arrived he was to be put to

death. Then the robbers also felt pity for him, and the captain tore up the letter and wrote another, saying that the youth, when he arrived, was to be married to the King's daughter. Then they let him sleep quietly on the bench till the morning, and when he awoke they gave him the letter and showed him the right way.

And when the Queen received the letter, she did as it commanded and had a splendid marriage feast prepared. And the King's daughter was given in marriage to the luck-child. Since he was both young and handsome, she lived with him in peace and joy. A little later the King came back to his palace and saw that the prophecy was fulfilled, and his daughter was married to the luck-child.

"How did this come to pass?" he said. "In my letter I gave another command."

Then the Queen handed him the letter, that he might see for himself what was written. The King then saw that it had been exchanged for the other, and he asked the youth what had become of the letter entrusted to him.

"I know nothing about it," he answered. "It must have been changed in the forest where I passed the night."

In a great rage the King said, "you shall not escape so easily. He who would have my daughter must fetch for me three golden hairs from the head of the giant. Bring me what I desire. Then shall you receive my daughter."

The King hoped in this way to get rid of him, but he answered, "The three golden hairs I will fetch, for I fear not the giant." And so he took leave and began his journey.

The road led him by a large town where the watchman at the gate asked him his trade and what he knew. "I know everything," replied the youth.

"Then you can do us a great kindness," the watchman

said. "Tell us why the fountain in our market place, from which wine used to flow, no longer gives even water."

"That you shall know," he answered. "But you must wait till I return."

Then he went on farther and came to another town, where the watchman asked him as before what was his trade and what he knew.

"I know everything," he answered.

"Then you can do us a great kindness, if you will tell us why a tree growing in our town, which once bore golden apples, no longer puts forth even leaves."

"That you shall know," he answered. "But you must wait till I return." And he went on farther till he came to a wide lake, over which he must pass. The ferryman then asked him what his trade was and what he knew.

"I know everything," he answered.

"Then," said the ferryman, "you can do me a great kindness, if you will tell me why I must always row backwards and forwards, and am never to be set free."

"You shall learn the reason why," he answered. "But you must wait till I return."

When he had reached the other side of the water, he found the entrance into the giant's kingdom. It was black and dismal, and the giant was not at home. But his grandmother was sitting there in a large armchair.

"What do you want?" said she, looking at him fixedly.

"I want three golden hairs from the head of the King of these regions," replied the youth, "or I cannot keep my bride."

"That is a bold request," said she, "for if he comes home and finds you here it will go badly with you. But still you may remain, and I will see if I can help you."

Then she changed him into an ant and said, "Creep into the folds of my gown, and there you will be quite safe."

"Yes," he said, "that is very well, but there are also three things I should like to know: why a fountain which once flowed with wine is now dry, and does not even give water; why a tree which once bore golden apples does not now have even leaves; and why a ferryman must always be rowing backwards and forwards, and is never set free?"

"Those are difficult questions," replied the old woman. "But you have only to keep quiet and pay attention to what the giant says when I pluck out the three golden hairs."

When evening came the giant returned home, and no sooner had he entered when he noticed that the air was not quite pure.

"I smell the flesh of man!" he cried. "All is not right here." Then he looked and searched into every corner but could not find anything.

Then his grandmother began to scold him, screaming, "It has all been swept and dusted and everything put in order! And now you are pulling things all about again. You have always man's flesh in your nose! Sit down and eat your supper."

When he had eaten and drunk he felt tired, and the old woman took his head in her lap and said she would comb his hair a bit. Soon he yawned, then he fell asleep, and at last snored. Then she plucked out a golden hair and laid it down beside her.

"Ouch!" cried the giant. "What are you about?"

"I have had a bad dream," answered the old woman, "and so I seized hold of your hair."

"What did you dream then?" he asked.

"I dreamt that a market fountain, that once flowed wine, is dried up and does not even give water. What is the cause of that, pray?"

"Well, if you must know," he answered, "a toad sits under a stone in the spring, and if they killed it, the wine would flow out as before."

Then the old woman went on combing till he went to sleep again and snored so that the windows shook. Then she pulled out a second hair.

"Ha! what are you doing?" cried the giant in a passion.

"Do not be angry," said she. "I did it in a dream."

"What did you dream this time?" he asked.

"I dreamt that in a certain kingdom there grew a fruit tree which once bore golden apples, but now has not a leaf upon it. What is the cause of it?"

"Why," replied the giant, "at the root a mouse is gnawing. But if they killed it, golden apples would grow again. But if the mouse gnaws much longer, the tree will wither altogether. But spare me any more of your dreams. If you wake me again you will get a box on the ear."

So the old woman rocked him gently again to sleep, quietly combing his hair the while. Then she plucked out a third golden hair. The giant jumped up, roared out in a fury, and would have treated her ill, but she pacified him and said, "Who can help bad dreams?"

"What was this dream then?" he asked, and was quite curious to know.

"I dreamt of a ferryman who must forever row backwards and forwards, and is never set free. What is the cause of it?"

"Ah, the simpleton!" answered the giant. "When someone comes who wants to cross over, he must put the oar into his hand. Then the other will have to row to and fro, and he will be free."

Now as the old woman had plucked the three golden hairs and had received answers to the three questions, she let the giant lie in peace and he slept on till daybreak.

As soon as he had gone out in the morning, the old woman took the ant out of the fold of her gown and gave him again his human form.

"Here are the three golden hairs from the giant's head," she said. "And I suppose you also heard what he replied to the three questions?"

"Yes," said he. "I have heard and will remember well." And thanking the old woman for her help, he left, well pleased that he had been so lucky in everything.

When he came to the ferryman he had to give him the promised answer. But he said, "First row me across, and then I will tell you how you may be freed." And when they reached the other side he gave him the giant's advice, saying, "When someone comes this way and wants to pass over, give him the oar in his hand."

Then he went on to the town where stood the barren tree, and where the watchman waited for an answer.

So he said to him, "Kill the mouse which gnaws at the root of the tree, and it will again bear golden apples." The watchman thanked him, and for a reward gave him two asses laden with gold, which followed him.

Last he came to the town where the dry fountain was, and he told the watchman as the giant had said, "Under a stone in the well sits a toad which you must find and kill, and then the wine will flow again as before."

The watchman thanked him and gave him two more asses laden with gold.

Now the lucky youth soon reached home, and his dear bride was very glad when she saw him return and heard how well everything had gone with him. He brought the King what he had desired—the three golden hairs from the head of the giant.

And when the King saw the four asses laden with gold he was quite pleased and said, "Now are all the conditions fulfilled and you may have my daughter. But tell me, dear son-in-law, whence comes all this gold? This is indeed a great treasure."

"I was rowed over a river," he answered, "and I picked it up there, where it lies on the shore like sand."

"Can I not fetch some as well?" asked the King greedily.

"As much as you like," said he. "There is a ferryman who will row you across, and then you can fill your sacks on the other side."

The greedy King set out in great haste upon his journey, and when he came to the river he beckoned to the ferryman to take him across. The man came and told him to step into the boat, and just as they reached the other shore, he put the oar into the King's hand and sprang on shore.

Henceforth, for his sins the King had to row back and forth forever. And perhaps he still is ferrying, for no one has yet taken the oar from him.

How Six Traveled
Through the World

THERE was once a man who understood all manner of arts. He had served in the army, where he had behaved very bravely, but when the war came to an end he received his discharge and three farthings for his services. "Wait a bit! This does not please me," said he. "If I find the right people, I will make the King give me the treasures of the whole kingdom."

Thereupon, inflamed with anger, he went into a forest, where he found a man who had just uprooted six trees as if they were straw, and he said to him, "Will you be my servant and travel with me?"

"Yes," replied the man. "But I will first take home to my mother this bundle of sticks." And taking up one of the trees, he wound it around the other five, and raising the bundle upon his shoulder, he bore it away.

Then he returned and his master said to him, "We two should travel well through the world!"

They had not gone far before they came up with a hunter who was kneeling upon one knee, and preparing to take aim with his gun. The master asked what he was going to shoot, and he replied, "Two miles from hence sits a fly upon the branch of an oak tree, whose left eye I wish to shoot out."

"Oh, come with me," said the man. "If we three are together we can pass easily through the world."

The huntsman consented and went with him, and soon they arrived at seven windmills, whose sails were going round at a great speed, although right or left there was **no** wind and not a leaf stirring.

At this sight the man said, "I wonder what drives these mills, for there is no breeze!" They went on, but they had not traveled more than two miles when they saw a man sitting up in a tree, who held one nostril shut while he blew out through the other.

"Good gracious!" said our hero. "What are you doing up there?"

"Did you not see," replied the man, "two miles from hence, seven windmills? It is upon those which I am blowing, that the sails may go round."

"Oh, then come with me," said our hero. "For if four people like us travel together, we shall soon get through the world."

So the blower got up and accompanied him, and in a short while they met with another man standing upon one leg, who had unbuckled the other leg and laid it by his side.

The leader of the others said, "You have done this, no doubt, to rest yourself?"

"Yes," replied the man. "I am a runner, and to keep myself from running along too quickly I have unbuckled one of my legs, for when I run with both I go faster than a bird can fly."

"Well, then, come with me," said our hero. "Five men such as we are will soon get through the world."

The five went on together and soon met a man who had a hat on, which he wore quite over one ear. The captain of the others said to him, "Manners! Manners! Don't hang your hat on one side like that. You look like a simpleton!"

"I dare not wear my hat straight," said the other. "For if I do there will come so sharp a frost that the birds in the sky will freeze and fall dead upon the ground."

"Then come with me," said our hero. "It would be odd if six fellows like us cannot travel quickly through the world."

These six new companions went into a city where the King had proclaimed that whoever should run a race with his daughter, and bear away the prize, should become her husband; but if he lost the race he should also lose his head. This was mentioned to our hero, who said that he would have his servant run for him. But the King told him that in that case he must agree that his servant's life as well as his own should be sacrificed if the wager were lost.

To this he agreed, and then he bade his runner buckle on his other leg, and told him to be careful and to make sure of winning. The wager was that whoever first brought back water from a distant spring should be victor. So the runner and the Princess both received a cup, and they both began to run at the same moment. But the Princess had not run many steps before the runner was quite out of sight, and it seemed as if but a puff of wind had passed.

In a short time he came to the spring, filled his cup, and turned back again. But now he did not go very far before he felt tired, set his cup down, and lay down to take a nap. He made his pillow of a horse's skull which lay upon the ground, thinking, from its being hard, that he would soon awake.

Meanwhile, the Princess, who was a better runner than many of the men at court, had arrived at the spring and was returning with her cup of water, when she perceived her opponent lying asleep. In great joy she exclaimed, "My enemy is given into my own hands!" And emptying his cup, she ran on faster still.

All would now have been lost, if by good luck the huntsman had not been standing atop the castle, looking with his sharp eyes. When he saw the Princess was gaining the advantage, he loaded his gun and shot so cleverly that he carried away the horse's skull under the runner's head, without doing the man any injury.

This awoke him, and jumping up he found his cup

empty and the Princess already far in advance. However, he did not lose courage, but ran back to the spring, and again filling his cup, returned home ten minutes earlier than his opponent. "Behold!" said he. "Only now I have used my legs. What I did before would not be called running."

The King was disgusted, and his daughter not less, that a common soldier should carry off the prize. So they took counsel how they should get rid of him and his companions.

At last the King said, "Do not distress yourself, my dear. I have found a way to prevent their return." Then he called to the six travelers and said to them, "You must now eat and drink and be merry." Then he led them into a room with a floor of iron, doors of iron, and the windows guarded with iron bars.

In the room was a table set with choice delicacies, and the King invited them to enter and refresh themselves. And as soon as they were inside he locked and bolted all the doors. Then he sent for the cook and commanded him to keep a fire lighted beneath the room till the iron was red-hot. The cook obeyed, and the six champions sitting at the table soon began to feel warm, and they at first thought it was the result of the hearty eating. But as it kept getting warmer and warmer, they rose to leave the room and found the doors and windows all fast. Then they perceived that the King had some wicked design in hand, and wished to suffocate them.

"But he shall not succeed!" cried the man with the hat. "I will summon such a frost as shall put to shame and crush this fire." And so saying, he set his hat on straight and immediately such a frost fell that all the heat disappeared, and even the meats upon the dishes began to freeze.

When two hours had passed, the King thought they would be stifled, and he caused the door to be opened and went in himself to see after them. But as soon as the door was opened, there stood all six fresh and lively, and said they would like to come out to warm themselves, for the cold in the room had been so intense that all the dishes were frozen.

In a great passion the King went down to the cook and scolded him, and asked why he had not obeyed his instructions.

The cook, however, pointing to the fire, said, "There is heat enough there, I should think." And the King was obliged to own there was, and he saw clearly that he should not be able to get rid of his visitors in that way.

The King now began to think afresh how he could free himself, and he caused their leader to be summoned and said, "Will you not take gold and give up your right to my daughter? If so, you shall have as much as you wish."

"Well, my lord King," replied the man, "just give me as much as my servant can carry, and you are welcome to keep your daughter."

This answer pleased the King very much, and our hero said that he would come and fetch the sum in fourteen days. During that time he collected all the tailors in the kingdom and made them sew him a sack, which took them all that time. As soon as it was ready, the strong man who had uprooted the trees took the sack upon his shoulder and carried it to the King.

At the sight of him the King said, "What a powerful fellow this must be, carrying this great sack upon his shoulders!" And sorely frightened, he wondered how much gold would be needed to fill it.

The King then commanded a ton of gold to be brought, which required sixteen strong men to lift. But the strong man, taking it up with one hand, shoved it into the sack, saying, "Why do you not bring more at a time? This scarcely covers the bottom of the sack."

Then by degrees the King caused all his treasures to be brought, which the strong man put in, and yet they did not half fill his sack. "Bring more!" said he. "These are only a couple of crumbs."

Then they were obliged to bring seven thousand wagons laden with gold, and all these the man pushed into his sack—gold, wagons, oxen, and all. Still it was not full, and the strong man offered to take whatever they brought, if they would but fill his sack. When everything that they could find was put in, the man said, "Well, I must make an end to this. And besides, if a sack is not quite full, it can be tied up so much the easier." And so saying, he hoisted it upon his back and went away, and his companions with him.

When the King saw this one man bearing away all the riches of his kingdom, he fell into a great rage, and ordered his cavalry to pursue the six men, and at all risks to bring back the strong man with the sack. Two regiments accordingly pursued them quickly and shouted out to them, "You are our prisoners. Lay down the sack of gold or you will be cut to pieces!"

"What is that you are saying?" cried the blower. "You will make us prisoners?" So saying, he held one nostril and with the other blew the two regiments right away into the blue sky, so that one regiment flew over the hills on the right side and the other on the left. One sergeant begged for mercy. He said he had nine wounds and was a brave fellow undeserving of such disgrace.

So the blower stopped a moment until he could come back down without harm, and then said to him, "Go back now to your King and tell him to send several more regiments so that I may blow them all away into the air."

When the King heard this message, he said, "Let the rascals go! They will meet with their deserts." So the six companions took home all the wealth of that kingdom, shared it with one another, and lived in contentment all the rest of their days.

Hansel and Gretel

   CLOSE to a large forest there lived a woodcutter with his wife and his two children. The boy was called Hansel and the girl Gretel. They were always very poor and had very little to live on. And at one time when there was famine in the land, he could no longer procure daily bread.

One night when he lay in bed worrying over his troubles, he sighed and said to his wife, "What is to become of us? How are we to feed our poor children when we have nothing for ourselves?"

"I'll tell you what, husband," answered the woman. "Tomorrow morning we will take the children out quite early into the thickest part of the forest. We will light a fire and give each of them a piece of bread. Then we will go to our work and leave them alone. They won't be able to find their way back, and so we shall be rid of them."

"Nay, wife," said the man, "we won't do that. I could never find it in my heart to leave my children alone in the forest. Wild animals would soon tear them to pieces."

"What a fool you are!" she said. "Then we must all four die of hunger. You may as well plane the boards for our coffins at once."

She gave him no peace till he consented. "But I grieve over the poor children all the same," said the man.

The two children could not go to sleep for hunger

either, and they heard what their stepmother said to their father.

Gretel wept bitterly and said, "All is over with us now."

"Be quiet, Gretel," said Hansel. "Don't cry! I will find some way out of it."

When the old people had gone to sleep, he got up, put on his little coat, opened the door, and slipped out. The moon was shining brightly and the white pebbles round the house shone like newly minted coins. Hansel stooped down and put as many into his pockets as they would hold.

Then he went back to Gretel and said, "Take comfort, little sister, and go to sleep. God won't forsake us." And then he went to bed again.

At daybreak, before the sun had risen, the woman came and said, "Get up, you lazybones! We are going into the forest to fetch wood."

Then she gave them each a piece of bread and said, "Here is something for your dinner, but don't eat it before then, for you'll get no more."

Gretel put the bread under her apron, for Hansel had the stones in his pockets. Then they all started for the forest. When they had gone a little way, Hansel stopped and looked back at the cottage, and he did the same thing again and again.

His father said, "Hansel, what are you stopping to look back at? Take care and put you best foot foremost."

"Oh, father," said Hansel, "I am looking at my white cat. It is sitting on the roof, wanting to say good-by to me."

"Little fool, that's no cat! It's the morning sun shining on the chimney," said the mother.

But Hansel had not been looking at the cat. He had dropped a pebble on the ground each time he stopped.

When they reached the middle of the forest, their father said, "Now, children, pick up some wood. I want to make a fire to warm you."

Hansel and Gretel gathered the twigs together and soon made a huge pile. Then the pile was lighted, and when it blazed up the woman said, "Now lie down by the fire and rest yourselves while we go and cut wood. When we have finished we will come back to fetch you."

Hansel and Gretel sat by the fire, and when dinner-time came they each ate their little bit of bread, and they thought their father was quite near because they could hear the sound of an ax. It was no ax, however, but a branch which the man had tied to a dead tree, and which blew backwards and forwards against it. They sat there so long a time that they got tired. Then their eyes began to close and they were soon fast asleep.

When they woke it was dark night. Gretel began to cry, "How shall we ever get out of the wood?"

But Hansel comforted her and said, "Wait a little while till the moon rises, and then we will find our way."

When the full moon rose, Hansel took his little sister's hand and they walked on, guided by the pebbles, which glittered like newly coined money. They walked the whole night, and at daybreak they found themselves back at their father's cottage.

They knocked at the door, and when the woman opened it and saw Hansel and Gretel she said, "You bad children, why did you sleep so long in the wood? We thought you did not mean to come back any more."

But their father was delighted, for it had gone to his heart to leave them behind alone.

Not long afterwards they were again in great destitution, and the children heard the woman at night in bed say to their father, "We have eaten up everything again but half a loaf, and then we will be at the end of everything. The children must go away! We will take them farther into the forest so that they won't be able to find their way back. There is nothing else to be done."

The man took it much to heart and said, "We had better share our last crust with the children."

But the woman would not listen to a word he said. She only scolded and reproached him. Anyone who once says A must also say B, and as the father had given in the first time he had to do so the second. The children were again wide awake and heard what was said.

When the old people went to sleep Hansel again got up, meaning to go out and get some more pebbles, but the woman had locked the door and he couldn't get out. But he consoled his little sister and said, "Don't cry, Gretel. Go to sleep. God will help us."

In the early morning the woman made the children get up and gave them each a piece of bread, but it was smaller than the last. On the way to the forest Hansel crumbled it up in his pocket, and stopped every now and then to throw a crumb onto the ground.

"Hansel, what are you stopping to look about you for?" asked his father.

"I am looking at my dove which is sitting on the roof and wants to say good-by to me," answered Hansel.

"Little fool," said the woman, "that is no dove! It is the morning sun shining on the chimney."

Nevertheless, Hansel strewed the crumbs from time to time on the ground. The woman led the children far into the forest, where they had never been before.

Again they made a big fire, and the woman said, "Stay where you are, children, and when you are tired you may go to sleep for a while. We are going further on to cut wood, and in the evening when we have finished we will come back and fetch you."

At dinnertime Gretel shared her bread with Hansel, for he had crumbled his upon the road. Then they went to sleep and the evening passed, but no one came to fetch the poor children.

It was quite dark when they woke up, and Hansel cheered his little sister. He said, "Wait a bit, Gretel, till the moon rises, and then we can see the bread crumbs which I scattered to show us the way home."

When the moon rose they started, but they found no bread crumbs, for all the thousands of birds in the forest had picked them up and eaten them.

Hansel said to Gretel, "We shall soon find the way." But they could not find it. They walked the whole night and all the next day from morning till night, but they could not get out of the wood.

They were very hungry, for they had nothing to eat but a few berries which they found. They were so tired that their legs would not carry them any farther, and they lay down under a tree and went to sleep.

When they woke in the morning, it was the third day since they had left their father's cottage. They started to walk again, but they only got deeper and deeper into the wood, and if no help came they must perish.

At midday they saw a beautiful snow-white bird sitting on a tree. It sang so beautifully that they stood still to listen to it. When it stopped, it fluttered its wings and flew around them. They followed it till they came to a little cottage, on the roof of which it settled down.

When they got quite near, they saw that the little house was made of bread and roofed with cake. The windows were transparent sugar.

"Here is something for us," said Hansel. "We will have a good meal. I will have a piece of the roof, Gretel, and you can have a bit of the window. It will be nice and sweet."

Hansel reached up and broke off a piece of the roof to see what it tasted like. Gretel went to the window and nibbled at that. A gentle voice called out from within:

> *"Nibbling, nibbling like a mouse,*
> *Who's nibbling at my little house?"*

The children answered:

> *"The wind, the wind doth blow*
> *From heaven to earth below."*

And they went on eating without disturbing themselves. Hansel, who found the roof very good, broke off a large piece for himself, and Gretel pushed a whole round pane out of the window and sat down on the ground to enjoy it.

All at once the door opened and an old, old woman, supporting herself on a crutch, came hobbling out. Hansel and Gretel were so frightened that they dropped what they held in their hands.

But the old woman only shook her head and said, "Ah, dear children, who brought you here? Come in and stay with me. You will come to no harm."

She took them by the hand and led them into the little house. A nice dinner was set before them: pancakes and sugar, milk, apples, and nuts. After this she showed them two little white beds into which they crept, and they felt as if they were in heaven.

Although the old woman appeared to be so friendly, she was really a wicked old witch who was on the watch for children, and she had built the bread house on purpose to lure them to her. Whenever she could get a child into her clutches she cooked it and ate it, and considered it a grand feast. Witches have red eyes and can't see very far, but they have keen noses like animals and can scent the approach of human beings.

When Hansel and Gretel came near her, she laughed wickedly to herself and said scornfully, "Now that I have them, they shan't escape me."

She got up early in the morning before the children were awake, and when she saw them sleeping, with their beautiful rosy cheeks, she murmured to herself, "They will be dainty morsels."

She seized Hansel with her bony hand and carried him off to a little stable, where she locked him up behind a barred door. He might shriek as loud as he liked, she took no notice of him.

Then she went to Gretel and shook her till she woke, and cried, "Get up, little lazybones! Fetch some water and cook something nice for your brother. He is in the stable and has to be fattened. When he is nice and fat, I will eat him."

Gretel began to cry bitterly, but it was no use; she had to obey the witch's orders. The best food was cooked for poor Hansel, but Gretel had only the shells of crayfish.

The old woman hobbled to the stable every morning and cried, "Hansel, put your finger out for me to feel how fat you are."

Hansel put out a knucklebone, and the old woman, whose eyes were too dim to see, thought it was his finger. And she was much astonished that he did not get fat.

When four weeks had passed and Hansel still kept thin, she became impatient and would wait no longer. "Now then, Gretel," she cried, "bustle along and fetch the water. Fat or thin, I will kill Hansel and eat him."

Oh, how his poor little sister grieved! As she carried the water, the tears streamed down her cheeks. "Dear God, help us!" she cried. "If only the wild animals in the forest had eaten us, we should at least have died together."

"You may spare your lamentations! They will do you no good," said the old woman.

Early in the morning Gretel had to go out to fill the kettle with water, and then she had to kindle a fire and hang the kettle over it.

"We will bake first," said the old witch. "I have heated the oven and kneaded the dough."

She pushed poor Gretel towards the oven and said, "Creep in and see if it is properly heated, and then we will put the bread in."

She meant, when Gretel had gone in, to shut the door and roast her, but Gretel saw her intention and said, "I don't know how to get in. How am I to manage it?"

"Stupid goose!" cried the witch. "The opening is big enough. You can see that I could get into it myself."

She hobbled up and stuck her head into the oven. But Gretel gave her a push which sent the witch right in, and then she banged the door and bolted it.

"Oh! oh!" the witch began to howl horribly. But Gretel ran away and left the wicked witch to perish miserably.

Gretel ran as fast as she could to the stable. She opened the door and cried, "Hansel, we are saved! The old witch is dead."

Hansel sprang out, like a bird out of a cage when the door is set open. How delighted they were. They fell upon each other's necks and kissed each other and danced about for joy.

As they had nothing more to fear, they went into the witch's house, and in every corner they found chests full of pearls and precious stones.

"These are better than pebbles," said Hansel, as he filled his pockets.

Gretel said, "I must take something home with me too." And she filled her apron.

"But now we must go," said Hansel, "so that we may get out of this enchanted wood."

Before they had gone very far, they came to a great piece of water.

"We can't get across it," said Hansel. "I see no stepping stones and no bridge."

"And there are no boats either," answered Gretel, "but there is a duck swimming. It will help us over if we ask it."

So she cried:

> "Little duck that cries quack, quack,
> Here Gretel and here Hansel stand.
> Quickly take us on your back,
> No path nor bridge is there at hand!"

The duck came swimming towards them, and Hansel got on its back and told his sister to sit on his knee.

"No," answered Gretel, "it will be too heavy for the duck. It must take us over one after the other."

The good creature did this, and when they had got safely over and walked for a while the wood seemed to grow more and more familiar to them, and at last they saw their father's cottage in the distance. They began to run, and rushed inside, where they threw their arms around their father's neck. The man had not had a single happy moment since he deserted his children in the wood, and in the meantime his wife had died.

Gretel shook her apron and scattered the pearls and precious stones all over the floor, and Hansel added handful after handful out of his pockets.

So all their troubles came to an end, and they lived together as happily as possible.

The Twelve Huntsmen

THERE was once a prince who was betrothed to a maiden, the daughter of a king, whom he loved very much. One day when they were together and very happy, a messenger came from the Prince's father, who was lying ill, to summon him home to see him before he died.

He said to his beloved, "I must go away and leave you now, but I give you this ring as a keepsake. When I am King, I will come and fetch you away."

Then he rode off, and when he got home he found his father on his deathbed. His father said, "My dear son, I wanted to see you once more before I die. Promise to marry the bride I have chosen for you." And he named a certain princess. His son was so sad that without reflecting he promised to do what his father wished, and thereupon the King closed his eyes and died.

Now when the Prince had been proclaimed king, and the period of mourning was past, the time came when he had to keep his promise to his father. He made his offer to the Princess and it was accepted. His betrothed heard of this and grieved so much over his faithlessness that she very nearly died. The King, her father, asked, "Dear child, why are you so sad? You shall have whatever you desire."

She thought a moment and said, "Dear father, I want eleven maidens exactly like me in face, figure, and height."

The King said, "If it is possible, your wish shall be fulfilled."

Then he caused a search to be made all over his kingdom till the eleven maidens were found, all exactly like his daughter. The Princess ordered twelve huntsmen's dresses to be made, which she commanded the maidens to wear, putting on the twelfth herself. Then she took leave of her father and rode away with the maidens to the court of her former bridegroom whom she loved so dearly. She asked him if he wanted any huntsmen, and whether he would take them all into his service. The King did not recognize her, but as they were all so handsome he said, yes, he would engage them. So they all entered the King's service.

Now the King had a lion which was a wonderful creature, for he knew all secret and hidden things. He said to the King one evening, "You fancy you have twelve huntsmen here, don't you?"

"Yes," said the King.

"You are mistaken," said the lion. "They are twelve maidens."

The King answered, "That can't be true! How can you prove it?"

"Oh, have some peas strewn in your anteroom tomorrow, and you will soon see. Men have a firm tread, and when they walk on peas, the peas don't move. But maidens trip and trot and slide, and make the peas roll about."

The King was pleased with the lion's advice and ordered the peas to be strewn on the floor.

There was, however, a servant of the King who favored the huntsmen, and when he heard that they were to be put to this test he went and told them all about it. He said, "The lion is going to prove to the King that you are maidens."

The Princess thanked him and said afterwards to her maidens, "Do your utmost to tread firmly on the peas."

Next morning when the King ordered them to be called, they walked into the antechamber with so firm a tread that not a pea moved. When they had gone away, the King said to the lion, "You lied. They walked just like men."

But the lion answered, "They had been warned of the test and were prepared for it. Just let twelve spinning wheels be brought into the antechamber, and they will be delighted at the sight as no man would be."

This plan also pleased the King and he ordered the spinning wheels. But again the kind servant warned the huntsmen of the plan. When they were alone, the Princess said to her maidens, "Control yourselves and don't so much as look at the spinning wheels."

When the King next morning sent for the huntsmen, they walked through the antechamber without even glancing at the spinning wheels.

Then the King said to the lion, "You lied to me. They *are* men. They never looked at the spinning wheels."

The lion answered, "They knew that they were on trial and restrained themselves."

But the King would not believe him any more.

The twelve huntsmen always went with the King on his hunting expeditions, and the longer he had them, the better he liked them. Now it happened one day when they were out hunting that the news came of the royal bride's approach.

When the true bride heard it, the shock was so great that her heart nearly stopped, and she fell down in a dead faint. The King, thinking something had happened to his favorite huntsman, ran to help him and pulled off his glove. Then he saw the ring which he had given to his first betrothed, and when he looked her in the face he recognized her. He was so moved that he kissed her, and when she opened her eyes he said, "Thou art mine and I am thine, and nobody in the world shall separate us."

Then he sent a messenger to the other bride and begged her to go home, as he already had a wife, and he who has an old dish does not need a new one. The marriage was then celebrated, and the lion was taken into favor again, because, after all, he had spoken the truth.

Faithful John

THERE was once an old king who, having fallen sick, thought to himself, "This is very likely my deathbed on which I am lying."

Then he said, "Let Faithful John be sent for."

Faithful John was his best-beloved servant, and was so called because he had served the King faithfully all his life long.

When he came near the bed, the King said to him, "Faithful John, I feel my end drawing near, and my only care is for my son. He is yet of tender years and does not always know how to shape his conduct. And unless you promise me to instruct him in all his actions and be a true foster father to him, I shall not be able to close my eyes in peace."

Then answered Faithful John, "I will never forsake him, and I will serve him faithfully even though it should cost me my life."

And the old King said, "Then I die, being of good cheer and at peace." And he went on to say, "After my death, you must lead him through the whole castle, into all the chambers, halls, and vaults, and show him the treasures that in them lie. But the last chamber in the long gallery, in which lies hidden the picture of the Princess of the Golden Palace, you must not show him. If he were to see that picture, he would directly fall into so great a love for her that he would faint with the strength of it. And afterwards for her sake he would run into great dangers. So you must guard him well."

And as Faithful John gave him his hand upon it, the old King became still and silent, laid his head upon the pillow, and died.

When the old King was laid in the grave, Faithful John told the young King what he had promised to his father on his deathbed, and said, "And I will certainly hold to my promise and be faithful to you, as I was faithful to him, even though it should cost me my life."

When the days of mourning were at an end, Faithful John said to the Prince, "It is now time that you should see your inheritance. I will show you all the paternal castle."

Then he led him over all the place, upstairs and downstairs, and showed him all the treasures and the splendid chambers. One chamber only he did not open, that in which the perilous picture hung. Now the picture was so placed that when the door opened it was the first thing to be seen, and it was so wonderfully painted that it seemed to breathe and move. In the whole world there was nothing more lovely or more beautiful.

The young King noticed how Faithful John always passed by this one door and asked, "Why do you not undo this door?"

"There is something inside that would terrify you," answered he.

But the King answered, "I have seen the whole castle, and I will know what is in here also." And he went forward and tried to open the door by force.

Then Faithful John called him back and said, "I

promised your father on his deathbed that you should not see what is in that room. It might bring great misfortune on you and me were I to break my promise."

But the young King answered, "I shall be undone if I do not go inside that room. I shall have no peace day or night until I have seen it with my own eyes, and I will not move from this place until you have unlocked it."

Then Faithful John saw there was no help for it, and he chose out the key from the big bunch with a heavy heart and many sighs. When the door was opened he walked in first. He thought that by standing in front of the King he might hide the picture from him. But that was no good: the King stood on tiptoe and looked over his shoulder. And when he saw the image of the lady that was so wonderfully beautiful and so glittering with gold and jewels, he fell on the ground powerless.

Faithful John helped him up, took him to his bed, and thought with sorrow, "Ah me! The evil has come to pass. What will become of us?"

Then he strengthened the King with wine until he came to himself. The first words that he said were, "Oh, the beautiful picture! Whose portrait is it?"

"It is the portrait of the Princess of the Golden Palace," answered Faithful John.

Then the King said, "My love for her is so great that if all the leaves of the forest were tongues they could not utter it. I stake my life on the chance of obtaining her. And you, my Faithful John, must stand by me."

The faithful servant considered for a long time how the business should be begun. It seemed to him that it would be difficult even to obtain only a sight of the Princess.

At last he thought out a way and said to the King, "All

that she has about her is of gold—tables, chairs, dishes, drinking cups, bowls, and all the household furniture. In your treasury are five tons of gold. Let the goldsmiths of your kingdom work it up into all kinds of vessels and implements, into all kinds of birds and wild creatures and wonderful beasts, such as may please her. Then we will carry them off with us and go and seek our fortune."

The King had all the goldsmiths fetched, and they worked day and night until at last some splendid things were prepared. When a ship had been loaded with them, Faithful John put on the garb of a merchant and so did the King, so as the more completely to disguise themselves. Then they journeyed over the sea, and went so far that at last they came to the city where the Princess of the Golden Palace dwelt.

Faithful John told the King to stay in the ship and to wait for him.

"Perhaps," said he, "I shall bring the Princess back with me, so take care that everything is in order. Let the golden vessels be placed about and the whole ship be adorned."

Then he gathered together in his apron some of the gold things, one of each kind, landed, and went up to the royal castle. And when he reached the courtyard of the castle, there stood by the well a pretty maiden who had two golden pails in her hand, and she was drawing water with them. And as she turned round to carry them away, she saw the strange man and asked him who he was.

He answered, "I am a merchant." And he opened his apron and let her look within it.

"Ah, what beautiful things!" cried she. And setting down her pails, she turned the golden toys over and looked at them one after another.

Then she said, "The Princess must see these. She takes so much pleasure in gold things that she will buy them all from you."

Then she took him by the hand and led him in, for she was the chambermaid.

When the Princess saw the golden wares she was very pleased and said, "All these are so finely worked that I should like to buy them of you."

But the Faithful John said, "I am only the servant of a rich merchant, and what I have here is nothing to what my master has in the ship. He has the cunningest and costliest things that ever were made of gold."

The Princess then wanted it all to be brought to her but he said, "That would take up many days. So great is the number of them and so much space would they occupy that there would not be enough room for them in your house."

But the Princess' curiosity and fancy grew so much that at last she said, "Lead me to the ship. I will myself go and see your master's treasures."

Then Faithful John led her to the ship joyfully, and the King, when he saw that her beauty was even greater than the picture had set forth, felt his heart leap at the sight. Then she climbed up into the ship and the King received her.

Faithful John stayed by the steersman and gave orders for the ship to push off, saying, "Spread all sail, that she may fly like a bird in the air."

So the King showed her all the golden things, each separately—the dishes, the bowls, the birds, the wild creatures, and the wonderful beasts. Many hours were passed in looking at them all, and in her pleasure the Princess never noticed that the ship was moving onwards. When she had examined the last, she thanked the merchant and prepared to return home. But when she came to the ship's side, she saw that they were on the high seas, far from land and speeding on under full sail.

"Ah!" cried she, full of terror. "I am betrayed and carried off by this merchant. Oh, that I had died rather than have fallen into his power!"

But the King took hold of her hand and said, "No merchant am I, but a king, and no baser of birth than your-self. It is because of my overmastering love for you that I have carried you off by cunning. The first time I saw your picture I fell fainting to the earth."

When the Princess of the Golden Palace heard this she became more trustful, and her heart inclined favorably to-wards him, so that she willingly consented to become his wife.

It happened, however, as they were still journeying on the open sea, that Faithful John, as he sat in the forepart of the ship and made music, caught sight of three ravens in the air flying overhead. Then he stopped playing and listened to what they said one to another, for he understood them quite well.

The first one cried, "Aye, there goes the beautiful Princess of the Golden Palace."

"Yes," answered the second. "But he has not got her safe yet."

And the third said, "He has her, though. She sits be-side him in the ship."

Then the first one spoke again, "What does that avail him? When they come on land a fox-red horse will spring towards them. Then will the King try to mount him, and

if he does, the horse will rise with him into the air so that
he will never see his bride again."

The second raven asked, "Is there no remedy?"

"Oh yes. If another man mounts quickly, and takes the
pistol out of the holster and shoots the horse dead with it,
he will save the young King. But who knows that? And
moreover he that knows and does it will become stone from
toe to knee."

Then said the second raven, "I know more. If the horse
should be killed, the young King will not even then be sure
of his bride. When they arrive at the castle there will lie a
wrought bridal shirt in a dish, and it will seem all woven of
gold and silver. But it is really of sulphur and pitch, and if
he puts it on it will burn him to the marrow of his bones."

The third raven said, "Is there no remedy?"

"Oh yes," answered the second. "If another man with
gloves on picks up the shirt and throws it into the fire, so
that it is consumed, then is the young King delivered. But
what avails that? He who knows and does it will be turned
into stone from his heart to his knee."

Then spoke the third, "I know yet more. Even when
the bridal shirt is burnt up, the King is not sure of his bride.
When at the wedding the dance begins and the young
Queen dances, she will suddenly grow pale and fall to the
earth as if she were dead. And unless someone lifts her up
and takes three drops of blood from her right breast, she
will die. But he that knows and does this will become stone
from the crown of his head to the sole of his foot."

When the ravens had spoken thus among themselves
they flew away. Faithful John had understood it all, and
from that time he remained quiet and sad, for he thought
to himself that were he to conceal what he had heard from

his master, misfortune would befall. Yet were he to reveal it his own life would be sacrificed.

At last, however, he said within himself, "I will save my master, though I myself should perish!"

So when they came on land, it happened just as the ravens had foretold: there sprang forward a splendid fox-red horse.

"Come on!" said the King. "He shall carry me to the castle." And he was going to mount, when Faithful John passed before him and mounted quickly, drew the pistol out of the holster, and shot the horse dead.

Then the other servants of the King cried out (for they did not wish well to Faithful John), "How shameful to kill that beautiful animal that was to have carried the King to his castle."

But the King said, "Hold your tongues, and let him be. He is my Faithful John. He knows what is the good of it."

Then they went up to the castle, and there stood in the hall a dish, and the wrought bridal shirt that lay on it shone like gold and silver. The young King went up to it and was going to put it on, but Faithful John pushed him away, picked it up with his gloved hands, threw it quickly on the fire, and there let it burn.

The other servants began grumbling again and said, "Look, he is even burning up the King's bridal shirt!"

But the young King said, "Who knows but that there may be a good reason for it? Let him be! He is my Faithful John."

Then the wedding feast was held, and the bride led the dance. Faithful John watched her carefully, and all at once she grew pale and fell down as if she were dead. Then he went quickly to her and carried her into a chamber hard by, laid her down, and, kneeling, took three drops of blood from her right breast. Immediately she drew breath again and raised herself up.

But the young King, witnessing all and not knowing why Faithful John had done this, grew very angry and cried out, "Throw him into prison!"

The next morning Faithful John was condemned to death and led to the gallows. And as he stood there ready to die, he said, "He who is about to die is permitted to speak once before his end. May I claim that right?"

"Yes," answered the King. "It is granted to you."

Then said Faithful John, "I have been condemned unjustly, for I have always been faithful." And he related how he had heard on the sea voyage the talk of the ravens, and how he had done all in order to save his master.

Then cried the King, "O my Faithful John, pardon! pardon! Lead him down!"

But Faithful John, as he spoke the last words, fell lifeless and became stone.

The King and Queen had great grief because of this and the King said, "Ah, how could I have rewarded such faithfulness with evil?" And he caused the stone image to be lifted up and put to stand in his sleeping room by the side of his bed. And as often as he saw it he wept and said, "Would that I could bring you back to life, my Faithful John!"

After some time the Queen bore twins—two little sons —that grew and thrived and were the joy of their parents. One day when the Queen was in church, the two children were sitting and playing with their father, and he gazed at the stone image full of sadness, sighed, and cried, "Oh, that I could bring you back to life, my Faithful John!"

Then the stone began to speak and said, "Yes, you can bring me back to life again, if you will bestow therefor your best-beloved."

Then cried the King, "All that I have in the world will I give up for you!"

The stone went on to say, "If you will cut off the heads of your two children with your own hand, and besmear me with their blood, I shall receive life again."

The King was horror-stricken at the thought that he must put his beloved children to death. But he remembered all John's faithfulness and how he had died for him, and he drew his sword and cut off his children's heads with his own hand. And when he had besmeared the stone with their blood, life returned to it, and Faithful John stood alive and well before him.

And he said to the King, "Your faithfulness shall not be unrewarded!" And taking up the heads of the children, he set them on again and besmeared the wound with their blood, upon which in a moment they were whole again, and jumped about and went on playing as if nothing had happened to them.

Now was the King full of joy, and when he saw the Queen coming he put the Faithful John and the two children in a great chest.

When she came in he said to her, "Have you prayed in church?"

"Yes," answered she. "But I was thinking all the while of Faithful John and how he came to such great misfortune through us."

"Then," said he, "dear wife, we can give him life again. But it will cost us both our little sons, whom we must sacrifice."

The Queen grew pale and sick at heart, but said, "We owe it him, because of his great faithfulness."

Then the King rejoiced because she thought as he did, and he went and unlocked the chest and took out the children and Faithful John, and said, "God be praised, he is delivered, and our little sons are ours again." And he related to her how it had come to pass.

After that they all lived together in happiness to their lives' end.

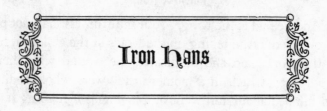

Iron Hans

THERE was once a king whose castle was surrounded by a forest full of game. One day he sent a huntsman out to shoot a deer, but he never came back.

"Perhaps an accident has happened to him," said the King.

Next day he sent out two more huntsmen to look for him, but they did not return either. On the third day he sent for all his huntsmen and said to them, "Search the whole forest without ceasing until you have found all three."

But not a single man of all these, nor one of the pack of hounds they took with them, ever came back. From this time forth no one would venture into the forest. So there it lay, wrapped in silence and solitude, with only an occasional eagle or hawk circling over it.

This continued for several years, and then one day a strange huntsman sought an audience of the King and offered to penetrate into the dangerous wood. The King, however, would not give him permission, and said, "It's not safe. And I am afraid if you go in that you will never come out again, any more than all the others."

The huntsman answered, "Sire, I will take the risk upon myself. I do not know fear."

So the huntsman went into the wood with his dog. Before long the dog started up some game and wanted to chase it, but hardly had he taken a few steps when he came to a deep pool and could go no farther. A naked arm appeared out of the water, seized him, and drew him down.

When the huntsman saw this, he went back and fetched three men with pails to empty the pool. When they got to the bottom they found a wild man whose body was as brown as rusty iron, and whose hair hung down over his face to his knees. They bound him with cords and carried him away to the castle. There was great excitement over the wild man, and the King had an iron cage made for him in the courtyard. He forbade anyone to open the door of the cage on pain of death, and the Queen had to keep the key in her own charge. After this anybody could walk in the forest with safety.

The King had a little son eight years old, and one day he was playing in the courtyard. In his play his golden ball fell into the cage. The boy ran up and said, "Give me back my ball."

"Not until you have opened the door," said the wild man.

"No, I can't do that," said the boy. "My father has forbidden it." And then he ran away.

Next day he came again and asked for his ball. The man said, "Open my door!" But he would not.

On the third day the King went out hunting, and the boy came again and said, "Even if I would, I could not open the door. I have not got the key."

Then the wild man said, "It is lying under your mother's pillow. You can easily get it."

The boy, who was very anxious to have his ball back, threw his scruples to the winds and fetched the key. The door was very stiff and he pinched his fingers in opening it. As soon as it was open the wild man came out, gave the boy his ball, and hurried away. The boy was now very frightened and cried out, "Oh wild man, don't go away, or I shall be beaten!"

The wild man turned back, picked up the boy, put him on his shoulder, and walked hurriedly off into the wood.

When the King came home he saw at once the empty cage and asked the Queen how it had come about. She knew nothing about it and went to look for the key, which was of course gone. They called the boy but there was no answer. The King sent people out into the fields to look for him, but all in vain. He was gone. The King easily guessed what had happened, and great grief fell on the royal household.

When the wild man got back into the depths of the dark forest, he took the boy down off his shoulder and said, "You will never see your father and mother again, but I will keep you here with me because you had pity on me and set me free. If you do as you are told, you will be well treated. I have treasures and gold enough and to spare, more than anybody in the world."

He made a bed of moss for the boy, on which he went to sleep. Next morning the man led him to a spring and said, "You see this golden well is bright and clear as crystal? You must sit by it and take care that nothing falls into it, or it will be contaminated. I shall come every evening to see if you have obeyed my orders."

The boy sat down on the edge of the spring to watch it. Sometimes he would see a golden fish or a golden snake darting through it, and he guarded it well so that nothing should fall into it. One day as he was sitting like this his finger pained him so much that involuntarily he dipped it into the water. He drew it out very quickly but saw that it was gilded, and although he tried hard to clean it, it remained golden. In the evening Iron Hans came back, looked at the boy, and said, "What has happened to the well today?"

"Nothing. Nothing," he answered, keeping his finger behind his back so that Iron Hans should not see it.

But he said, "You have dipped your finger into the water. It does not matter this time, but take care that nothing of the kind occurs again."

Early next morning the boy took his seat by the spring again to watch. His finger still hurt very much and he put his hand up above his head, but unfortunately in so doing he brushed a hair into the well. He quickly took it out, but it was already gilded. When Iron Hans came in the evening, he knew very well what had happened.

"You have let a hair fall into the well," he said. "I will overlook it once more, but if it happens for the third time, the well will be polluted, and you can no longer stay with me."

On the third day the boy again sat by the well, but he took good care not to move his finger, however much it might hurt. The time seemed very long to him as he looked at his face reflected in the water. As he bent over further and further to look into his eyes, his long hair fell over his shoulder right into the water. He started up at once, but not before his whole head of hair had become golden and glittered like the sun. You may imagine how frightened the poor boy was. He took his pocket handkerchief and tied it over his head, so that Iron Hans should not see it. But he knew all about it before he came and at once said,

"Take that handkerchief off your head." And then all the golden hair tumbled out.

All the poor boy's excuses were no good. "You have not stood the test and you can no longer stay here. You must go out into the world, and there you will learn the meaning of poverty. But as your heart is not bad, and as I wish you well, I will grant you one thing. When you are in great need, go to the forest and cry 'Iron Hans,' and I will come and help you. My power is great, greater than you think, and I have gold and silver in abundance."

So the King's son left the forest and wandered over trodden and untrodden paths till he reached a great city. He tried to get work, but he could not find any. Besides he knew no trade by which to make a living. At last he went to the castle and asked if they would employ him. The courtiers did not know what use they could make of him, but they were taken with his appearance and said he might stay. At last the cook took him into his service, and said he might carry wood and water for him and sweep up the ashes.

One day, as there was no one else at hand, the cook ordered him to carry the food up to the royal table. As he did not want his golden hair to be seen, he kept his cap on. Nothing of the sort had ever happened in the presence of the King before, and he said, "When you come into the royal presence, you must take your cap off."

"Alas, Sire," he said, "I cannot take it off. I have a bad wound on my head."

Then the King ordered the cook to be called, and asked how he could take such a boy into his service, and ordered him to be sent away at once. But the cook was sorry for him and exchanged him for the gardener's boy.

Now the boy had to dig and hoe, plant and water, in every kind of weather. One day in the summer when he was working alone in the garden, it was very hot and he took off his cap for the fresh air to cool his head. When the sun shone on his hair it glittered so that the beams penetrated right into the Princess' bedroom, and she sprang up to see what it was. She discovered the youth and called to him, "Bring me a nosegay, young man."

He hurriedly put on his cap, picked a lot of wild flowers, and tied them up. On his way up to the Princess, the gardener met him and said, "How can you take such poor flowers to the Princess? Cut another bouquet quickly, and be sure they are the choicest and rarest flowers."

"Oh no," said the youth. "The wild flowers have a sweeter scent than the garden flowers and will please the Princess better."

As soon as he went into the room the Princess said, "Take off your cap. It is not proper for you to wear it before me."

He answered again, "I may not take it off because I have a wound on my head."

But she took hold of the cap and pulled it off, and all his golden hair tumbled over his shoulders in a shower. It was quite a sight. He tried to get away, but she took hold of his arm and gave him a handful of ducats. He took them, but he cared nothing for the gold and gave it to the gardener for his children to play with.

Next day the Princess again called him to bring her a bunch of wild flowers. When he brought it she immediately clutched at his cap to pull it off, but he held it on with both hands. Again she gave him a handful of ducats, but he would not keep them, and gave them to the gardener's children. The third day the same thing happened, but she could not take off his cap, and he would not keep the gold.

Not long after this the kingdom was invaded. The King assembled his warriors. He did not know whether they would be able to conquer his enemies or not, as they were very powerful and had a mighty army. Then the gardener's assistant said, "I have been brought up to fight. Give me a horse and I will go too."

The others laughed and said, "When we are gone, find one for yourself. We will leave one behind in the stable for you."

When they were gone, he went and got the horse out. It was lame in one leg and hobbled along, humpety-hump, humpety-hump. Nevertheless, he mounted it and rode away to the dark forest. When he came to the edge of it, he called three times, "Iron Hans," as loud as he could, till the rocks and trees resounded with it.

The wild man appeared immediately and said, "What do you want?"

"I want a strong horse to go to the war."

"You shall have it, and more besides."

The wild man went back into the wood, and before long a groom came out, leading a fiery charger with snorting nostrils. Behind him followed a great body of warriors, all in armor and their swords gleaming in the sun. The youth handed over his three-legged steed to the groom, mounted the other, and rode away at the head of the troop.

When he approached the battlefield a great many of the King's men had already fallen, and before long the rest would have to give in. Then the youth, at the head of his iron troop, charged and bore down the enemy like a mighty wind, smiting everything which came in their way. They tried to flee, but the youth fell upon them and did not stop while one remained alive.

Instead of joining the King, he led his troop straight back to the wood and called Iron Hans again.

"What do you want?" asked the wild man.

"Take back your charger and your troop, and give me back my three-legged steed."

His request was granted and he rode his three-legged steed home.

When the King returned to the castle, his daughter met him at the gate and congratulated him on his victory.

"It was not I who won it," he said, "but a strange knight who came to my assistance with his troop." His daughter asked who the strange knight was, but the King did not know. He said, "He pursued the enemy and I have not seen him since."

She asked the gardener about his assistant, but he laughed and said, "He has just come home on his three-legged horse, and the others made fun of him and said, 'Here comes our hobbler back again,' and asked which hedge he had been sleeping under. He answered, 'I did my best, and without me things would have gone badly.' Then they laughed at him more than ever."

The King said to his daughter, "I will give a great feast lasting three days, and you shall throw a golden apple. Perhaps the unknown knight will come among the others to try and catch it."

When notice was given of the feast, the youth went to the wood and called Iron Hans.

"What do you want?" asked the wild man.

"I want to secure the King's golden apple."

"It is as good as yours already," answered Iron Hans. "You shall have a tawny suit and ride a proud chestnut."

When the day arrived the youth took his place among the other knights, but no one knew him. The Princess stepped forward and threw the apple among the knights, and he was the only one who could catch it. As soon as he had it he rode away.

On the second day Iron Hans fitted him out as a white knight riding a gallant gray. Again he caught the apple, and he did not stay a minute, but hurried away as before.

The King now grew angry and said, "This must not be. He must come before me and give me his name."

He gave an order that if the knight made off again he was to be pursued and brought back.

On the third day the youth received from Iron Hans a black outfit and a fiery black charger.

Again he caught the apple, but as he was riding off with it the King's people chased him, and one came so near that he wounded him in the leg. Still he escaped, but his horse galloped so fast that his helmet fell off, and they all saw that he had golden hair. So they rode back and told the King what they had seen.

Next day the Princess asked the gardener about his assistant.

"He is working in the garden. The queer fellow went to the feast, and he came back only last night. He has shown my children three golden apples which he won."

The King ordered him to be brought before him. When he appeared he still wore his cap, but the Princess went up to him and took it off. Then all his golden hair fell over his shoulders, and it was so beautiful that they were all amazed by it.

"Are you the knight who came to the feast every day in a different color, and who caught the three golden apples?" asked the King.

"Yes," he answered. "And here are the apples," he said, bringing them out of his pocket and giving them to the King. "If you want further proof, here is the wound in my leg given me by your people when they pursued me. But I am also the knight who helped you to conquer the enemy."

"If you can do such deeds you are no gardener's boy. Tell me who is your father?"

"My father is a powerful king, and I have plenty of gold —as much as ever I want."

"I see very well," said the King, "that we owe you many thanks. Can I make you a gift or do anything to please you?"

"Yes," he answered, "indeed, you can. Give me your daughter to be my wife!"

The maiden laughed and said, "He does not beat about the bush! But I saw long ago that he was no gardener's boy."

Then she went up to him and kissed him.

His father and mother came to the wedding, and they were full of joy for they had long given up all hope of ever seeing their dear son again.

As they were all sitting at the wedding feast, the music suddenly stopped, the doors flew open, and a proud king walked in at the head of a great following. He went up to the bridegroom, embraced him, and said, "I am Iron Hans, who was bewitched and changed into a wild man, but you have broken the spell and set me free. All the treasure that I have is now your own."

The Lady and the Lion

THERE was once a man who had to take a long journey, and when he was saying good-by to his daughters he asked what he should bring back to them.

The eldest wanted pearls, the second diamonds, but the third said, "Dear father, I should like a singing, soaring lark."

The father said, "Very well, if I can manage it you shall have it." And he kissed all three and set off. He bought pearls and diamonds for the two eldest, but he had searched everywhere in vain for the singing, soaring lark, and this worried him for his youngest daughter was his favorite child.

Once his way led through a wood, in the midst of which was a splendid castle. Near it stood a tree, and right up at the top he saw a lark singing and soaring.

"Ah," he said, "I have come across you in the nick of time." And he called to his servant to dismount and catch the little creature. But as he approached the tree, a lion sprang out from underneath and shook himself and roared so that the leaves on the tree trembled. "Who dares to steal my lark?" said he. "I will eat up the thief."

Then the man said, "I didn't know that the bird was yours. I will make up for my fault by paying a heavy ransom. Only spare my life."

But the lion said, "Nothing can save you, unless you promise to give me whatever first meets you when you get home. If you consent, I will give you your life and the bird into the bargain."

But the man hesitated and said, "Suppose my youngest and favorite daughter were to come running to meet me when I go home!"

But the servant was afraid and said, "Your daughter will not necessarily be the first to come to meet you. It might just as well be a cat or a dog."

So the man let himself be persuaded, took the lark, and promised to the lion for his own whatever first met him on his return home. When he reached home and entered his house, the first person who met him was none other than his youngest daughter. She came running up and kissed and caressed him, and when she saw that he had brought the singing, soaring lark she was beside herself with joy.

But her father could not rejoice. He began to cry and said, "My dear child, it has cost me dear for I have had to promise you to a lion. He will tear you in pieces when he has you in his power." And he told her all that had happened and begged her not to go, come what might.

But she consoled him, saying, "Dear father, what you have promised must be performed. I will go, and I will soon soften the lion's heart so that I shall come back safe and sound." The next morning the way was shown to her, and she said good-by and went confidently into the forest.

Now the lion was an enchanted prince, who was a lion by day, and all his followers were lions too. But by night they reassumed their human form. On her arrival she was kindly received and conducted to the castle. When night fell, the lion turned into a handsome man, and their wedding was celebrated with due magnificence. They lived happily together, sitting up at night and sleeping by day.

One day he came to her and said, "Tomorrow there is a festival at your father's house to celebrate your eldest sister's wedding. If you would like to go my lions shall escort you."

She answered that she was very eager to see her father again, so she went away accompanied by the lions.

There was great rejoicing on her coming, for they all thought that she had been torn to pieces and had long been dead. But she told them what a handsome husband she had and how well she fared, and she stayed with them as long as the wedding festivities lasted. Then she went back again into the wood.

When the second daughter married and the youngest was again invited to the wedding, she said to the lion, "This time I will not go alone. You must come too."

But the lion said it would be too dangerous, for if a gleam of light touched him he would be changed into a dove and would have to fly about for seven years.

"Ah," said she, "only go with me, and I will protect you and keep off every ray of light."

So they went away together and took their little child with them too. They had a hall built with such thick walls that no ray could penetrate, and thither the lion was to retire when the wedding torches were kindled. But the door was made of fresh wood which split and caused a little crack which no one noticed.

Now the wedding was celebrated with great splendor. But when the procession came back from church with a large number of torches and lights, a ray of light no broader than a hair fell upon the Prince, and the minute this ray touched him he was changed. And when his wife came in and looked for him, she saw nothing but a white dove sitting there.

The dove said to her, "For seven years I must fly about the world. Every seventh step I will let fall a drop of blood, and a white feather which will show you the way. If you will follow the track you can free me."

Thereupon the dove flew out of the door. She followed it, and every seventh step it let fall a drop of blood and a little white feather to show her the way. So she wandered about the world, and never rested till the seven years were nearly passed. Then she rejoiced, thinking that she would soon be free of her troubles, but she was still far from release. One day as they were journeying on in the accustomed way, the feather and the drop of blood ceased falling, and when she looked up the dove had vanished.

"Man cannot help me," she thought. So she climbed up to the sun and said to it, "You shine upon all the valleys and mountain peaks. Have you not seen a white dove flying by?"

"No," said the sun, "I have not seen one, but I will give you a little casket. Open it when you are in need."

She thanked the sun and went on till night, when the moon shone out. "You shine all night," she said, "over field and forest. Have you seen a white dove flying by?"

"No," answered the moon, "I have seen none, but here is an egg. Break it when you are in great need."

She thanked the moon and went on till the night wind blew upon her. "You blow among all the trees and leaves. Have not you seen a white dove?" she asked.

"No," said the night wind, "I have not seen one, but I will ask the other three winds, who may perhaps have seen it."

The east wind and the west wind came, but they had seen no dove. Only the south wind said, "I have seen the white dove. It has flown away to the Red Sea, where it has again become a lion, since the seven years are over. And the lion is ever fighting with a dragon who is an enchanted princess."

Then the night wind said, "I will advise you. Go to the Red Sea. You will find tall reeds growing on the right bank. Count them and cut down the eleventh. Strike the dragon with it and then the lion will be able to master it, and both will regain human shape. Next, look round and you will see the winged griffin who dwells by the Red Sea. Leap upon its back with your beloved and it will carry you across the sea. Here is a nut: drop it when you come to mid-ocean. It will open immediately and a tall nut tree will grow up out of the water, on which the griffin will settle. Could it not rest, it would not be strong enough to carry you across. If you forget to drop the nut, it will let you fall into the sea."

Then she journeyed on and found everything as the night wind had said. She counted the reeds by the sea and cut off the eleventh, struck the dragon with it, and the lion mastered it. Immediately both regained human form. But when the Princess who had been a dragon was free from enchantment, she took the Prince in her arms, seated herself on the griffin's back, and carried him off. And the poor wanderer, again forsaken, sat down and cried. At last she took courage and said to herself, "Wherever the winds blow I will go, and as long as cocks crow I will search till I find him."

So she went on a long, long way till she came to the castle where the Prince and Princess were living. There she heard that there was to be a festival to celebrate their wedding. Then she said to herself, "Heaven help me," and she opened the casket which the sun had given her. Inside it was a dress, as brilliant as the sun itself. She took it out, put it on, and went into the castle, where everyone, including the bride, looked at her with amazement. The dress pleased the bride so much that she asked if it was to be bought.

"Not with gold or goods," she answered, "but with flesh and blood."

The bride asked what she meant and she answered, "Let me speak with the bridegroom in his chamber to-night."

The bride refused. However, she wanted the dress so much that at last she consented, but the chamberlain was ordered to give the Prince a sleeping draught.

At night, when the Prince was asleep, she was taken to his room. She sat down and said, "For seven years I have followed you. I have been to the sun and the moon and the four winds to look for you. I have helped you against the dragon, and will you now quite forget me?"

But the Prince slept so soundly that he thought it was only the rustling of the wind among the pine trees. When morning came, she was taken away and had to give up the dress. And as it had not helped her she was very sad and went into a meadow and cried. While sitting there, she remembered the egg which the moon had given her. She broke it open and out came a hen and twelve chickens all of gold, who ran about chirping and then crept back under their mother's wings. A prettier sight could not be seen.

She got up and drove them about the meadow, till the bride saw them from the window. The chickens pleased her so much that she asked if they were for sale. "Not for gold and goods, but for flesh and blood. Let me speak with the bridegroom in his chamber once more."

The bride said "Yes," intending to deceive her as before, but when the Prince went to his room he asked the chamberlain what all the murmuring and rustling in the night meant. Then the chamberlain told him how he had been ordered to give him a sleeping draught because a poor girl had been concealed in his room, and that night he was to do the same again.

"Pour out the drink and put it near my bed," said the Prince.

At night she was brought in again. And when she began to relate her sad fortunes he recognized the voice of his dear wife, sprang up, and said, "Now I am really free for the first time. All has been as a dream, for the foreign princess cast a spell over me so that I was forced to forget you. But heaven in a happy hour has taken away my blindness."

Then they both stole out of the castle, for they feared the Princess' father, because he was a sorcerer. They mounted the griffin, who bore them over the Red Sea, and when they got to mid-ocean she dropped the nut. On the spot a fine nut tree sprang up, on which the bird rested. Then it took them home, where they found their child grown tall and beautiful, and they lived happily till the end.

THE BEAUTIFUL
Illustrated Junior Library
EDITIONS